A FIELD GUIDE TO
ARMAGEDDON

A FIELD GUIDE TO ARMAGEDDON

GARY ALEXANDER

Encircle Publications, LLC
Farmington, Maine U.S.A.

*I know not with what World War III will be fought, but
World War IV will be fought with sticks and stones.*
Albert Einstein

All reactionaries are paper tigers.
Mao Tse-tung

OTHER BOOKS BY GARY ALEXANDER

Pigeon Blood
Unfunny Money
Deadly Drought
Kiet and the Opium War
Kiet and the Golden Peacock
Kiet Goes West
Blood Sacrifice
Dead Dinosaurs
Dragon Lady
Disappeared
Zillionaire
Interlock
Loot
Gold
A Book of Facts a novel
Father's Day
Damn Near Broke
Bad Elements
Humpty Dumpty Goes Kersplat
Harry Saves The World
Numerous short stories

JANUARY 1, 1963

PROLOGUE

The Air France flight from Paris touched down at Zurich's Kloten Airport on what looked to the sole Chinese passenger like sheer ice, not concrete.

He clung to the bottom of his seat, as if that would help stick the aircraft to the surface. But the landing was perfect and the pilots kept the twin-engine Caravelle decelerating dead center on the runway, turning off onto an apron that led to the terminal.

He was met inside by an expensively-dressed Swiss banker: Savile Row, wearing a handmade wool topcoat..Ruddy, fiftyish and heavyset, the banker noted with relief that the Chinese wore a business suit, tie and topcoat, not the absurdly-ascetic tunic favored by Chairman Mao Tse-tung and his toadies. A tasteless statement of proletarian unity.

They shook hands, but no names were exchanged. Each knew *what* the other was, so *who* was unnecessary. The Chinese was roughly the banker's age. He too was well-fed, a sign, the banker thought, of privilege after so many instances of mismanagement and famine. In a socialist paradise, all but the elite were permitted to starve equally.

On the way to the baggage station and out of the terminal to the parking lot, they exchanged small talk—the visitor's flight experience from Peking, the weather so similar this time of year to Zurich's, et cetera—until they reached the host's car, a Mercedes-Benz300SE sedan. A light snow began to fall.

There was no chauffeur. That his host was driving was an indication that they would discuss business wherever they had privacy, the Chinese knew.

"How many banks are there in Zurich?" the Chinese asked as the Mercedes' tires crunched over snow.

Here it comes, the banker thought. A rant on capitalist decadence. The influence of the U.S. imperialists and their running-dog lackeys. Topped off with a windy lecture on Marx and Engels and dialectical materialism. Zealots of any stripe could talk for hours and say nothing.

He smiled and played along. "So many I have lost count."

The Chinese forced a laugh, demonstrating as ordered a Western sense of humor. He believed that neutral Switzerland had been an economic whore of Nazi Germany during the Second World War. How much of the gold he was purchasing was taken from occupied countries and from jewelry and dental fillings of Jews in their holocaust camps? The Swiss were pliable and like this banker worshipped only money.

No matter. Once gold was melted down into ingots, gold was gold. The beauteous metal had no conscience.

They pulled up in front of an imposing stone and glass structure. The street was lined with similarly pretentious buildings and shops displaying all manner of luxury goods. Breathe deeply, the Chinese thought, and you would inhale money. So unlike the egalitarian People's Republic of China.

Two men in uniform rushed from the steps of the bank to open their car doors. They were dressed like cavalry officers from the last century. Was there no end to the pomp in this city?

"If you wish, we can leave your luggage in the trunk," the banker said. "I can drive you to your hotel later."

"I am not staying tonight. You can drive me to the airport, though, if you would please. I am catching a late flight out."

"As you wish, sir," he said.

The banker hadn't known this when he made reservations at Zurich's finest hotel, but it suited him. Considering who the man represented and what they were doing, the sooner the Chinese was out of his hair, the better. Although it was a Tuesday, it was New Year's Day. The meeting had been timed with the holiday in mind.

The banker escorted his guest through the unoccupied bank, going by teller windows and offices to a brushed-steel vault. A younger banker stood by nervously.

The banker twirled a finger. The younger man nodded and worked a large dial, then twisted a handle. The door swung open. The banker excused himself before he walked in with the Chinese.

In the rear was a stack of gold ingots—each the size of a brick—the dimensions of a small kitchen stove. It weighed almost ten metric tons.

The banker said, "The last payment arrived six days ago. As your people promised."

By unknown means, the Chinese government had paid in American dollars. Red Chinese money was worthless outside of their sphere of influence. How they had converted it into hard currency was none of the banker's business. His experts had verified that it wasn't counterfeit.

The Chinese looked at the gold and smiled. An impressive monument to the imperialist worship of a metal. A devotion that will be their undoing, theirs and the traitorous revisionists in Moscow.

Total value at $35.25 US per troy ounce: $10,000,000 US.

The banker waited for approval. The man's hesitations throughout their conversation—was this indecision or an element of their fabled inscrutability?

The Chinese finally nodded and said, "Yes. This is good."

"Accurate to the last ounce," the banker said.

The Chinese nodded again. A criminal process known in the decadent West as "money laundering" had been implemented to gather and transfer ten million American dollars to the bank. It had not been easy.

He handed the banker a slip of paper and said, "The password."

"Very good."

"And according to our agreement, until the gold is claimed, you will receive an annual fee and the negotiated percentage when the value of gold rises. Today's transaction will not be altered even in the event of regime changes, nor will your secrecy rules be loosened."

Thinking that the price of gold will rise was typically naïve of the Eastern bloc, the banker thought. Communists had no concept of free-world economics. Gold hadn't risen above forty-three dollars per ounce since 1934. If this fellow and his masters were planning on a big profit, they were going to be disappointed.

"Excellent," he said, looking at the nine-digit password and a word at the end.

"Do you have an idea when it may be claimed, sir?"

"It may be soon, by a family known to us. It may not be claimed soon by them or by others."

East is east, west is west. Rudyard Kipling's assertion was correct. Without question, Orientals were inscrutable.

The banker said, "The key word following the nine numbers is, frankly, troubling."

"It is a word found in your Christian Bible," the Chinese said, deadpan.

"Yes, well," the banker replied, leaving it at that, unwilling to encourage a longwinded argument supporting Marx's "religion is the opium of the masses" quote.

"The numerical password may be issued to the correct party at the correct moment. I have no control how this is done, if it is done. Or has been done. Future events will decide."

That rang of some insipid quotation from their beloved Chairman Mao Tse-tung's little red book. The banker desperately wanted to be done with this. To go home to a crackling fireplace and a full snifter of cognac.

"Again, I'm sorry, but that word—"

"It may or may not be the word itself or the act. You will know."

The banker looked at him.

"Chairman Mao said in his great book that political power grows out of a barrel of a gun. He menaces nobody with that quotation. He is stating a historical fact. The event, the act, will be the doing of others. The warmongers have excluded us. They will pay."

"Excluded you?"

"It is ironic."

"How so?"

"We invented gunpowder in the seventh century, but modern pyrotechnic science has left us behind."

"Dare I ask?"

"We are endangered by a former ally and by an enemy. We will catch up, but taking in account global tensions, we may be too late."

The banker began walking the Chinese back through the bank.

"You appear worried."

"Me?" the banker lied. "No."

"The gold, its purpose?"

"If you wish to reveal it," the banker said, hoping he would not.

"Let me say that the Cuban Missile Crisis last October was at once frustrating and inspirational."

The United States and the Soviet Union, fingers on their nuclear triggers until the missiles were removed from Cuba. That was inspirational?

The banker tensed at the front door.

The Chinese smiled. "You continue to fret over the key word. Please be at ease. It is only a word that completes the code giving access to the gold."

"Yes. I will try," was all the banker could summon.

Nine numbers and *Armageddon.*

He badly needed the restroom.

The Chinese clapped the banker on a shoulder. "On second thought, we have concluded our business so quickly and efficiently, I shall take the hotel room as you offered. To clean up and rest."

There was something in the Chinese's eyes, a man-to-man acknowledgment. Mao Tse-tung, the banker had read, loved the company of women, many of them.

He offered, "If you desire companionship—"

"If it is not too much trouble."

The banker smiled. The man was human after all.

NOVEMBER 22, 1963

1

The man known to some as Fred Miller fidgeted in his third-floor perch. The CLOSED sign was on the front door, the blinds were shut, and the window was cracked the height of a rifle barrel and a homemade suppressor.

He had memorized every detail he knew in advance. He had committed to memory every detail he didn't know but might encounter. Exits that may or may not be locked, variations in seating arrangements, security personnel in and out of uniform. Every possible possibility. Imagining people coming and going, seeing them in his dreams.

This was how he worked. This was what kept him out of jail and the morgue.

This assignment had made him edgy from the outset. He had accepted it on November fifteenth, one short week ago. They'd told him on the phone that they had not known the venue until that day, until it was announced as the Dallas Trade Mart.

Fred Miller had said no dice if it was who he thought it was. They promised it wasn't *him*.

Given the hoopla of the event, all the attention, the political friction, Miller demanded and received triple his normal fee, take it or leave it, not the way you talked to these people.

He said to think it over and call him in the next ten minutes at a phone booth a block away, yea or nay. Payment upon satisfactory completion of said task.

Per his procedure, rolls of nickels in his pockets, on the fifteenth of each month, Miller drove or flew to a city he picked at random, called from one phone booth, then gave them another at which to reply. If there was a lot to talk about, he'd give them the number of another. Leapfrogging pay phones kept them from homing in on him. If the deal wasn't done in twenty minutes, he was in his car or on a plane, headed out of town, writing it off. He had declined jobs enough times that they knew he was serious.

When he got to the booth, the phone was already ringing. That they agreed without a word of argument was to say the least, troubling. Highly troubling. Although he had never personally met them, he knew they were people who, if you gave them lip face-to-face, they'd have the last word while garroting you.

In the brief time between arriving in Dallas and the here and now, Miller had practically lived in libraries, devouring newspaper articles and photostats. When not getting eyestrain, he was driving the route, checking it and the destination, major thoroughfares on a gas-station road map of the city he committed to memory. The research was not comforting.

He knew the Dallas Trade Mart was already overrun with Secret Service agents. Sure, the motorcade route would be worrisome for them because of the buildings they passed and the thousands of windows in them and people crowding the sidewalks, but the limousine was in motion. A moving target, agents on all sides. The president would be safe en route.

The Dallas Trade Mart was a different story, a true security nightmare. It was a four-story square donut centered by a large atrium. The sides were filled with offices and showrooms, hundreds of which could be a sharpshooter's nest. The atrium, the Grand Courtyard, was set up for a luncheon and speech by President John F. Kennedy who was arriving shortly with his lovely wife, Jacqueline.

The agents were hard to miss with their dark suits, twice-weekly haircuts, and eyes that never stopped moving. No less than five times had Fred Miller held his breath as he heard footsteps in the walkway.

Miller looked out and downward at The Grand Courtyard, now two-thirds full. He was in the third-floor showroom that belonged to Harry's Hattery, to a maker and retailer of Western hats. He had reconnoitered the day before yesterday, learning that the hatter was out of town because of a family emergency.

Harry's Hattery was a one-man band, with a counter, shelving behind it, and a faint aroma of leather. Miller knew he'd have the shop to himself.

He stuck a Harry's Hattery business card in his shirt pocket, so if someone in authority demanded entry, he might be able to talk himself out of a jam, waving the card, claiming he was a customer in for a selection and a fitting, annoyed as all get-out because he hadn't been told the shop was closed.

Regardless of the fuss downstairs, it was a Friday, springboard to the weekend. If you didn't get your hat today, you'd have to wait till Monday. And the big family barbeque was Sunday, the cousin he hadn't seen in ten years attending with two young nieces he'd never seen.

So what are you doing inside the shop if it was closed, wise guy? Fred Miller would throw his hands in the air and in exasperation say that the door was unlocked, Harry's problem, not his. If he found a suitable hat and left cash and a note, was that a crime? Weak and lame, but all he had.

I must be out of my gourd taking this job.

Fred Miller checked his watch: 12:32. The motorcade route from Love Field to here was nine-point-five miles, so it should be arriving any second, no later than 12:35 or 12:36. He chambered a round. It wasn't the standard full-metal-jacket cartridge. In his home workshop, Miller had hollowed out lead slugs until they were almost translucent.

Soft lead that would strike its target hard enough to pierce the skull and mushroom, turning gray matter into porridge.

Killing bad people for bad people doesn't necessarily make you a bad person, does it? Aren't you performing a public service?

If Fred Miller was lucky, the target would land on his side or back, the entry wound not visible. By the time anyone realized that the unfortunate hadn't suffered a heart attack or stroke, Miller would be long gone.

He did not like what he saw. He especially did not like what he didn't see. The atrium and its twenty-six hundred seats were filling fast. But nobody yet on the podium.

Hands perspiring inside surgeon's gloves, he checked his watch again: 12:34. Occupants of the motorcade's lead cars should be arriving. Vice President Johnson, Governor Connolly, and other dignitaries.

They weren't.

His target had just sat down in his assigned seat, second row from the rear, fourth seat from the right. All Miller knew of him was that he matched the seat and description. The assignment was not young or trim. He had a gray crew cut and was wearing a green sport jacket a size too small. Fred had been given no name.

His plan had been to pop him when the President and his wife first entered. All attention, including the Secret Service's, would be on the Kennedys, guests on their feet applauding, his target well positioned for his fatal seizure.

They had their reasons for wanting him dead. Like any other job, that's all he needed to know.

He checked his watch: 12:37.

Something was haywire. Fred Miller's paranoia was bursting into full bloom.

Miller stood and edged backward. He turned his attention and his weapon toward the service door, debating whether to go through with it or go through that door, calling it a day. Harry's Hattery was on a corner, so it would be a quick trip to the stairs or the elevator, then out of the building.

Not fifteen seconds later, he heard similar clicking noises he'd made when he'd picked the lock. Similar, but not the same. This was made by a key.

Two men rushed in, revolvers drawn, one carrying a long, narrow zippered bag.

Miller swung his rifle around and pressed it to the first man's ear.

"Drop the guns, boys," he said quietly.

They froze. Fred kicked the door shut.

"A basic fact. A round will travel through one lame brain to the other in a hundredth of a second. Second and last request. Drop the guns. Your bag too."

They dropped their weapons and the bag. Miller kicked the handguns aside and stepped back.

"Maybe I'm wrong, but I can't picture you clowns as hat makers."

"You are making big mistake," one replied. "We are Secret Service."

Fred Miller sized them up. In their thirties, in wrinkled slacks and sport coats, not too tall, not too short, not fat, not skinny. Brown hair, green eyes. If you passed them on the street, you couldn't describe them five minutes later. They were average in all respects, perhaps too average. The speaker's grammar was imperfect and he had no accent, words learned in an English-language class for foreigners.

"Turn around slowly. Back up against that side wall beside the door, "Miller said, gesturing with his rifle. "If you're Secret Service, I'm Elvis."

He patted them down and found nothing except a wallet on one. Nothing whatsoever on the other.

"Traveling light, boys?" Fred Miller asked.

He didn't expect an answer and didn't receive one.

The contents of the wallet raised a mountain range of goose bumps. He didn't know Russian, but he knew Cyrillic characters when he saw them. Some letters were the same as English, some like English seen through a mirror, some completely foreign. Screwy.

And the symbol of the KGB(KT) on one of the cards. The wallet was the property of a V. I. Larrionov. The KGB ID had an embossed picture—Fred Miller's own.

When was it taken? A year or two ago? Not much background around his face and it was fuzzy, likely taken from a distance with a telephoto lens.

He shifted the rifle to the nearest guy's crotch, raising it hard, raising him onto his tiptoes.

He knelt and unzipped the bag with his free hand. The contents fell out with a hard clunk.

Fred Miller knew his weaponry. The visitors had brought a Soviet-made Dragunov to the party. It was a newer model, an original design, a semi-automatic, gas-operated sniper rifle that fired a 7.62 mm round. It was fitted with a 4X PSO-1 scope and silencer. The Dragunov had a soft two-pound trigger pull and a free-floating firing pin. Maximum rate of fire: thirty rounds per minute. Effective firing range: eight-hundred meters.

One of the finest weapons in the Eastern Bloc, Miller knew. With it, he could shoot a wing off a fly anywhere in this building.

Miller's own weapon, brought in a precisely-compartmentalized attaché case, was an all-American buffet of parts, sans serial numbers—barrel, breech, scope, fold-up stock—fashioned in his backyard workshop, to be disposed of in individual pieces after completion of the assignment. No match for the Russki rifle, though.

Presumably, his guests' plan was for him to swallow the barrel of *his* Dragunov after *he* had killed John Fitzgerald Kennedy, thirty-fifth president of the United States of America.

His body would be discovered later. An assassination-suicide. His fingerprints had never been taken, so his KGB ID would be an easy sell.

A KGB agent assassinates an American president.

Let the Commies deny it, lying through their teeth like they do.

We aren't gonna stand still for that.

Threats and counter-threats.

The generals hollering for a preemptive nuclear strike.

Launching the ICBMs and away we go.

World War III?

Why not? They asked for it.

No thanks, Fred Miller thought. Not today.

He had killed seventeen men, the last sixteen for money, but he had some scruples. Not to mention well-honed survival instincts.

Miller looked around, thinking fast. At one side, behind the counter: cowboy hats stacked high, empty boxes, and a hand truck.

"Off with your clothes, gentlemen."

"Now, you wait a second, sir. Please. This cannot be done."

Miller raised his rifle barrel and jammed it against his neck so hard it had to hurt. "Last chance, comrades, or the coroner will do the undressing."

While they obeyed, Miller put the largest box on the hand truck, then their guns in it. Then every stitch of their clothing.

They faced him, covering their private parts.

"Please, "said the one doing the talking.

Miller understood their concern, their dilemma. Dallas, Texas was not the best of all worlds for two naked men caught together in a public place overlooking a presidential appearance.

Speaking of President Kennedy, where the hell was he?

There was a growing murmur downstairs, puzzled glances, eyes on watches and on the doors behind the podium.

Miller's watch: 12:40.

His rifle still trained on his captives, Miller backed to the door, opened it a crack and looked outside. All clear.

Into the hallway he went with the hand truck. Breathing evenly, like he belonged there.

2

The 1958 Chevrolet Impala was a one-of-a-kind model. It was the first GM product to be designated as an Impala, with a body style that was marketed for only one year. Although one-hundred-and-eighty-one thousand coupes and convertibles were manufactured, the '58wasregarded as too subdued for the era. Its quarter panels were muted, curved at the ends, as if there had been a change of heart about adding tailfins. That flaw was corrected in the 1959 Impala, with fins that seemed ready, willing and able to launch the two-ton beast into the stratosphere.

To make innocuous conversation on the drive to Dallas, the history of that automobile was provided to Mother Hen by Mr. C, the younger one of the two, who had signed her up in Lawton, Oklahoma.

The Impala had been chosen for her, he said, because even if its uniqueness made it stand out, it wouldn't stand out because they would be on the alert for total anonymity.

They?

Total anonymity, standing out or not?

For what purpose?

Dare she ask any of this?

She did not. Generosity had its price.

Now, parked in the Dallas Trade Mart lot, the woman who had been tagged by Mr. C the Younger as Mother Hen sat behind the wheel of the oatmeal-white '58 Impala coupe. Mr. C the Younger (her tag for him) said that after her job was done, the car was hers, with a full tank of gas, plenty to get her back home. No looking back, even through the mirrors, please.

This was serious, see-no-evil serious, but she was in no position to look a gift horse in the mouth.

Mother Hen was trying to appear calm and patient. She was pretending to touch up her nails with a file, right hand working on the left, eyes really on the hands of her watch: 12:33.

She was waiting for her two unnamed Chicks. The older Mr. C said to think of them as chicks, under her protective wings. They should be here soon. Then again, how could they be? The presidential motorcade hadn't arrived. She tapped her watch and held it to her ear, listening to see if it still ticked.

She had learned of the presidential visit by sneaking out for a newspaper. They had sequestered her in her motel room upon her arrival, for the past three days. No radio, no TV, meals delivered or out with her Chicks, then back. But this was a lady with a mind of her own. The money she was being paid, well, something had to be fishy. Yes, she was a see-no-evil kind of gal, but there were limits to everything.

Mother Hen wore a blondish beehive and horn-rimmed glasses on a chain. A biddy, not young, not old. Look at her and you'd see a librarian taking the day off to catch a glimpse of her President, albeit a man generally despised in the state of Texas as a rich, pretty-boy, East Coast pinko, a fellow traveler with a silver spoon in his mouth.

The younger Mr. C had recruited her outside the Lawton unemployment office, initiating a conversation with her as she was wiping a tear. The clerks had turned her away, accusing of her lying and falsifying forms to collect beyond the weeks allowed. A little white lie at the worst when you considered the bums and loafers and coloreds who lived on the government tit.

And here she was, abandoned by her latest husband, an Army sergeant, who ran off with an Oriental GI-bride, a divorcée who tended bar, no better than a common whore.

Mr. C had been vague about the job other than she was to drive and supervise two young men of limited intelligence. Mother Hen was not young or pretty, but he didn't seem the sort to send girls out onto the street in short skirts.

She had worried at the moment that he was feeding her a line, indecisive, and just for a moment, before she hopped into his brand-spanking-new metallic-blue Cadillac, that he was the boss of a white slavery ring, shipping white ladies off to A-rabs and Mau-Maus, who cared most of all about the skin and eye color of their concubines. Mr. C wore a nice business suit, though, not a zoot suit she understood pimps to wear like uniforms.

There was plenty of security in and by the parking lots. Police standing by the building. Police cruising through the parking areas and nearby streets. Gobs and gobs of police. Sooner or later, one will politely inquire why she was sitting in her car so long, doing her nails, something of that nature.

She had no Texas accent. She was a refined and cultured gal from the north—suburban Chicago, if you must know—not southern white trash, thank you. If they became impolite and nosy, she wasn't a librarian. She was visiting her maiden aunt who lived right here in a respectable Dallas neighborhood. If they cared to check her story, by the time they did, she'd be long gone.

If truth be told, she was a deserted wife and an unemployed grocery store checker, whose joblessness (so they all said) was her attitude. How she couldn't control her temper or keep her big yap shut. Didn't they understand that the customer wasn't *always* right? To give her lip for being slow or hitting the wrong keys and overcharging, lying like a rug, you shouldn't have to put up with that and she didn't.

Four times in divorce court and the no-good bastards walked out winners, selling the judge a bill of goods about her screaming rages and thrown dishes and silent sulks that went on for days. Married to those louses, who wouldn't be a little testy?

"Oh goodness, officer," she'd prattle as rehearsed. "While I'm in town, I just have to sneak a peek at her. I do so adore fashionable ladies. Mrs. Kennedy. Him? Am I here for *him?* Please. That is understandable, so I shall not be insulted. I am a Republican through and through, but a lady appreciative of high fashion."

A scrape with the file on her pinky and: 12:35.

Sirens.

Mother Hen adjusted her mirror.

Sirens and more sirens.

A caravan flew by behind her. Cars, most or all black. Perhaps a limousine. A man stretched out on top of the limo, on the trunk, like a movie stunt man? Was she seeing things?

More sirens and more sirens.

Parkland Hospital wasn't far and they were headed in that direction. She peeked around, as far as the car windows and her bony neck would permit, searching for billowing smoke. An industrial fire, something of that extent? All the crude oil they pumped around here. What else could it be?

But no smoke. How strange.

Police cars were leaving the Dallas Trade Mart, tires spinning and burning, some racing left, some racing to the right.

No Chicks.

Mr. C the Younger and Mr. C the Elder will be beside themselves, not good news for her.

A young fella two spaces away got into a car, also a Chevy, but a bland coupe. He was lean and supple, clean-cut and matter-of-factly. Nice haircut, college-boy clothes, sweet innocent face .Like one of those popular singers from *The Beach Boys or The Kingston Trio.*

She sighed. If any of her wretched husbands had been like him, how differently her life may have turned out.

She thought of calling out to him, asking him if he knew what the fuss was all about, but he certainly wouldn't know. The young fella hadn't even looked in the direction of the sirens. Was he deaf?

Mother Hen sat up, started her car, and backed out.

She drove to a far corner of the lot, stopped, and removed a three-by-five index card from her purse.

She remembered the identical three-by-five card Mr. C the Elder gave her when they first met at the motel. He had made her read it, memorize it, and recite to him, like she was a dummy.

MISSION STATEMENT
We need to start over. And we will.

"What does the card mean to you?" Mr. C the Elder had asked, standing closer to her than the social distance.

"Goodness, it's all too deep for me," she'd answered truthfully. "Starting over and everything, whatever it is you stopped so you could start over, I have not the foggiest notion."

He looked at her as if she were a retarded child, her a woman who had graduated from high school with a solid C-average.

"You have not a foggiest notion why you were hired in another state by a total stranger, but away you went? If I confirm your employment, will you be motivated by ideology or money?"

"Well, Mr. C, with your generous offer, money, money, money. I've been treated horribly by men who drained my finances and cavorted with loose women and lied in the courtroom—"

"That is what I like to hear."

"Yes, well, thank you," she said, relieved.

"I've shown you my mission statement simply to implicate you."

"Sir?"

"Once again, the job was offered in Lawton, Oklahoma and accepted by you. No ifs, ands or buts. With the vaguest knowledge of the job, you climbed into a car with a complete stranger."

"Well—"

"Meaning that if you fail or are ever tempted to talk to anyone at any time, present or future, there will be—consequences. Dire consequences. You have been sworn to a sacred confidence."

"Well, yes."

He tore the card out of her hand and held it to her mouth.

"Swallow it, bit-by-bit."

She had done so, tearing it into tiny pieces and forcing it down. Like an initiation ceremony into some icky cult.

The boy had been so nice, but that man was a meanie. He scared her to half to death. When she was done, he smiled for the only time in her presence, an icy grin.

She peeked around him at the youngster. His face was no longer fresh and kindly, it was a blank mask, with something simmering under the surface. A Jeckyl and Hyde?

"You see," Mr. C the Elder said, "the mission statement and you have become one."

What sort of craziness had she gotten herself into?

The zillionth check of her watch: 1:02. People were streaming out, looks of confusion and sorrow on their faces. People crying and hugging. None among them were her Chicks.

She wasn't born yesterday. She'd had a hunch they were up to no good, but, goodness, they wouldn't be able to get close enough to shoot President Kennedy with those little pistols of theirs, if that was what they had in their suit coats.

At the very worst, they were there to create a commotion. A protest or something, on behalf of God-fearing, Commie-hating Texans, exercising their Constitutional rights of free expression. They would stand by the nearest door, shoot in the air, and pile back into the car. They'd be out on the road before anyone could react.

This was her take on it, what she dearly hoped it was. If she hadn't needed the money so badly—

Mother Hen moved onto the street and parked out of sight of the Dallas Trade Mart, unsure what to do next, thinking of Mr. C's promise of consequences.

3

Leaving the Dallas Trade Mart, the pseudonymous Fred Miller lifted the box of clothing and the Dragunov rifle into the nearest trash receptacles, conveniently located by each stairwell. Into the next bin went parts of his rifle, into the next and the next and the next the remainder. His gloves and empty attaché casein the next.

Six trash cans later, he walked outside, an ordinary, law-abiding citizen.

Miller heard the wail of sirens all around. He climbed into his pale-blue 1963 Chevrolet Biscayne two-door, a rental car as blandly all-American as its driver.

Hurrying without hurrying, looking without obviously looking, he had noticed nobody but a woman in the driver's seat of a white '58 Impala two spaces away. Doing her nails, paying no attention to him or the sirens.

Was she deaf?

He started the car, listening to the last of stereophonic sirens, thinking that it must be one hell of a fire, but he should be seeing smoke. Or something to do with JFK, who was running very late. As he'd first walked out of the building, out a corner of an eye, he thought he'd seen cars speeding past in the direction of Parkland Hospital.

Presidents didn't run late, he thought. Their itineraries were scheduled down to the minute, not the hour. They were that busy. This was not good.

Fred Miller was twenty-eight-years-old, clean-cut and blandly handsome in his pressed suntans and Madras shirt. He had an athletic build. Neatly-trimmed hair, and white teeth. He was harmless, boy-next-doorish, with a nice smile.

Miller could approach his objectives point-blank with his baby pistol and later stroll past police without tripping red flares. He had smelled onions on the breath of his last assignment, a labor union boss.

On his way to Love Field, he tuned in the radio, curious about the sirens. After sputtering static as the vacuum tubes warmed up, the first words he heard were "yet unconfirmed, but believed to be dead."

Miller turned up the volume.

The announcer's voice was shaky as he reported that President Kennedy had been shot and taken to Parkland Hospital.

Miller twisted the knob from one station to another. All carried the story, elaborating as time passed. President Kennedy had been shot in the head by an unknown gunman as he passed through Dealey Plaza. Condition unknown, but presumed serious, even critical. Everything yet unconfirmed.

Dealey Plaza, Miller thought, picturing the city map he had memorized and the streets he had driven. Dealey was approximately three miles and five minutes from the Dallas Trade Mart. He recalled a tall brick building at Dealey Plaza and a couple of sharp turns—Houston Street turning onto Elm Street—where a big limo would have to take it slow.

Why were they setting him up as the fall guy when they had shot President Kennedy elsewhere? The right hand not knowing what the left hand was doing. Nothing made any sense.

In the locked glove box was a set of ID for Don Lester, a driver's license and Social Security card. He'd use it if he had to, though he didn't know why he would, not until later, if at all. Fred Miller prepared for every contingency, regardless how remote.

Fred pulled into a supermarket lot and parked far from other cars, beside a storm drain. He noticed sale banners on the front of the store, hung by the doors. Colby cheese at thirty-nine cents a pound. Judy loved grilled cheese sandwiches made of Colby on Wonder Bread. It was one of her first solid foods.

Boneless ham was on special for forty-nine cents a pound, ice cream at seventy-nine cents for a half gallon, things he and Betty loved too. Too bad he couldn't take advantage of the sales and bring some home.

He perused the fall-guy wallet. Three pieces of plastic-laminated ID for him as Comrade V.I. Larrionov. An unknown amount of currency with Khrushchev's ugly mug on it—rubles, he thought they were called—and one-hundred-and-eighty-seven American dollars.

Miller was absolutely-positively sure that he, a Soviet assassin-suicide, was to be Comrade Larrionov. His true identity may eventually be revealed, but not before the war to end all wars.

He'd be vindicated by historians in the Twenty-first Century. Maybe. If there were historians then. Or anyone else.

Miller stuffed the dollars into his own wallet and opened the driver's door, to drop the wallet into the storm drain. After sticking the Russian funny money through the slots, he closed the door, deciding to keep the wallet for reasons he would never fully understand. He'd pack it in his suitcase before he turned in the rental car.

He listened to the radio until he reached the airport. The police were in pursuit of an unnamed suspect. Miller's assignment was probably still at the Trade Mart, stunned by the assassination like everyone else.

As Don Lester, he dropped off the car at the rental agency. As Larry Meyer, he flew Braniff Airlines to Tulsa. He chose names that were bland but not too bland, as he himself was.

At Tulsa, Phil Hayes checked the first departure board he came to, looking for a westward flight set to go soon, went to the Frontier desk, bought a ticket to Salt Lake, where Dan Jackson repeated the process to Denver, on a vibrating DC-4 as old as he was, then TWA to San Francisco, where Western Airlines flew Neil Johnson to his final destination in a shiny new Boeing 707jet—Seattle-Tacoma International Airport and his parked car.

The trip home had taken forever, but it was tedious ordeal versus increased risk. The man known by some as Fred Miller et al was not sloppy or careless.

He'd had a lot of time to think as he hopscotched home. When the 707touched down at Sea-Tac, he made up his mind. Once and for all. Even if they gave him a let-bygones-be-bygones pitch, blaming it on others, crossed signals, a mix-up, he was through.

As best as he could establish without sticking his nose into places where it might be chopped off, the outfit that assigned him jobs was a clearinghouse of sorts, with layers and firewalls between them and those who had quarrels with people they wanted eliminated.

Whoever had placed this order may have also hired Tweedledee and Tweedledum with their choppy English and the incriminating wallet. Fred Miller smiled, imagining those meatheads covering their privates with Harry's Hattery cowboy hats. Like burlesque dancers teasing the crowd.

Was it personal or had he been picked at random?

That he was to be the deceased patsy in a presidential assassination meant he was disposable too. Always had been. He knew that one day he'd be given his walking papers, but he didn't think they'd be served in such a spectacular fashion. When he outlived his usefulness, if they had their way, his gold watch would be a bullet to the head or a midnight swim wearing concrete water wings.

Knowing this day was inevitable, he had built so many protective layers. His clients had no idea who he was and where he lived, and didn't care so long as he performed. And he had.

Payment was made to post office boxes, scores of which he'd rented with a smorgasbord of names, in cities and towns within a four hundred mile radius of home, careful that he wasn't being watched when he picked up his money.

Said payments were in advance, except for this last one. They apologized—a suspiciously rare event—saying that the time squeeze made it impossible.

Made sense then, even more now. He seriously doubted if a thick envelope awaited Jerry Keith at a Pendleton, Oregon post office for today's job. He sure as hell wasn't going there to find out.

Betty was standing on the front porch when he pulled into the driveway of Seattle's Columbia City neighborhood. It was middle-class, predominantly white, though a few Negros were sticking a toe in from the Central Area where most of them lived. This was fine with him. Live and let live.

Fred Miller, the man who was known at home as Jonathon Smith, jumped the white picket fence and rushed into her arms. His wife was pert, blonde and youthful, a mien closer to class officer than cheerleader.

You would think she had been raised by loving parents in affluent suburbia. You would be wrong.

A friend once said that the family could model casual wear in a Sears catalog, another said that they were a match for the Cleaver family in *Leave it to Beaver*, house and all. It embarrassed the Smiths, but they knew the remarks weren't facetious.

"I've missed you so much," Elizabeth (Betty) Smith said. "You'd said you were going to Dallas. I was so worried after I heard the news."

"And I've missed you even more."

They went inside. Their brand-new Raytheon 21" TV was on, the sound turned low. It was time for *The Twilight Zone*, but Jonathon knew it wouldn't be on. That station and every other had preempted regular programming because of President Kennedy's assassination. Tomorrow was *Lawrence Welk*, their favorite. Miller hoped it wouldn't be bumped too.

"Isn't it horrible?" Betty said. "The Texas governor, John Connally, was in the limo in front of the Kennedys. One of the bullets passed by or through JFK and wounded Connally, but he's expected to recover.

I'm glad they caught the creep who did it. They got him in a movie theater right after he shot a Dallas policeman who stopped him outside it for questioning. At least they think it's him."

"Terrible," Jonathon Smith agreed. "You're sure Kennedy is dead."

"Walter Cronkite was on about three-thirty. He said the President was dead. If Mr. Cronkite says he's dead, he's dead. I will always remember where I was on this day."

"Me too. For many reasons," he said. "Judy's in bed?"

"She is and has been much of the day. The poor baby has a cough and a fever."

"The day I left, you said her throat was scratchy. Kids and colds."

"She's improving. All she's had today is chicken broth and baby aspirin."

This solidified his decision. Betty had been urging him to get out without being pushy.

He said, "I wish I'd been here for you and her."

"You have to make a living. She's very smart for her age, and asks where Daddy is when you're gone."

"She is one smart little cookie, that girl of ours."

"I tell her that you're away on business. She understands that you have to make money to pay for groceries and clothing and oil for the furnace. Not many kids her age do."

"You know," he said. "We've put away a little money."

"More than a little," Betty said grinning, as they cuddled on the couch. "Your ha-ha consulting business pays so well."

"Not this trip."

She looked at him. "They were paying triple, you said."

He said nothing.

"Them paying so much. You smelled a rat. Me too. Going to Dallas, were you caught in the middle somehow?"

Other than the city, it was his practice never to reveal a single detail when he left on a job. If it went sour and she was grilled afterward, Betty could honestly say she knew nothing about it. At times, upon completion of the job and it was especially gory or a close call, he also said little or nothing. Like the thief who had stolen from thieves, and the severed carotid mess he'd left.

He told Betty exactly what had happened in Dallas at the Trade Mart. Every minute detail.

"Oh my God. I was right to worry this time."

"I should've made excuses." He laughed. "Called in sick."

"We both know they aren't the type that tolerate excuses, "Judy said, "Those two Russians or whatever they are with the guns, do you think they'll spill the beans when they're nabbed?"

Jonathon replied, "They are in so much trouble by now with the Dallas police and whoever hired them, if they talk they're dead."

"Naked as jaybirds, if they were Negroes, they'd be lynched if they ran for it."

"No doubt."

"Remember that *Twilight Zone* episode?" she asked.

"Let me guess. Burgess Meredith starred. It was three or four years ago."

"That's the one," Betty said."Meredith played a bank teller. A real square and a bookworm with glasses as thick as magnifying glasses. One day he takes his lunch break in the bank vault. He comes out after an H-bomb wiped out all humanity. He stumbles around in the rubble and finds a library with thousands of books for him to read without being pestered. At the end, he trips and his glasses break. Every book in the world is at his disposal and he can't read a one."

He paused. "Apropos to my day. My very own *Twilight Zone* episode, except that I changed the script for the last act."

"Please say that this is really, really, really the end of it, dear."

Jonathon raised his right hand. "All right. I swear. I'm retired. Period. Not that I have a choice. If our savings are invested right, we should be okay. Shouldn't we? That's your department."

"We'll look at it in a moment, after you tell me one more time that you're done."

"Done, done, absolutely done. I need to be a family man and I'd like to participate in the community. Volunteer for this and that. Not right away, naturally, but after a safe interval."

"How long?"

"A year or— I don't know. We'll talk it over."

She nodded. "That would be good. Should we move, do you think? To another city or state?"

He thought for a minute and said, "No. We love it here, for one. Second, we'd be attracting attention if we pack up and move in a big hurry. Hiding in plain sight is a risk, but assuming the worst, that they've narrowed me down to a few cities, if they want to get me out of the picture, they'll be checking real estate activity. We have to think that they don't know who I am. I can't keep my head in a burrow if we're out digging a new one. And there's the government to think about too, investigating the assassination, covering all angles."

"Every word you said is logical," Betty said.

"This isn't an ordinary client of theirs either, wanting someone eliminated for love or money or power. Hitler and Stalin slaughtered people in increments, not in one fell swoop. These monsters, what the hell are they, who are they?"

"You threw a monkey wrench into a plan that's the work of a maniac. A demon who wants a war that will kill half the people in the world."

"The garden too. I miss working with the soil, watching things grow," he said, thinking that the "not right away, naturally" would end when he was satisfied they they'd given up hunting for him.

She smiled, moved onto his lap, and said, "That is so wonderful, dear. Even if it went well, I was worried that you'd be given another assignment and be gone next week for Thanksgiving. You've missed the last two. I was carrying Judy on the first one, big as a house."

"Cute then as ever."

"You're a wonderful husband and daddy, Judy's first words were 'da da'."

"An ordinary and loving family man and sociopath."

She gently cuffed his forehead. "Oh bosh. You're no sociopath. You're a man doing a job that has to be done. Name one of your assignments that wasn't a terrible person."

"I can't. Especially the first one I did for free."

"So there you are. You're doing a public service. If you didn't, someone else would. Or the assignment would be arrested, thrown in jail, and cost us taxpayers a fortune."

"We don't pay taxes."

"You know good and well what I mean, buster. Are you sure this is it?"

"Worry not and ask me as many time as you want. My retirement is official. All that's missing is a gold watch."

"This calls for a drink," she said, standing up and going into the kitchen.

It wouldn't be her first. Betty smelled of wine. But who was he to criticize? Him out on a high-wire act, a capital offense if caught by the law or if backfired, either way, and her not knowing if she'd ever see him again.

Her as an accessory too. Easily proven too after a thorough search of the tool shed. Judy in an orphanage—all too horrific to contemplate.

When he first had the opportunity to do what he did, they spent a couple of days hashing it out. Well into the night too.

The practical reasons. The risks and procedures to avoid undue risk. And last but not least, the morality of it:

Killing bad people for bad people doesn't necessarily make you a bad person, does it? Aren't you performing a public service?

They had spoken those words or close facsimiles not a few times. The entitlement of pay for killing a human being was a weak rationalization, but they didn't dwell on it.

"We've talked about a second child," she said, returning with two glasses, one with red wine for her, the other, bourbon, 7 Up and ice, for him, her glass fuller than his.

They clinked glasses.

"We have," he said.

She kissed his forehead. "If we have a boy, our own Cleaver family will be complete."

The *Leave It To Beaver* comparison amused the Smiths and they loved the show. They had lamented its cancellation. Its last episode was in September. In that time slot this season, they watched *McHale's Navy* and *My Three Sons*. They were entertaining, but it wasn't the same.

"It will be," he agreed.

"I forget. What was the Beaver's real name?"

He thought for a moment. "Theodore?"

"Theodore. That's right. Theodore Cleaver. A great name for a boy. Our boy. He'd grow up to be a prominent doctor or a lawyer or a scientist."

She said, "Who knows, he may become a Rhodes Scholar."

He replied, "Phi Beta Kappa for sure."

She said, "A brain surgeon. Or an engineer or scientist or chief executive of a big corporation. The sky's the limit."

She stopped, her eyes glassy. "President Kennedy promised that we'd have a man on the moon before the end of the decade."

"Theodore will be too young to design the rocket or make the trip. Mars, though, in forty or fifty years."

"Those canals on the planet," Betty said. "Are they real? I think not."

"Me too, along with the three-headed gondoliers," Jonathon said.

"They're saying that isn't so, none of it. Mars is like the moon. They're building a rocket that they'll send to find out. When you were last gone, I saw a story on TV. Mariner 4, it's called. It'll blast off next year and whiz by Mars taking pictures."

Sometimes when she was drinking, Jonathan thought, her conversation could veer off into orbit too.

He said, "I predict that Judy will be homecoming queen in high school. She'll have high grades and go to college too."

She added, "Community college and maybe even on to a four-year school. We'll start her on ballet lessons in a year or two."

He said, "A degree in teaching or nursing."

She said, "When grown up, she'll marry a prominent doctor or lawyer, with a fulfilling hobby like watercolor painting. She already draws well for her age. We'll get kits and supplies to encourage her."

He said, "Yeah, she'll be a volunteer who makes the society page in the paper. You got As and Bs in art, so your talent was passed on to her. She can do landscapes and flower arrangements. They'll sell like hotcakes at charity auctions."

"But that can't happen if you're gone in a terrible place making license plates waiting for them to hang you."

"I do like my neck the way it is."

"Me too," she said, stroking it. "Dear, will you bring the adding machine out here? It weighs a ton."

With both hands on its sides, Jonathon lugged it in from the spare bedroom closet and set it carefully on the coffee table. A hefty black device with a hand crank, it didn't weigh a ton, but it was a good ten pounds and awkward.

Betty went to the hall closet for bank statements hidden under loose floorboards and laid them out, side by side. Eight or nine or ten different banks under different names. He wasn't sure of the fine details as she handled business, every bit of it.

Entering each current balance with number keys a crank of the handle, she pulled off the tape, and handed it to him:65,775.81.

He whistled. "That's dollars?"

"Yes sir. And eighty-one cents."

"You're very, very good with money," he told her. "The bookkeeping classes you took in high school are really paying off."

"Money or no money, not to sound like a broken record, but Judy's getting older and she is extremely bright."

He nodded.

"If you kept going away on quote-unquote business, she'd be

wanting to know what kind of business. You work as a consultant, I was planning on telling her. Then I'd have to figure out how to explain what a consultant is."

He nodded again. "I mean it, kiddo, I am done. Finished. Retired."

"You know, an aeronautical engineer at Boeing makes as much as nine thousand dollars a year, a very comfortable living. We've saved over seven times that. If we didn't invest a dime, the principal and interest would let us live as well as they do for"—she paused—"ten or eleven years. I can explore investments to stretch out that amount. I have some ideas."

He said, "For certain. No turning back. No reason to. Never ever."

"Uh huh. We can't. Not after today. This wasn't just a contract they double-crossed you on, them and their phony-baloney triple pay."

"Don't I know."

"It's settled then."

Being repetitive, like she didn't believe him one-hundred-percent. He didn't blame her. She knew that besides the money, he got a charge out of the risks. Like a high-wire act at the circus. Today cured him of the derring-do bug, but only time would convince her.

"We'll give Judy and whoever else comes along the childhood we didn't have."

Her childhood in particular, he thought. "We will."

"I can't just putter around the house and yard waiting until the coast is clear," he said. "I'll go crazy if I don't do something else too."

"Go back to school. To college."

"I could. Yeah."

"I've been thinking for awhile. There are new kinds of businesses I can invest some of our money in, you know."

"Like?"

"Those big computer machines, they're coming out with. IBM and Univac and companies like that. This adding machine makes me think of them. They might become a big thing."

"Yeah, they might be. I've read about them."

She tapped the top of the adding machine and said, "They make computers now as small as two chest freezers. They're fully electrical and do calculations a thousand times as big as this thing will, automatically, a thousand times as fast, and they're improving by the day. You feed punch cards into them, push buttons, and the computer does the rest. It spits out sheets of paper with your answer. The government and all the major corporations use them now. While you're hitting the books, I'll dig into it. Computer jobs will multiply. Why, Judy could be a punch card operator if she doesn't want to go to college. Those gals make pretty good money."

"You're the expert," he said. "It's in your good hands."

She replied, "Take your time deciding what you want to do. I do like school as a possibility."

"Me too. After today, history will be on my mind. How one thing can alter it forever."

She held a thumb and forefinger an inch apart. "You came that close to making it, mister."

"Don't I know. I could graduate with a degree and teach it. With a passion."

"I like that. I like that a whole lot."

"I'll send away for college catalogs"

"Oh, by the way," she said. "I've had my eye on a new fire-engine-red Chevy Impala. I saw an ad in a magazine."

"We can afford to splurge, but wait until next year, hon. We can't have all eyes on us. Not right away. A hot chick like you behind the wheel, yabba dabba doo."

She tickled him in various places.

"I'll plant a garden this spring and start college in the fall. I do miss getting my hands dirty," he said, immediately regretting the wording.

"Judy would love to help you."

"I'd love her help."

She smiled, moved onto his lap again, and said, "It's past our bedtime."

4

After a pleasurable effort to plant the seed of Judy's sibling, an attempt that unknown to them had proven to be successful, the now-retired professional assassin slipped out of bed and out the back door with a transistor radio and a pack of cigarettes.

Jonathon did not smoke in the house. Experts were saying cigarettes might be bad for one's health. He smoked the same brand as the Marlboro Man, who by the looks of him was doing just fine. But smoke made Betty's eyes water and made Judy sneeze, so outside it was, even in the winter, freezing his butt off. He considered quitting. He'd tried before and failed, the end result a nicotine fit. It was no fun at all, but the next time he'd make it work. If Betty got pregnant, he promised himself he'd quit for sure.

It was a cool evening, but not so chilly that he could see his breath, so he lit up by his workshop rather than going inside it. He thought of the Browning .25 automatic he kept in a workbench drawer, part of his arsenal. He had used it for nine assignments, including the union boss.

It was a baby pistol, a deadly toy of a gun, but he'd start carrying it, just for peace of mind, just in case they were overly optimistic about being home free. Betty had encouraged him to, day and night, just to be on the safe side.

Bless her, she'd named it Baby, as the Browning brothers had when they designed the weapon. Thinking about the tiny pistol, he had an idea for Betty's next birthday present.

Jonathon turned on the radio, keeping the volume low, the speaker close to an ear. There was only one story.

Nothing made complete sense yet, but the pieces were coming together. Dallas was full of Kennedy-hating rednecks and everyone had a houseful of guns. Half the town ached to empty a clip into the head of the com symp rich-boy President with the Ivy League hair and beautiful wife.

Who did JFK think he was, they were thinking? He was gracing their fair city and others like Fort Worth for one reason and one reason alone—hoping he'd carry Texas in the 1964 election.

Funny thing was, they had arrested a suspect who was nothing like his image of a Texan. The guy had assassinated JFK while the motorcade was on its way to the Dallas Trade Mart, shooting down from an upper floor of a building that stored schoolbooks. While on the lam, as the TV reporter said, he had killed a Dallas cop too, and was captured near that shooting, inside a movie theatre.

Jonathon Smith heard the name "Oswald," but didn't catch whether it was his first or last. There was an unconfirmed report that this Oswald had lived in the Soviet Union, had a Russian wife, and worshipped Fidel Castro. The opposite in every way to a Texas redneck.

Screwy.

Jonathon looked upward. He saw stars between patches of thin clouds. Dallas had been partly cloudy too, though somewhat warmer.

What if their plan had worked? Whoever they were.

What sort of sky would there be in a week or so?

And if the desired ending was a nuclear shitstorm, who profited? If you collect a billion dollars for the caper, you can't spend it in Antarctica.

He flicked his cigarette into the alley, thinking that the world was upside down and sideways.

5

Jonathon and Elizabeth (Betty) Smith were having a far more enjoyable day than Mother Hen.

She was back in her motel room, seated stiffly at the edge of her bed, doing as she was told—waiting. *Exactly* as she'd been told. God knows, the AWOL Chicks were not *her* fault. She had told Mr. C the Younger this, tapping her watch crystal, telling him how long she hung around the Dallas Trade Mart, not leaving until all the hullabaloo, when she was absolutely sure they weren't returning.

He seemed to understand. Seemed to. He had listened without interruption and calmly told her to go to her room and wait.

Mother Hen occupied half of a two-bedroom unit, a "suite" the rat-faced desk clerk had said, an unintentional joke on his part. The sad excuse for a suite was in the rear of a U-shaped motor court closer to Fort Worth than Dallas. She'd lived in better, she'd lived in worse.

The parking slots out front were a third full. In the center of the lot was a "park," as the clerk called it, a scrubby rectangle with picnic tables composed of rotting planks.

She had been instructed by Mr. C the Younger to rent it for a week as Debra Davis Johnson, paying in advance, but advised her that she probably wouldn't be staying that long. Upon arrival from Lawton, Oklahoma, he had given her a generous wad of cash, so money wasn't a problem.

The Chicks had one room in the suite, her the other. Mother Hen-Debra Davis Johnson had kept the adjoining door locked, latching the chain too, a precaution in the event her Chicks wanted to play around with a biddy. They were very strange young men, flat-faced and mute. She could not imagine their tastes in that regard, for sure depraved. They had no names and she had too many.

She had overheard them whispering to each other in an evil, godless, communistic language like Polack. She didn't understand a word, but she knew what she was hearing and plugged her ears, as she habitually did as a barrier to overheard filth of any nature. The Chicks hadn't said five words to Mother Hen, essentially Neanderthal grunts. Fine with her. Besides locking and latching her door last night, she'd shoved the dresser against it, and didn't hear a peep thereafter.

She was no imbecile, so she had a very good idea after listening to clicking sounds that they doing something with firearms. Playing with them was more accurate. As if playing with themselves judging by the hungry looks on their faces when they got into the car this morning carrying a zippered nag and wearing jackets with bulges in them.

Mr. C the Younger had given her instructions. Drive them to the Dallas Trade Mart. Drop them off, pick them up, nothing more, nothing less. Aside from that, the trip was none of her concern. He had issued his orders with his empty nothing of a stare again. The man was not the sympathetic sweetheart who had scooped her up in Lawton.

She had been sitting and waiting for an hour or two after her return from the fiasco when Mr. C. the Elder walked in without even knocking. He was in his forties, her age, big and strong and ruggedly handsome in a creepy context, dark hair slicked back and a crooked sneer where a smile should have been. His eyes saw nothing and everything.

He locked the door and asked her if she minded doing the dirty deed. Just like that. Well, she didn't mind, not at all, and slid backward on the bed. Yes, she was a lady, but a lady with normal urges and desires.

However, foreplay to him was shoving her down flat on her back, and taking down his pants. He tore off her best pink panties, pounced on her, and used his thing in her like a battering ram. As he thrusted violently, she told herself that she was being well paid. She did enjoy a little pain when they got frisky, but he was taking it too far.

While Mr. C the Elder was on top of her, huffing and puffing and grunting, lifting her off the bed, he was in essence reminding her that he owned her, the whole kit and caboodle. He had the right to do what he wanted, when and how he wanted to.

"Need me to clarify ownership?" Mr. C asked as he rolled off her without so much as a peck on the cheek, pulling up and fastening his trousers before his feet hit the floor.

"Oh no, sir. I understand."

"I'll do it anyway if you don't mind," Mr. C the Elder said. "When you read, memorized, and consumed our mission statement, you became one of us."

"Oh, yes sir," she said, sitting up, primly fluffing up her hair.

Of course, it was all irrelevant now. She was not going to be sharing the "suite" with the Chicks. They had fallen out of their nest before they could spread their wings. And nothing else had gone as it should have.

It was obvious why they'd recruited her out of nowhere. If things went terribly wrong, as they apparently had, she, a virtual stranger, would be holding the bag, so unfairly blamed. The story of her life.

Headed back here from the Dallas Trade Mart, all by her lonesome, every station on the car radio told the tale. Gun shots from a tall building. The president murdered. Putting two and two together, she understood what the sirens and the speeding limousine were about. The Chicks had to be players in some regard and she was in a pickle that was not her doing.

Mr. C the Elder said, "You stay the fuck in this room until you're told otherwise. Meals will be brought to you. Don't you fucking think of setting foot out the door. Got it?"

"Yes sir."

"When you do go, nothing happened today. Nothing."

"Yes sir."

"We may have some new identification for you in case we need you again."

All her married names, now names and nicknames not hers. So confusing.

"Yes sir."

Mr. C the Elder stormed out and slammed the door behind him so hard that a cheesy landscape print hanging on the adjoining wall fell, setting off a puff of dust.

He was in a big tizzy, unlike normal men who were angry when they were denied the treasure between her legs, not when they weren't. In her opinion, use of the F-word in the company of a lady was highly rude and disrespectful too.

He was a horrid, horrid man.

Sore and stinging in her private area, Mother Hen got up gingerly, put on her panties, and peeped between the curtains.

Mr. C the Elder's right-out-of-the-showroom Cadillac was a twin of Younger's, the 1964 model, metallic blue with subtle tailfins, and a mile long.

When he wasn't pacing around the lot with clenched jaw and fists, he was inside the Caddy listening to a shortwave radio he had turned up loud.

Even in her room, she could hear snippets. The police frequency, it sounded like.

Mr. C the Elder grabbed a handful of gravel and flung it. Rocks pinged off parked cars.

"It's all ruined. That shooter ruined everything. Everything's ruined. We have to start over. It's all fucking shot to shit."

Mr. C the Younger said, "I checked at the hospital ten minutes ago. Sharon's in labor. I thought you'd like to know."

"Don't bother me with petty shit, boy. It's ruined," said his father. "Tell me, what's this Texas School Book Depository have to do with anything?"

"It's a seven-story brick building. Not far from the Trade Mart. Someone on the news said the guy worked there. They're trying to dope out what—"

"Where is he? Do you think?"

"The shooter?"

"I don't give a flying fuck about that shooter. They have that asshole in jail. Nabbed him in some movie theatre. I mean the guy we set up."

"No sign of him."

"I should've had my head examined letting the fucking gorillas pick those two retards and the hit man. The guy who must've been trailing the hit man too."

"We were careful not to let anyone know."

"Those fucking Chinamen, they have their ways to avoid paying. They're behind it."

"All three. Gone to who knows where."

"He did the morons before they could do him. That's the only thing I can—"

"There's been nothing on the news."

"There hasn't been, not they we've heard."

"We have to find him," Mr. C the Elder said. "He was tipped off. He was paid to fuck us over. Had to be."

"The guys who provided him to us, they claim they don't know anything about him."

"The lying motherfuckers, they vouched for him, swore by him. Said they used him a lot of times. They vouched for those retards too. What a fucking joke."

"Being in that business, they aren't decent citizens, none of them. We know that."

"They'd peddle their grandmothers' asses to syphilitic midgets."

Mr. C the Younger shrugged. "He could've gotten the drop on the monkeys. They said he was the best they had."

Mr. C the Elder kicked a Cadillac door so hard he left a small dent. Mother Hen flinched.

"He won't talk. I don't think he will. Wherever he is. He won't if he knows what's good for him. He'll have it figured out and hide."

"That fat fucking Chinaman," Mr. C the Elder screamed.

"Those Orientals, they are shifty."

"The slant-eyed cocksucker, everything I did for him during the war. He was short on tungsten, I got him tungsten. He was short on tin. The Japs controlled the tin, but I got him tin. I could've gotten twenty years if I'd been caught. We looked each other in the eye and all the time he was lying through his teeth."

"He got cold feet and this was how he backed out. Or he got a better offer."

"Him and his stupid fucking quotes. 'Imperialism will not last long because it always does evil things'. He treated me to that one in person, him and his gold, the hypocritical motherfucker."

"Sharon—"

"Okay, okay, Sharon. She's due. A good omen."

"An omen?"

"Think about it. This date. Like the day I was born."

"If she has it before midnight."

"Make sure she does. Have them cut her open. A caesarian."

"Good idea. I'll get on over there."

"We have so much money invested in this, we're in a bind. I'd like to cut off that fat gook's wart with pruning shears."

Mr. C the Younger said, "The gold is still there waiting for us in Zurich. Ten-million bucks worth. We'll have other chances."

"Unless somebody beats us to the punch. We can't let that happen. Ever."

"The guy who nailed Kennedy from the book place, he's in on it?"

"Has to be. The Chinamen, the sneaky slopehead, they had him hit Kennedy to be sure we were left out in the cold."

They began walking away, so she heard no more.

Where do I fit in now, Mother Hen wondered? Was she going to be the scapegoat? Her essentially a prisoner. And where did his mysterious fat Chinaman of theirs come in? The Chinamen she had seen were in chop suey restaurants and they were beanpoles.

Until she was plucked out of thin air in Lawton, she was down to her last hundred bucks, about to be evicted from an apartment that made this dump look like the Ritz. She had rotten ex-husbands, no children or close relatives or friends. She hadn't a pot or a window.

They knew this, didn't they? Mr. C the Younger hadn't picked her at random.

Like they say in the movies, *You know too much.*

Mother Hen ran to the bathroom before she peed her blood-speckled panties.

NOW

6

"**M**r. Jonathon Smith, I presume."

Jonathon Smith, age eighty-two, held his hose nozzle like a pistol and said, "I've been expecting you. You're running late, boy."

The man in the alley reminded Jonathon Smith of himself when he was that age, roughly forty. Clean-cut, bright-eyed, fit. Dressed like he was on the golf course, he could be a physician or an Army major.

Momentarily taken aback, the man in the alley said, "Well, the line at the rental car counter was long."

The old man laughed. "No, no. I mean fifty-plus years late. In excess of half a century."

"Uh, you've been out here watering plastic flowers," he said, surprised and then some.

"Ever since I began seeing you near sundown, cruising by in different rental cars, new but cheap base models. Dull colors. Walking on the sidewalks, in the alley, coming from different directions. That dog you were walking so you wouldn't appear suspicious, where is it?"

"Back where it came from."

"You rented it?"

"No, not exactly. I had it on approval from a pet shop, to see if it got along with my other pets. I asked for a mongrel nobody would remember. The purebreds and the hyperactive little muffy dogs, they wouldn't have let one out of the shop, and they were too yippy-yappy anyway. They were happy to be rid of the mutt."

"A Heinz 57. To answer your next question, I can water plastic flowers for as long and often as I want without drenching them or overwatering the root systems they don't have. My vegetable garden back by the fence, not so. Even the pole beans and tomatoes, they'd have root rot before you know it."

"How do you know who I am? What I am? Who and what you think I am?"

"I didn't know for certain, but I thought I did."

"How?"

"Your persistence. You looking at every house but ours."

"I was that obvious?"

"You were. You are."

"I'll have to work on my technique."

"You do this regularly?"

"I could be a new neighbor, a block or two over, you know."

"You aren't. We've lived here for ages, as you may know. We know everybody in a two-block radius in person or by sight, even the newbies."

"You do think you know who I am?"

"Who you represent. A sense of who you're beholden to."

"A sixth sense?"he asked.

"Call it what you like. Do you have a name?"

"My real name?"

"You'd be a fool to give it to me and I doubt if you're a fool."

"Will Robin work?"

"First name or last?"

"You pick."

"Robin it is. Would you like to come in for coffee, Robin? A drink?"

"That's kind of you, Jonathon, but I'd disturb Betty. Early to bed, late to rise. At her age, eighty-one years young, an octogenarian like yourself, and a functioning alcoholic to boot. I sincerely admire that in a senior. One DUI, seven years ago, where she hopped a sidewalk, ran over a parking meter, and nosed into a display of men's clothing. The old senior-citizen ploy of a sticky gas pedal didn't fly. She blew a point-one-seven. Your daughter's law firm bulldozed the charge through court to a not-guilty. It was like OJ's dream team in action."

Jonathon Smith looked at him.

"I do my homework. In the olden days, on the job, you did yours too, did it well."

Jonathon wasn't born and raised in the Pacific Northwest, but the Seattle coffee gene had attached itself due to his long residence here. Even though it had been unseasonably warm for late-June, a cup of hot java would hit the spot.

"There's a coffee shop four blocks from here. It's not the megabrand. This place, their coffee is better. Cheaper too."

Robin said, "I'm game."

They walked out of the alley to Rainier Avenue and an intersecting street. Along with the neighborhood, the businesses along Rainier had gentrified, although not yet to overpriced cutesiness. In the shops and cafés and bars, you received good value for your money.

The inside was as usual crowded, but not so crowded that they couldn't find a table that afforded privacy if they kept their voices down. There were no kids on laptops, wearing headphones. Jonathon Smith exchanged nods and hellos with several patrons, acquaintances whose names he didn't recall.

They ordered at the counter, a medium Americano and blueberry muffin for each, and took a corner table.

"Witnesses," Robin said. "Clever of you."

"Witnesses to what?"

"Just an expression. Please don't make something out of it."

"They're friends and casual acquaintances and strangers, mostly the latter two. I'm a homebody. As you know."

Robin said, "It doesn't appear to be a younger crowd, with their mandatory tablets and laptops and smarty-pants phones."

"The owner was sick and tired of them nursing a latte while taking up one of his seats and tables as a home office. He shut off his Wi-Fi when they outnumbered real customers. They've taken the hint."

"Smart," Robin said.

"I have to admit that my familiarity with locals is lessening. The real estate market is wild. People are selling, making a bundle. People who can't afford to live closer to downtown are buying hereabouts."

"You're talkative, Jonathon. Does that come from all those years standing up in front of high school kids?"

Jonathon Smith didn't reply.

Robin raised his cup in toast. "You and I are probably the only ones in this coffee house who drink straight coffees. These frappru-cappu-whipped cream concoctions. If I want a milkshake, I'll go to the Dairy Queen."

Jonathon didn't raise his cup. "I don't suppose you'll tell me who hired you."

"Even if I knew, it'd be highly unprofessional. Oh, I met the boss briefly, the gentleman who hired me, the patriarch of the current generation of a family concern. Beyond that—"

He lifted a shoulder.

"Layers?" Jonathon Smith said. "Layers and firewalls?"

"Good for all parties, especially us. You know that, don't you? You had the technique nailed. *Perfecto.* Some things are immutable."

They sipped their coffee. Jonathon Smith left his muffin untouched, but Robin finished his in three bites.

"You know, Jonathon, once they zeroed in on you, I did my own research. It wasn't encouraged but I am a curious sort. Until early-1964, as far as I could tell, Mr. and Mrs. Jonathon Smith didn't exist. You were born as adults in your twenties with one child and another on the way. As if you'd materialized from a spaceship. Is that your actual name?"

"Back to names again. Is Robin yours?"

Robin smiled.

"I was known to some as Fred Miller back then, but you know that."

"I do. You have to do your homework, now as then. The only difference is the technology," Robin said.

"They are persistent. After all these years. How long have they known who and where I am?"

Another lifted shoulder. "A while. I had the impression they were on top of things."

"Why now, after all these years?"

"Please, Jonathon, my visit isn't ominous. They want their records brought up to date. That is all."

"Records?"

"What people from their past are up to. Why at this time they sent me to you, they didn't say. Trust me, sir, it's only a bureaucratic deal. Ducks in a row."

Jonathon said nothing, resisting the temptation to tell Robin that his nose was growing.

"*After all those years* being in that nineteen-sixties era, you're saying. You've been a solid citizen ever since you emerged from the womb in your twenties as Jonathon Smith."

Jonathon took a risk, hoping to shed light on this visit, to give him a chance to plan a move. "Would you like to hear a story? You may or may not know. It pertains to a November day in Dallas, nineteen-sixty-three."

"I know in summary only, and rumors and wild tales and a hint of long-standing frustrations and anger. I'm listening."

Jonathon Smith spoke in detail of his adventure on November 22, 1963 in Dallas.

Robin grew flushed. "Goodness. Well, that clarifies many things. You sure spoiled somebody's fun."

"I did. Your father's or grandfather's too. If they came from, say, Leningrad. There's no family resemblance, but maybe you were adopted"

"No, no. Not me. Those two inept rascals with the Russian rifle. Nobody in my family tree. Honestly, Jonathon, I'm just a hired hand, a working stiff."

"Hired to do what?"

"Please believe me, my instructions were to check you out, to ascertain that you were living your new life to the fullest, with no intention of ever stirring up the past. Believe me, that's it, the bottom line. Updating records."

"Your bosses aren't cooking something up, are they?"

"Not to the best of my knowledge. I detected no urgency, no instructions other than what I've told you. In all candor."

Robin seemed to be working too hard at making sincere, gee-whiz eye contact.

Jonathon said, "This may sound strange, but Lee Harvey Oswald saved my life. The president being late, raising my suspicions, my paranoia, putting me on alert for shenanigans."

"I believe you. It makes perfect sense and it's probably no exaggeration that you prevented World War Three. The prelude to Armageddon, which by definition is the final and conclusive battle between the forces of good and evil. In the real world, I'd say it's evil versus evil. If you're launching nukes, you cannot be pristine."

"Much to the dismay of your employers and their forebears?"

Robin didn't answer.

"It that was their mission, it was beyond sick."

Again, Robin remained silent.

"I have to ask again. Why are you here, Robin? Over half a century later. I was upfront with you. Is something in the works? You here cleaning up loose ends?"

"Between you and me and the gatepost, you deserve to be in the history books, Jonathon. You should have been teaching those kids about yourself. A Nobel Peace Prize laureate. Accolades from here, there and everywhere."

"Anonymity is okay by me. I knew when I tiptoed out of Harry's Hattery that I'd annoyed somebody. Severely"

Robin furrowed his brow. "You may've saved the world as you were saving yourself. Understandable"

Jonathon Smith said, "The older gent in the next to last row at the Dallas Trade Mart, was he picked at random so I wouldn't suspect the real reason why I was there?"

Robin said, "As you explained everything, yes, I'd say it was a strong possibility he was, an easy target for an expert marksman like yourself. Here again, I'm just an ordinary guy on a payroll. I'm not privy to the inside dope, but I do thank you for enlightening me."

"I wasn't anonymous enough. Obviously."

Robin sipped his coffee and scavenged crumbs from his plate.

"Know what I think, Robin? You know the answer to that and everything else I've told you."

Robin answered with a question. "How many, um, completions before you retired?"

"Presuming I did what you do for a living?"

Robin smiled. "Lots of hypotheticals laid out today."

Jonathon Smith said, "I was candid with you."

"Okay, quid pro quo. You first."

"Sixteen for pay, the seventeenth not. The eighteenth in Dallas, as I explained, I whiffed on it."

"Care to elaborate or the earlier ones?"

"No point in it, is there?"

"I'd love to hear, even the pro bono hit. Now, that might be intriguing."

"How about yourself? Care to recite your résumé?"

"At the risk of sounding nebulous, no, except to say that I'm opposed to the taking of a human life, so please stop worrying. How I was recruited is troubling, though. I'm a field agent with an indefinite future. I envy you, and all your happy and productive years."

"Go on," Jonathon Smith said. "Let's hear your story."

Robin leaned back, stretched and said, "Are you a spiritual person, Jonathon?"

"Not lately. You?"

"Oh yes. Past tense. Once upon a time, I was a Protestant minister, hard-shell through and through. Fire and brimstone. The apocalypse, Armageddon. The upcoming end of the world, the Rapture. Bad times await the heathen, the nonbeliever. Us believers, we were smug, as eager for the hell-bound as our eternal paradise. Schadenfreude came to mind as I preached what they wanted to hear."

"Schadenfreude. Taking pleasure in the woes of others," Jonathon said.

"You and I know the word. My congregation didn't, as well as the definition of many other words. I operated barely in an environment one intellectual level above the Holy Rollers."

"My sister-in-law is in one of those, some cult or another. The Rapture and the rest of it."

"I was defrocked. Know why?"

See if we can get a rise out of him, Jonathon thought; see if he'll blow his top, and attract some attention. "Exposing yourself to eight-year-old boys?"

No dice. Robin shook his head slowly and calmly.

"We were having such a proper, gentlemanly conversation, Jonathon. Then you have to spoil it. I am in a forgiving mood, though, as you spared us Armageddon on that fateful day. I wouldn't even be here or anywhere else if you hadn't."

"Go on with your story. I won't interrupt again unless I do."

"I'll accept that as an apology. To continue, my faith was gradually seeping away. My ministry, my dogma, was feeling—forgive me, Lord—science fictional, a complete fantasy.

"I had become two-faced to my congregation and to the Lord, and not solely for the diminishment of my faith. I was drinking and fornicating like a madman.

"Well, one fine Sunday morning, a bee flew into my bonnet. I stood before my flock, melodramatically flung aside my sermon notes, scattering them at and above the choir, and stated what I believed earlier and what I believed then."

Robin drew in a deep breath and said, "Religion, this religion, and most others, exist simply because *we cannot accept the finality of death.* Your God, his earthly son, the rest of it, they're no more bona fide than the security blankets we cuddled with as children."

Jonathon smiled. "As far as I'm concerned, you hit the nail on the head. I'll bet it went over well."

"If I may be permitted a vulgarity, it went over like a turd in a punch bowl. After a moment of apoplexy, they began filing out. Singly, then in couples, then entire rows, accompanied by hurt, angry stares and a few unChristian shouts. On Wednesday, my superiors paid me a visit and I was *gone.* My tight-assed wife too. Two days later, I received a divorce summons."

"A busy week."

"None of it was my fault."

"Really?"

"Really. I can accurately blame my childhood. My father was a drunken, whoring, alcoholic, abusive fundamentalist preacher who regularly laid into us with his belt. Any slight whatsoever after he stumbled through the door and he'd say *vengeance is mine Sayeth the Lord* as he unbuckled. I have the scars to prove it. The congregation should have known better than to hire someone in that gene pool, but they got me cheap. Me, a chip off the old block."

Jonathon's instinct was to offer condolences, but he didn't care, wasn't sorry for Robin, even if the story was true. He was inclined to believe it was, but Jonathon had his own considerable problems.

A pro would have taken him out without the surveillance or this coffee and muffin interlude. Wham bam. No muss, no fuss, no chitchat. He didn't know who gave him jobs when he was in the trade, didn't want to know. Robin was different. He didn't take orders from no-necks. But from whom?

In one breath, Robin was hinting he was the Grim Reaper, in the next a messenger boy, and a newfound buddy. Keeping me off-balance, Jonathon thought. A trick learned in preacher school to draw his flock in, on the edge of their seats, waiting for the punch line, their ticket to the Pearly gates.

Jonathon finished his coffee and muffin.

"My present employers visited before the end of the next week and recruited me. How they knew of my plight is anyone's guess."

"Convenient."

"It was," Robin said. "Please. Your pro bono hit? Practice? A grudge settled?"

"Leave it be, Robin."

"I give up. But as I'd said, technology. In your day, doing what you did, it was rudimentary. Hands-on and mechanical."

Jonathon looked at him. "Tale of two assassins, you and I paraphrasing Dickens. I doubt that he'd approve."

"You've done well in the intervening years, Jonathon. Comfortable, but not overtly wealthy, not ostentatious. You didn't move out of the middle class and attract attention. In 1968, you graduated from college. Why did you wait a year to start after you retired? You must've been terribly bored. Wait, let me guess. You'd been hiding in plain sight and wanted a year to pass to be confident you were in the clear."

Jonathon Smith sipped from his empty cup.

"You're a retired high school history teacher. Your special interest was war. And who could blame you. You designed a course, Warfare Through the Ages, and won awards for it. You were cautionary without being didactic. Santayana's famous quote, how does it go?"

"Those who do not remember the past are condemned to repeat it," Jonathon answered.

"You created a generation of pacifists, a wonderful legacy."

"An exaggeration."

"You volunteer in the community, teaching ESL at the senior center. You and Betty raised two lovely children. Judy, a highly-impressive overachiever who rules a powerful and allegedly shady law firm empire. Driven, she is."

"Where do you get off calling her shady?"

"Allegedly, that loveliest of all lawyer words. It's what we hear. And your son, Theodore, a painter. Abstract expressionism for a time. Abandoned in favor of a passion for Edward Hopper, a genre in its own right.

"Theodore Cleaver Smith, a chaser of artistic trends in his younger days, but too late, too mediocre. A boy with the ability to master engineering or pre-law or pre-med in college, dashing your dreams for him when he didn't. A boy who studied fine arts before dropping out. So sad."

Jonathon said nothing.

"Your children rebelled against your expectations for them, reversing their mandated roles. Not unusual, but extreme."

"I trust that you have no plans for my family, Mr. Robin. If you do, I'm going to throw a tantrum. Right here and now. That will be the end of it for you."

Robin displayed his palms. "No, no. I don't pester anybody I'm not paid to pester."

From updating of records to pestering. Touching his pants pocket with his left hand, Jonathon nodded.

"Oh, if you do make a fuss and I'm arrested or detained, you'll not be able to say why the bother, will you?"

Jonathon stared at him, a statue.

"Very well. Cards on the table. They'll be miffed and send somebody else. They won't be harmless interviewers like me. You know they won't. You won't know where or when. You're not young and the anxiety will age you. Prematurely, if that's not an oxymoron. An odd choice of wording, all things considered, but there you are. And if they choose to act while you're not alone, say with your family, well, who can say?"

"Why now? You've known about me for a long, long while, haven't you?"

"I, myself, have not known. Not until I was given my marching orders. They tell me to go, brief me, and I go. Let's say they've had a file on you. For whatever reason, they believe the time is right to ask you to keep your head down and mouth shut. That is the gist of my message."

"This is becoming a circular, zigzag, repetitive conversation, you know."

"That's an overstatement, Jonathon."

"Are they ideologues of any stripe, with strong political views?"

"Doubtfully."

"Back then, I thought it was all about money. It took money to set things up, an investment. Luxurious retirement somewhere out of the way of a nuclear winter."

"There you are," Robin said. "I agree. Deep pockets desiring to be deeper. The timing is important to them for motivations unknown to me. A stab in the dark, though, I'm thinking there's a golden goose yet unclaimed."

"I'm an old man, no threat to anyone or anything but aphids on my plastic roses."

"As you inquired, you may be a loose end," Robin said. "That's in their thinking, I suppose. They'll be glad we had this friendly chat. I'll give a glowing report on your cooperation."

"You plan well, Robin. All contingencies."

"You've lived a good, long life, Jonathon. What's the average lifespan for the American male now? Seventy-seven or thereabouts. You've beaten the numbers. Because you've fallen in line, you'll live many more happy years."

"I feel a whole lot better. Where does homicide rank in cause of death?"

"Odd that you should ask, albeit irrelevant and, frankly, insulting and needlessly morbid. Number fifteen in this country," Robin said. "I looked it up. But, heck, as the clichés go, we all have to go sometime and nothing lasts forever. Five billion years from now, the sun will enter a red-giant phase and we'll be fried to a crisp. Unless we've left, emigrated, and are on another world orbiting an Alpha Centauri star or wherever."

Thinking, puzzling, formulating what to do, Jonathon Smith glanced at his watch.

"It's been interesting, Robin, but it's late and if Betty wakes up and I'm gone, she'll worry."

They stood and Robin said, "It's dark now. I'll walk you home."

Jonathon replied, "Thanks, but I know the way."

"No trouble," Robin said. "Really. This isn't an insult, Jonathon, but you oldsters tend to fall in the dark. The pavement in this old neighborhood is uneven. Even senior citizens as spry as you are. That's a known fact. Invariably, you break a hip. Why a hip? They're light on calcium and brittle, or you land that way? Who knows? I don't."

Jonathon decided to play along, let the son of a bitch think he'd caved in. Accepted his fate. But at age eighty-two or even age one-eighty-two, he'd be goddamned if he give up without a fight. The old college try.

He had Betty to think about too. A few years back, looking ahead to an eventuality such as this, he'd probed her about selling the house, buying an RV, and hitting the open road, seeing the country. Before they were too old.

She'd been noncommittal as she was about many things.

"Okay. Sure. What the hell."

As they walked out, he let his left hand brush his pocket, against Baby. Never leave home without it: Betty had insisted. He didn't. Baby was as imprinted in his wardrobe as his drawers.

"When are you going back to Dallas?"

"I apologize if I've led you astray. I've never been to Dallas. You couldn't make me go there this time of the year. It's one-ten in the shade and there isn't any shade."

"So where do you turn in your glowing report about me? Having updated the records."

"I'm told that they're pop-up."

"Pop-up?"

"Here and there, temporarily. Pop-ups, like restaurants you see on those cooking shows, Jonathon, setting up where practicable. We go where we have to go. No addresses, no roots."

"It's *we* now, not *they*."

"Plural pronouns. They're very often confused."

"Pop-up. You've popped up in Seattle for how long, you and they?"

"I'd only have to fib."

Entering the alley, Jonathon Smith thought of begging Robin not to do it in the face, distracting him while he was drawing Baby. But Robin had slowed and had slipped behind him.

"Jonathon."

Jonathon turned and saw Robin's outstretched hand, as if to shake his.

"This is where we part company. It's been a pleasure."

Jonathon Smith did not take Robin's hand. He reached into his pocket to withdraw his .25 caliber "Baby" Browning Automatic Pistol with the hollowed-out slugs. But before he could raise it level to Robin's chest, he felt a sting in his other wrist.

"Jonathon, I want you to know it isn't personal, and I do feel terrible. Everybody has a conscience at some level, even a sociopath."

He then saw the tiny syringe that Robin was withdrawing. He saw and felt little after that, as Robin gently moved him backward and seated him in the lawn chair by Tony and Bev Horton's single-car garage. Bev made Tony sit out there when he smoked.

It was where Jonathon Smith had planned to seat Robin after the .25 round had mushroomed and shredded his heart.

Robin had taken Baby from him. "Shame on you, Jonathon. I thought we were friends."

Jonathon Smith looked at him, seeing nothing.

"There there, Jonathon. If you believe in God, I'm so sorry, God doesn't love you. If you believe in Jesus, Jesus is in step with his mythical father. Nonetheless, Armageddon may be on the horizon, though not the Biblical version. Give thanks that you won't be around to experience it.

"No deity forgives you for your sins, but Mr. C the Three and Mr. C the Deuce forgive you now that you're dying. You and your family have embittered Mr. C the Deuce for reasons unknown to me. Please accept my apologies. I did what I had to do," Robin said, adjusting him gently and closing his eyes, careful to position him upright. "There, there."

There, there.

The last words Jonathon Smith heard.

7

The Saturday following his death and two days after his cremation, friends and family said goodbye to Jonathon Smith at the local senior center, where he had volunteered, teaching ESL to over-fifty immigrants.

Dad's will hadn't been read, but in a cover sheet he had requested that any final words be secular, comments and arrangements at the discretion of his loved ones. Anyone in attendance who deviated and offered a prayer or the ubiquitous 23rd Psalm would be haunted. A dollop of levity from beyond the grave.

Some wrinkly-faced people were offended, but I liked it. Liked it a lot, Dad at his finest.

It was SRO. Roughly one hundred and fifty people were seated on folding chairs in the social hall, twenty to twenty-five more standing against the back and side walls. He'd been well-liked and well-loved.

Elizabeth (Betty) Smith sat in the front row, flanked by her children, Judith Ann (professionally, Judy to family and friends) Smith and yours truly, Theodore Cleaver (Call Me Theo, but *please* not Theodore or Beaver or The Beav) Smith. We held hands throughout.

My girlfriend, Quetzal Adams, love of my life for real this time, was in the Midwest, visiting her parents, a trip arranged weeks ago. My mind drifted to Quetzal, as it did much of every day. Her father, the Reverend Adams, was an alcoholic fundamentalist-Christian missionary who had gone to Yucatán Mexico to do "language studies," the bullshit buzz phrase given to the practice of making nuisances of themselves, preaching the True Word of God to the savages in haranguing English, which few understood or cared to understand.

Somehow, while overstaying his welcome in a remote village by the ancient ruin of Cobá and given the green light by the Lord (?), he had impregnated Quetzal's mother, a strong woman with the ancient Maya profile seen on limestone glyphs.

To spite him, we think, she had insisted over his ranting objections that the child be named after the Toltec and Aztec false God of "wind and learning," Quetzalcoatl. A feathered serpent, no less. The Mayan equivalent was Kukulkan, but Quetzalcoatl was deemed a catchier and more appropriate name for a girl.

When Mrs. Adams was well into adulthood, she confided in her daughter that, no, she had *not* named her little girl after some rival deity, a male of the species at that, but for the resplendent quetzal, the Maya holy bird. In ancient times, to kill or to defeather the beauteous quetzal was a capital offense. Your beating heart was removed from your chest and not by a transplant surgeon but by a holy man with an obsidian knife.

At that point in time, Quetzal's mother was not to be contradicted, certainly not by a pickled preacher. So Quetzal she was.

The Reverend Adams, driven mad by mescal and Jesus, had drunkenly ranted once too often and loudly to the wrong people on the subject of Eternal Damnation, so he had been recalled by his superiors and retired to his hometown, a windblown highway crossing which I thought of on my one and only visit as West Corn Tassel, Nebraska. If offered a gas station, a grain elevator and little else.

Quetzal is an infinitely lovable and deceptively tough, a fiftyish bleached blonde with a gorgeous Mesoamerican profile. A two-time matrimonial loser, there was little chance that she would once again wed until divorce did her part. Certainly not to me, a confirmed (by choice and otherwise) bachelor with a shaky income, downscale prospects, and age-fifty in the rear-view mirror.

I kept in regular touch with her on burner phones I'd taken from my employer, the Happy-Happy Convenience Store. I regarded them as performance bonuses.

"The old man and I have irreconcilable differences," she said on her last call.

"You usually do."

"We'd been civil, a long-standing truce, but yesterday was too much. It's your fault too."

"Why?"

"Out of nowhere, he started on me on our cohabitation. Mom allows him a pint of hootch a day to keep him calm, but he obviously exceeded the limit."

"We only semi-cohabitate."

"Same diff to him. Fornication without benefit of clergy is a sin. End of story."

"Fornicating? That's what we're doing?"

"His word, not mine, which places us on his Heavenly shit list. He was wound up, telling me that premarital sex is dirty and filthy. I went, it is if you're doing it right."

"Oops."

"He's not speaking to me, the answer to my prayers."

"How's your mom?"

"She's hanging in there."

Quetzal's long-suffering mother was the *only* reason she visited. At 4' 10½", she was holding her own with her crazy husband, a florid roly-poly man twice her size, whose face was a road map of burst capillaries, a map that could be of Mexico City.

Quetzal, Mom and Judy had hit it off immediately and became fast friends. Both Judy and my mother were unanimous that Quetzal was too good for me. Yeah, they were right, but it still stung.

Our romance flourished, I believed, by the ongoing freshness of living separately. I slept over in her downtown condo close to her prospering CPA office, but declined to move in and be a kept man, even if the offer had been forthcoming.

She refused to put down roots in my "Black Hole of Calcutta" that reeked of linseed oil and dirty socks, mostly-unfinished Edward Hopperesque canvases scattered willy-nilly, being a reverse kept woman. My studio apartment/art studio was so foul, suggestive of a hot-sheet motel or the Naugahyde back seat of a 1960s car, that our sex was incredibly intense. So frenzied were we that my resplendent Quetzal said it wasn't sex, it was *fucking*.

Quetzal wasn't certain how long it'd take to get the hell out of West Corn Tassel hell with minimal guilt, but she would give me her flight number and ETA as soon as she could.

Seated next to me at the service were Christopher Theodore Polk and Tyler Lee Taylor, duded up in their notion of formal wear, semi-clean blue jeans and tight black T-shirts that covered fifty-percent of their tattoos. They were Judy's sons, one from each of her disastrous marriages. The primary affection I felt for my nephews was that thanks to them I wasn't the only black sheep in the Smith clan, and arguably not the blackest of the herd.

Dad's wholesome, milk-fed, all-American looks had jumped a generation to the boys. You'd never know it, though, with those tattoos. Chris's barbed wire around his neck for one. Ty was off parole for residential burglary—a cat burglar with two left paws—and was no longer required to wear an anklet, but he had that career-criminal look about him. He complained of itching, how the thing had either implanted cancer or a microchip that sent out radio signals. I told him to use calamine lotion and to stop whining like a baby.

The boys had a demeanor that made one consider crossing the street if they were coming. In one of my many, many lectures, I'd said fine, keep fucking up and the anklets will sure-as-hell go again; you can start a jewelry line of them.

Bonded by DNA and a free-floating alienation from mainstream society, Chris and Ty returned my dubious affection. Judy and her powerhouse law firm employed them in a largely make-work position as Correspondence Supervisors (read mail clerks, messengers and delivery boys).

She stored them in a bare-bones condo seven blocks south of her office that belonged to her or to one of her unnamed clients who was persona non communicado. She let it be known that she'd had the place wired for sight and sound. Whether or not this was a bluff, it throttled back the debauchery. Slightly. Their lady friends did not parade in the nude during daylight hours.

My familial chore was to keep an eye on them, to keep them out of mischief. In other words, I played devoted uncle/mentor/babysitter/unindicted coconspirator. We got along too. I liked the little shits and they sort of looked up to me, seeing some of themselves.

Sartorially, I set a pathetic example. My favored fashion statement was the tie-dye shirt. I kept myself fit, so I could pull it off. For the funeral, though, I was as spruced up as I've been since high school graduation: new jeans, blue shirt, sport jacket, long graying hair tied up in a ponytail.

When I scolded the boys about almost anything, they'd rebut with something such as, "Like Uncle T, you never poached a hubcap a long time ago when you were a kid?"

Nobody in our surviving family was estranged from another, nor were we particularly close. Dad had been the glue.

The chairs faced a white board, which Mr. Jonathon Smith used when he taught ESL. Anyone who wished to say a word was invited to, standing where they sat or in front of the board.

Before he broke down, Tony Horton said that when he went out back for a puff and saw Jonathon in his chair, he looked like he'd stopped for a snooze, he looked so peaceful. But when he didn't move an inch or speak—

Bev Horton helped her husband back into his seat, saying that yeah, no fooling, whatever it was, stroke or heart attack, they were fairly sure he hadn't felt a thing.

Others spoke briefly, many of them former high-school students and present ESL students, a common theme being that though they didn't know Mr. Smith well, that frankly he was a difficult man to know, they admired and loved him. He'd given them so much.

As the ceremony wrapped up, I delivered a nonverbal eulogy, one atheist to another: *Dad, you and Mom suppressed your disappointment in me, skepticism at my career choice, my shortcomings, but I loved you for trying and I know you loved Judy and me equally.*

After hugs all around, we filed out. Judy gave teary, rapid-fire hugs to mourners and was the first one gone in her Porsche 911. On to her office, I knew. A funereal Saturday was still a routine workday.

I had a moment outside with the boys. All three of us had glassy eyes. As the masculine contingent, us guys fought our unmanly tears. This in spite of being the weakest links in our tribe.

"I'd like to get my hands on the motherfucker who did this," Ty said.

"I'd stomp him into a fucking grease spot," Chris added, pounding a fist into a palm.

Everyone but Mom was satisfied that old age had taken him, Dad's system shutting down. She insisted that it was murder. Mom's imagination could do aerobatics after a few drinks, so we hoped she'd let it drop. The boys may not have believed either. They wanted vengeance even if none was warranted; violence cured all.

"Easy with the language, boys," I said. "If your kind-of Aunt Quetzal was here, she'd wash your mouths out with soap."

"Yeah, shit, sorry, but Gramma says it wasn't natural causes."

"I know," I said, not adding that it might be the merlot talking.

Chris said, "I believe her. She acts like she knows something."

"I'm open-minded on that," I said, giving each a quick, manly hug, then catching up to Mom and walking her to her car.

"I have a confession to make in behalf of your father," she said before I could get a word out. "He'd want me to clear the air."

I tensed and waited. Judy and I knew they kept secrets from us. Early on, the birds and the bees, sure. Why they named me after a sitcom character. Others from then until now that defied even an educated guess. Dad's locked shed in the backyard he hadn't used for years at the top of the list.

"When you wanted a kitten for your seventh birthday?"

"For my eighth, ninth, tenth and eleventh too, After that, I gave up."

Ignoring my sarcasm, she said, "Your father saying he was allergic to cats. Well, it was a lie. He didn't like kitties and thought they were for sissies and girls. I want to go on record as saying I disagreed and wouldn't have minded it. I think cats are cute, a secret I kept from him. Married as long as we were, you learn to compromise."

"Well, thanks for letting me know, Mom."

"Will you be there for the get-together?"

It was scheduled in an hour at her home, Judy's and my childhood home. Judy, the responsible, organized one had gone ahead to be sure everything was set up properly in time for the guests. Professionally catered, of course. She's make an appearance, albeit brief.

"I'm already late for work," I said.

"Work," she said, leaving unsaid *if you can call that a job.*

"We're shorthanded,"I said with an apologetic shrug. "Par for the course."

She didn't reply, but allowed me to help her into her car, a bright-red 1965 Chevy Impala with 94,512.6 actual miles on the odometer.

Defending Mom's spectacular DUI, Judy's lawyers steamrolled the justice system into a not-guilty verdict. Her attorneys brought to the stand a barrage of experts, and in cross-examination hammered the arresting officer. They attacked everyone else in the justice system, and anything remotely imaginable. They blamed the car manufacturer, the city's traffic system, blinding reflections from store windows, improperly placed and installed parking meters.

After the acquittal, Judy paid for every penny of property damage so Mom's insurance company wouldn't drop her. She had the Impala taken to a shop where they installed an ignition interlock system that required the driver to blow into it before the car would start. If Mom had brought her best gal pal, Ms. Merri Merlot, along for the ride, there would be no ride. Additionally, the shop installed a three-point seat-belt and harness which was linked to the ignition too.

Mom complained that "all your fanciness destroyed the collectability and authenticity of a classic car." Judy told her to live with it or take the bus.

Elizabeth (Betty) Smith offered her cheek for a kiss and asked, not for the first time, "Did you talk to Judy about the blood test and her private eye?"

The police refused to order an autopsy. Humoring her, they had conducted a perfunctory investigation, canvassing the immediate neighborhood and found nothing suspicious. Dad was seen at a nearby coffee shop having a cup and a conversation with an unknown man, but it was cordial. This wasn't unusual. To Jonathon Smith, there was no such thing as a stranger. And don't forget, this was a man of eighty-two, peacefully passing without any sign of trauma. End of story.

"Nothing yet. She'll keep after them."

"I know she will," Mom said.

I got into my 1989 Chevy Corsica and started it, always grateful that it turned over. A car older than half the population on the planet, twenty-four years newer than my mother's, and worth one-percent as much. I'd removed the back seat to make room for my paintings that I was seldom invited to bring to galleries. The vehicle looked like living quarters for the homeless.

Driving to my job, I thought of last night, having a few in the dive across the street from the dump I called home. It was an establishment where eye contact was not prudent, but the drinks were strong and cheap.

Who was our father? Really. Other than biological. The old man was always there for us. Soccer games, concerts, parent-teacher conferences, trips to the dentist and zoo. Like today's eulogizers, I did not know Jonathon Smith well.

Nor Jonathon Smith me.

Since becoming the star finger painter in kindergarten, I had never wanted to do anything but paint. A job drifter, to make ends meet in order to do so, among other things I had worked as a butcher and a baker. When I was feeling sorry for myself, I'd wonder if candlestick makers were hiring.

My career income was the same as a poet's. In thirty-five years, my total earnings came to $27,755. It was further depressing that the IRS totally ignored me.

In my late forties, I'd taken an especially humiliating and disheartening job at a park-and-fly lot, shuttling passengers to the airport. At the wheel of the airporter, a tip cup mounted beside me as if an alms bowl, I was taking people to the first step of a journey. They were going places and I was going nowhere.

Fifty-four years old now, I was receiving junk mail from cremation outfits and manufacturers of chairs that rotate forward to help the infirm get in and out, like slow-motion ejection seats.

I was tall, lean and fit, so even at my age I could pull off the long hair and tie-dyes. I don't know how to describe myself further than take-your pick. Through the eyes of others, I was an antique hippie (accurate), loser (painfully true), immature (so?), and a dilettante (nope, make that dirt-poor and obsessed).

An ex-girlfriend said I looked like an actor whose name escaped her. A leading man like Clint Eastwood, I asked? No way. The villain who Clint wasted in the last act.

As 1960s infants, little was expected of Judith, a girl, but much from me, a boy. It was no more complicated than that. The reverse had occurred stunningly. It had started when I was a squirt, even before the finger-painting triumph, dabbling with Judy's watercolor kits and supplies, which she had given me unused.

*   *   *   *   *

My present day job was partly a night job. I worked swing shift, arriving in daylight and leaving in the dark. I refused to work graveyard, as that could become a ticket to one. Consequently, due to personnel problems, the Happy-Happy Convenience Store was open sixteen/seven as often as twenty-four/seven.

The Happy-Happy Convenience Store was ten minutes south of the senior center and ten minutes from my apartment. It wasn't on the city's best street, nor its worst. The Happy-Happy was in the heart of a quote-unquote multiethnic neighborhood, a melting pot that had its share of police activity.

To many outsiders *multiethnic* automatically meant *dangerous*. In my mind, it wasn't. Like people anywhere, the majority kept their disputes to themselves, disputes that made the news because they could not afford lawyers to keep them hushed.

Convenience stores were examples of democracy in action, I felt. The clerk on duty could be robbed and shot in a C-store in any neighborhood. The stolen getaway cars in tonier areas were newer and nicer; that was the sole distinction.

Across the street from the Happy-Happy was a thrift shop and a usury mill aka a payday loan joint. Rob one or borrow from the other, and come on in for a pack of smokes or a deal on off-brand beer, the only things we ever offered on sale. Your basic harmonic convergence.

I got behind the counter, replacing Lil, the heavyset and heavily-tattooed assistant store manager. I'd tell her I was at my father's funeral and she'd say, yeah, I heard that one before. So I said nothing, returning Lil's glare with a cheery smile. Good help was hard to find. Mediocre help too.

Mr. Singh, the store owner, would never fire me. I had tenure on all employees, tenure on every employee *combined.* I had been on the payroll for an unprecedented fifty-one months. In dog and cat years, that was equivalent to fifty-one *years* at GM or Boeing.

I had experienced three robberies. In the first two, I had done as recommended and docilely handed over the contents of the till.

By the third, eight months ago, I'd had a bellyful. Instead of cash, I drew from under the register an old .38 Special I had acquired at a gun show. It had a cracked wooden handle and a two-inch barrel. The thing was manufactured in a country with a name full of consonants. Annie Oakley couldn't've hit an elephant five feet away with it.

The robber had wild, dumb eyes, the rotted teeth of a meth addict, and a firearm as excellent as my own. He closely resembled some of the attendees at that aforementioned gun show.

In the standoff, squinting and firing wildly, somehow I shot the gun from the robber's hand without harming him, a la The Lone Ranger.

Ping. Off it flew, from his hand into a display of empty-calorie snacks.

The goof stared at his palm, then ran outside, into the waiting arms of the police, who were in pursuit of him for a gas station robbery two blocks away, which had netted him forty-four dollars and change.

Theodore Cleaver Smith achieved minor celebrity for the shootout, and the threat of jail and a fine for carrying an unregistered firearm. Intervention by lawyers at Judy's firm—Smith, Hurlbert and Kraus, LLC, Attorneys-at-law—made the threat go away pronto. I was an innocent man, exercising my Second Amendment right to bear arms when no well-regulated militia was present.

It didn't hurt that two local TV news stations sent out talking haircuts to do thirty-second filler pieces on me and my Gunfight at Happy-Happy Corral. I'd been for an eyeblink an Internet celebrity too.

Mr. Singh was delighted at my stand in behalf of his property and the resultant publicity, which had caused a temporary bump in business similar to the store having sold a winning lotto ticket. He had taken to calling me "Kemo Sabe," him a Subcontinent Indian impersonating a 1950s TV version of an American Indian, everybody being a comedian.

"Oh, the most worthy of all Kodak moments," he had rhapsodized.

Had the notoriety been good enough to win me a raise? If merely a dollar per hour?

"Oh, Kemo Sabe," Mt. Singh told me. "I would so much love to do so, even in excess of one dollar. You would weep if you knew how small my profit margin is and how large my financial responsibilities are."

"Yeah," I said. "That your 7-Series BMW is a year old is making me misty-eyed."

I went into the store safe and brought my legally-registered weapon under the counter, hoping it didn't accidentally go off, and put on my apron, ready to sell wrinkly hot dogs, salty chips, smokes and beer.

Or get robbed. Whichever came first.

8

Bright and early Sunday morning, around ten, Judith Ann Smith's call awakened me.

Without preamble, Judy said, "Can you get over right away, Theo? Security has been notified and will let you in."

Meaning she was at her office. Deeper into her fifties than me by three years and exponentially richer, she was as driven as she had ever been. Judy powered through the University of Washington on a full ride, then Harvard Law School, top third of her class. And then, she sledgehammered one glass ceiling after another until reaching the top floor of her office building, which she occupied exclusively. Sporadically, I considered whipping a lawyer joke on her, but lacked the balls.

"Right away" to Judy was ten minutes ago.

"What's up?" I said through a cotton-mouthed yawn, that I blamed on an inferior brand of whiskey I'd drank after work while watching night owl infomercials—wrinkle-shrinking salves by blond cuties who had not a wrinkle one, get-rich-quick schemes by human oil slicks, exercise equipment and diet aids demonstrated by beachwear models who didn't need any of it.

"I'll show, not tell," she said.

"A hint??I asked.

"Go into our garage. I'll validate. Hurry," she said, then hung up.

After splashing water on my face, I dressed while glancing at my life's work, not necessarily admiringly, but for a finished triptych I

74

could not bring myself to attempt peddling.

There was a clutter of unfinished faux Edward Hoppers, one on an easel, others leaning against walls. Perhaps it was his craftsmanship, perhaps his story-telling on canvas that drew me in. You could add a comic-strip balloon on each and begin a four-hundred page novel.

I'd modernized his venues of automats and trains with junk-food emporiums and airport misery. So there they were, leaning, oil pigments long since dried, awaiting narrative hooks and endings.

Hopper, dead for over fifty years, didn't haunt me, but he sure did taunt me. Don't ask me to make sense of that. I can't.

Take *Nighthawks, 1942.* A bored-looking couple sitting at a lunch counter, smoking and drinking coffee. The counter guy looking up from the sink, saying something serious to them, very serious. Could be anything. A threat, a warning, the weather. Add a balloon and away we go.

And one of my favorites, *New York Movie, 1939.* To the left, the movie is playing. To the right, a pensive, young blond usherette staring down at nothing. As in a large number of his works, Hopper's wife was the model. In her usherette's uniform and holding a flashlight, her mind wasn't on her job. Had she missed her period, thinking how to break the news to her boyfriend and her family?

I had wadded up half the pages in a sketchpad, a failed start to *Multiplex, 2015.*

The story of Edward and Theodore.

*   *   *   *   *

I negotiated the Corsica the ten miles from a poorer edge of the city to the moneyed epicenter of downtown Seattle, to Judy's office tower and its parking garage.

I'll validate. A good thing. For the price of parking in there, you could rent a studio apartment in my neighborhood; three days in the garage and the tab would exceed the value of my car.

A guard was waiting as promised. He looked at my ride as if it was something he'd stepped on, but raised the gate and punched in a code that let me into Judy's private elevator. I parked and rode to the fifty-sixth and top floor, and Smith, Hurlbert and Kraus LLC, Attorneys-at-law.

I knew little about her firm's partnership structure other than that five years ago, dead drunk, the late James Kraus crossed a centerline and wound up dead.

Three years ago, Ralph Hurlbert's had been broken up into cubicles. He'd specialized in—something—and was seldom mentioned by Judy. She once let it slip that Ralph fancied himself as a ladies' man. Me and my dirty mind imagined Hurlbert's zipper unzipping where it shouldn't have. A homicidal husband bribed and Ralph exiled to a branch office, perhaps. She did have other offices, so perhaps Ralph was transferred to one, or bought off and shown the door.

Which left Big Sis as the Big Boss, which she had been anyhow.

I knew not the specifics of her clientele, but I knew that Judy and her staff didn't troll courthouse hallways for unrepresented perps and skells, nor advertise on the sides of buses for the whiplashed. Her clientele on the surface was silk-stocking, town dads, respected businessmen. Her firm did high-profile pro bono too; woe be it if you were a slumlord caught in her crosshairs. You'd make the five o'clock news.

The cynic in me believed this all to be a façade for clients much less transparent and far more lucrative. These clients owned islands and politicians. Categories that in my mind were semi-genteel forms of organized crime, gangsters who had been to college and enunciated properly. Whenever I'd probe who some of them were, Sis waved the red flag of attorney-client confidentiality.

"Don't let them own you, Sis," was my rejoinder, earning myself a laser stare.

She had offices in Denver, Minneapolis and Charlotte too, roughly two hundred attorneys total. I'd kidded her that if she opened up shops in Porto, Mumbai and Brisbane, the sun would never set on the Judith Ann Smith Empire. She was mildly amused, but I could hear the wheels turning.

I walked through the reception area that was larger than my apartment, glass tabletops with *Smithsonian* and the *Wall Street Journal* and *The New Yorker* fanned out, nary a *People* or *National Enquirer* in sight. Being the Sabbath, Inge, the blond Ice Princess/Praetorian guard behind the front desk was absent. She was a six-foot-tall knockout who I'd failed to thaw with my winning leer. I knew zero about her personal life, but supposed her significant other was an MBA who played a major college sport.

Big Sis caught me once and told me to stop drooling, she wasn't my type. I desperately wanted to know what Inge's type was, so I could remake myself. She shook her head and laughed.

I went into her corner office, into floor-to-ceiling windows, into nothing but blue skies and neighboring office towers, and looked down at fluffy dumplings of breaking fog. Judith Ann was high enough to have her own weather.

No greetings were exchanged. This was not animus; it was a habit dating to adolescence. So it went with us, from the time I could speak, brother and sister. Half friendly, half resentful. Our competitiveness ended when I was eight or nine and we both knew that it was hopeless on my part. Our parents had thrown in the towel too.

I sat across from her at a hardwood desk you could play shuffleboard on, a single polished slab for which some tropical tree gave its life. Counting the rings, I thought, you might be able to date it to the Millard Fillmore Administration.

An endangered species, I had goaded her. From a tree already knocked down by a cyclone, Judy countered, as if you care an iota about the environment. Spoken like a brilliant trial attorney, I'd said.

Covering a third of a side wall, providing the only color in the room, hung a Theodore Cleaver Smith work done in my Minimalism phase, an interpretation of nothing that I'd perhaps taken too far, a color field of pale yellow and a diagonal reddish stripe, a la Mark Rothko, a pity purchase when I was between day jobs. She'd paid the exact amount, to the dollar, that chased off the pit bulls that the collection agencies sent. Big Sis possessed the tools to learn many things and she never underestimated the power of money.

Judy was seated at right angles with a sixtyish man in a cheap suit two sizes too small. Retired cop cum private eye, I thought.

Judith Ann Smith was accepting middle-age gracefully, applying *nada* to her graying hair but shampoo. Slim and maintaining her weight to the ounce, with high cheekbones and blue eyes that saw everything she wanted them to see. She was a vegetarian and until the age of forty-five a triathlete.

Judy's business suit was worth twice as much as my car. Conversely, I was dressed in my standard summer ensemble… Today's tie-dyes were speckled with paint, adding pigments that dazzled even further. My jeans were likewise colored, in my opinion transforming discount-store-made-in-China denims into designer category. An opinion not shared by her.

Judy was like the fine-wine cliché. She'd never been homecoming-queen material, but she wasn't "mildly unattractive" as one of her asshole exes had tagged her.

He was Ty's old man, an all-purpose sleaze and a pussy hound. She had taken him to the cleaners in the divorce, rendering him one income level above Dumpster diver. The guy deserved every lick including info to the bar association that got him disbarred. One did not butt antlers with my sister.

If she has had a boy-girl personal life since, it was news to me.

"Well," I said.

"Theo, this is Richard. Richard, Theo. Richard does some work for the firm and has uncovered some interesting things regarding Father on the night it—happened."

I doubted if Richard went by Richard when on the force. Too

formal. Dick or Rich or Richie. Richard opened a notebook and cleared his throat.

"Well, the homicide boys wrote off Mr. Smith's death as age-related, which was logical, I guess. I can't fault them for that. He was just sitting there on that bench, not breathing or anything."

"Let's move on, Richard."

Richard made an expanding spiral with a fingertip. "I canvassed the close-by neighbors first. It was after dark, so nobody saw him. Then I fanned out. Still nothing. I was gonna bag it when I tried a coffee shop in business strip on Rainier Avenue, four blocks away from his residence. There were several folks who knew him by sight, but didn't really know him personally, you know. Mr. Smith had been in there that evening, having coffee and a muffin with a guy."

"A guy?" I asked.

"A guy. That's all anyone remembered. Just a guy. A younger guy, thirty-five or forty or forty-five, you know, not too young, not too old. Clean-cut was the best description they gave. They were leaning forward toward each other as they talked, him and Mr. Smith, like not wanting to be overheard. It was kind of intense, but not unfriendly. I went, if I brought in a sketch artist. They all said no, a waste of our time and your money."

Richard closed his notebook.

"Interesting," I said. "Most of this we already know. Did they come in together or leave together?"

"Good question," Richard said. "A couple of folks I talked to said no, a couple said yeah. A couple said maybe."

"They came in together or left together or came in and left together?"

Richard shrugged. "These people I talked to. It's all over the board. This guy who was with him, he's a needle in a haystack."

Judy said, "A needle is shiny silver and substantially heavier than dry herbage, Richard. Remove the hay in increments from the top down and shake it as you do. When the hay's completely gone, there the shiny needle is, on the bottom."

Richard nodded tightly, reddening. He had just been lectured and didn't like it, not one little bit, especially by a girl lawyer.

Judy first lectured me when I was six or seven, as I dug down into my Cracker Jacks box for the prize, a haystack needle in its own right. Explaining patiently and logically, telling me to pour out the contents on a plate if I was in such a big hurry. I was pissed and did pour the contents out, not caring that half of it went on the floor.

"Sure, okay, I get it. I'll keep looking," Richard said, as he glanced at me for support, which I knew better than to give.

Richard realized that it was fruitless, but he presumably billed by the hour. And his client was good for it.

"Thank you, Richard," Judy said.

Richard and his Sunday-go-to-meeting suit took the hint, which was a dismissal. Judy had that down pat. You'd be out the door and on the elevator before it dawned on you that you'd been given the boot.

After Richard was gone, I said, "Coffee and a doughnut with Joe Anonymous. Is that enough to back up Mom's suspicions?"

"Coffee and a muffin."

"Pardon me."

Judy opened a folder.

"They remembered the muffin but very little about the guy."

"That's not all I wanted to run by you."

"The blood test?"

"The report's in. I'm delighted that Mother pushed us on this. If delighted is the right word. I was able to have the sample taken—just in the nick of time."

Before Dad's trip into the oven, thinking that it was best left unsaid.

"Tincture of aconite. The report took so long because they had to go through several levels or protocols to isolate the substance. To say the least, aconite is uncommon."

"'Tincture-of' means in a solution of alcohol."

"It does."

"Dad didn't drink."

"He didn't."

"You lost me on the other. This acolyte?"

"Aconite. Aconite or aconitum is in a family of over two-hundred-and-fifty flowering plants." She paused and looked at the report again. "The family Ranunculaceae."

"Not a controlled substance?" I asked. "But not an herb you'd sprinkle on your pasta."

"True. In olden times, aconite was used to poison spears and arrows for warfare and hunting large animals. It did the job.

"You could go out in the woods and pick it, like an afternoon out gathering huckleberries, instead of ordering it on online where there'd be a record. It doesn't take a skilled chemist to turn it into a liquid solution, but you'd have to know what you're doing, or get it from somebody who did."

I said, "Someone who'd done it before or knew somebody who did"

"Exactly," Judy said.

"Introduced directly into the bloodstream?"

"The lab believes so. The alcohol wasn't processed by the liver. In smaller doses, death can occur in between one and six hours. The symptoms aren't pleasant."

"In a large dose.?

"Within seconds. Twenty to forty milliliters of the tincture can prove fatal."

"By syringe?" I asked. "Poison spears are unwieldy."

Judy stared at him, letting Theo's inappropriate sarcasm pass, her kid brother and his wise-ass remarks compensating for a life of frustration.

From the time she was in junior high school, she knew that Mother wasn't a social drinker, and knew of fetal alcohol syndrome, she had wondered if Theodore was a victim of a mild case of FAS. However, the physical characteristics—short stumpy body, flat face, small eye openings— weren't there.

Theodore's IQ was in the 95th percentile, so FAS may or may not have contributed to his behavioral problems. If he was one-up on the rest of the family, it was in physical conditioning. He ran, jogged, and played pickup basketball well into his forties, though as a kid he never went out for sports. His erraticism and inability to settle down and make something out of himself, stubbornly chasing an unrealistic dream to be A Painter. A cop-out or a true passion? To steer clear of devoting hard work to a meaningful career or an unshakable obsession? She remained uncertain. The poor man's career earnings were that of the stereotypical starving artist.

He was taller and darker than the family norm, with the beginning of a gut, though not like so many who looked like they were candidates for an emergency caesarian. Theo could unpredictably behave like a defiant adolescent. That and/or suppressed anger at being named after a sitcom character.

Judy thought of him as a polymath without portfolio. Not untalented with a brush and canvas either, a better-than-average amateur, and even better than that after his Edward Hopper fixation, a painter she too admired, a man who told a tale on every canvas. Unfortunately for Theo, thousands of other painters were on that almost-professional tier.

She had never slapped his face with her FAS theory. He may have harbored one of his own, she thought. His boyhood idol was an old-time baseball star named Hack Wilson, who may have had it. Theo, who didn't much care for baseball, had painted Hack into a triptych that hung in his dilapidated home studio.

If he had FAS, she often wondered, how had Mother's drinking affected her *in the womb? One of her exs, Christopher's father, had screamed in her face that she was a frigid, driven harpy who had sold her soul for a client list that was a multiple incarnation of the devil. That was difficult to dispute when she accepted calls from St. Petersburg clients in the middle of the night, Pacific Daylight Time, tendering advice and billing them in the morning.*

After an uncomfortable silence, Judy said, "Injected by a syringe right in the alley, close to Tony Horton's smoking chair. The medical examiners may have done a cursory examination, but at his age and as active as he was, he had all sorts of blemishes and age spots. Small cuts and scrapes from gardening or tinkering around the house. A pinprick from the needle would be easily missed."

"The man in the coffee shop with no face," I said. "When are we telling Mom?"

Judy closed the folder. "After the reading of the will. Mother's not revealing all she knows, is she?"

"Mom seldom does," I offered.

"I'll arrange security for her."

I smiled. "We'll blackmail her if she doesn't come clean."

"Excuse me?"

"By telling her that we'll ship her off to live with Aunt Leah."

Judy smiled too. Leah was their mother's older sister, the only other surviving family member. Married to a retired farm equipment mechanic, their Aunt Leah lived in Sioux Falls, South Dakota.

The sisters hadn't spoken for years, after Leah joined an apocalyptic religious cult that went door-to-door handing out semi-literate pamphlets, warning that if they didn't repent, the end was coming any second and they were going to spend eternity in a bad, hot place.

She had mailed pamphlets to us when we were kids, until Mom found out, had a cow, and either intercepted them at the mailbox or got on the phone and put a stop to them.

If you weren't "saved," Aunt Leah's way, you could look forward to the imminent end of the world, to famine and ten-point-oh earthquakes, oceans turning to blood, plagues, demons, fire-breathing monsters. Your ticket would not be punched for The Rapture. The same message as Quetzal's daddy's, the same but different, each being the only true path. Batshit crazy, all of them.

I remembered Aunt Leah as silver-haired, with the posture and demeanor of a drill sergeant.

"Let's hope it doesn't come to that," Judy said.

9

Darwin Meade was a small-town lawyer who practiced on the south outskirts of Seattle in a suburban blur of cul-de-sacs and strip malls. It was a small, unincorporated town when he began his practice. I'd have to hunt for it on a 1970s street map to be any more specific.

Our family met with him as scheduled at his office in a two-story professional building. Darwin was sandwiched between a dentist and proctologist. When it was quiet as it was now, the buzz of a dental drill could be heard. Visitors occasionally thought they heard screams on one side or the other, but that may have been power of suggestion.

Paying homage to progress, his original office that I remembered as a tyke had been bulldozed with other storefronts on the town's vanished main drag. In its replacement, Darwin had retained the furnishings, the dark wood paneling and shelving that groaned under the weight of leather-bound law books. I pretended there was no big box store across the way, but the old five-and-dime and ice cream shop.

Darwin Meade was a graduate of a state university's law school in the Great Plains. He had been the Smith family attorney long before Harvard Law was a gleam in Judy's eye.

I didn't think he had anything against Judy personally, probably adoring her as an ultra-precocious child, but he used his words with care in her Ivy-League company, intimidated, I believed, so not to make a picayune boo-boo. We all felt he was a good man who practiced with integrity.

Judy knew how he felt about her and did her best to be acquiescent, bordering on timid, an unnatural emotion for her. Big Sis was a courtroom killer who could shrink the gonads of the smuggest, booming baritone, leonine opponent to the size of BBs. Deep, deep down, I was so proud of her in situations like this and wondered where she came from as I often wondered where I came from.

Jonathon Smith's last will and testament was in boilerplate language and brief. To nobody's surprise, the bulk of the estate went to Elizabeth (Betty) Smith, his beloved wife of fifty-eight years.

After Meade finished reading the will aloud, he distributed envelopes: a large manila to Judith Ann Smith, one a bit smaller and bulging to me, Theodore Cleaver Smith. Letter-sized ones to Christopher Theodore Polk and Tyler Lee Taylor.

Judy's offspring tore into theirs as if children on Christmas morning, then made faces. By their expressions their bequests weren't paths to easy street. Sis glared at them and glanced pleadingly at me.

I mouthed *okay*; I'd do my scoutmaster duty later. Have them over for a drink and perform my role as shoulder to cry on/mentor/fellow loser. After telling them for the umpteenth time to cease behaving like infantile pissants.

When it was over, us heirs exchanged the smallest of small talk and obligatory hugs, mimicking the aftermath of Dad's funeral. Before leaving the parking lot, I sat in my 1989 Chevy Corsica and examined the contents of my inheritance: Five grand in hundreds and a smaller sealed envelope that was responsible for the bulge.

That envelope contained an old wallet, three pieces of plastic-laminated ID for a V.I. Larrionov of the former Soviet Union and a yellowed, pre-ZIP code business card for a Dallas, Texas hat shop named Harry's Hattery. Nothing else.

Puzzled, I guessed that all the stuff dated from the 1960s. The old man hadn't been one to hang on to sentimental artifacts. Come to think of it, there was nothing in their home that predated the mid-1960s. Furniture, wall hangings, dishware, trinkets, nothing stored and forgotten in the basement or garage.

Seated on a mix of duct tape and frayed upholstery, worn to the consistency of rat fur, I recounted the money, thinking that I could upgrade my transportation with the five grand.

I picked up the Larrionov ID again and gave it a closer look. The KGB piece had a small photo that I'd overlooked.

V.I. Larrionov was Dad as a young man.

So there it was, I thought. The old man was finally getting in my face. From the great beyond. Giving me a challenge. To work to my potential. Doing something meaningful. Whatever the hell it was.

Hands shaking, after fumbling and dropping my phone twice, I called my sister. We planned to break the aconite news to Mom later today anyway.

We'd best do it now.

10

Seattle was hilly, picturesquely bumpy. God's country, should that abstract deity exist to claim credit for it.

By golly, you can look from one hilltop and see another and another. The man known to some as Robin—designated as such by Mr. C the Three—enjoyed sightseeing and he enjoyed spectacular views, even while on business.

Belvedere Park in West Seattle offered such views. It wasn't as glorious as Florence's Belvedere (in travelogues and in his dreams), but it was worth a sightseer's trip, as mandated by Mr. C the Three.

In the midst of old trees, flowerbeds and freshly-cut grass, with his top-quality German binoculars, Robin had a panoramic sweep of the Seattle's skyline. On his far left, the trademark Space Needle, built for the city's 1962 World's Fair. To his far right, now an art-deco dwarf, the Smith Tower, at thirty-eight stories and four-hundred-and-sixty-two feet, the tallest building west of the Mississippi when completed in 1914. Between them, the fast, fast, fast-growing Seattle skyline, sprouting as if glass and steel dandelions.

The Very UnReverend Robin (as Mr. C the Three had mockingly tagged him) had no interest in downtown skyscrapers or cityscapes, nor tourism per se.

Two weeks after Robin's Fall From Grace, a man had knocked on the door of his studio apartment just as he was about to flavor his breakfast coffee with two thick fingers of bourbon. The roach-infested cubbyhole was provided by the church and he had one week to vacate.

The man didn't ask to come in or offer his name.

He introduced himself by handing Robin a money clip holding folded cash.

"How would you like to change careers, Reverend?"

He laughed and said, "Who do I have to kill?"

The visitor didn't laugh. He gave the soon-to-be Robin another wad of folded cash and said, "Nobody you know. When can you leave?"

He had replied by opening a suitcase.

Robin focused on his right and below, at Harbor Island, one of the nation's busiest container ports. Just bursting with trivia, he knew from tourism literature that when completed in 1909, Harbor Island was the largest artificial island in the world. Composed of twenty-four million cubic yards of landfill, you'd certainly think so.

Depending on the statistics one read, the Port of Seattle-Tacoma was the fourth, fifth, seventh or eighth busiest in the United States. One stat had them at thirty-sixth in the world, trailing a majority of ports in Asia.

Asia, where their ship was steaming in from. And here it was, right on the money, stacked high with containers. It was the *Bamsan Kiet*, Liberian registry, address a Panama City P.O. box that likely received no mail.

Robin found it peculiar that a ship with an Oriental name had an official home in Central America by way of darkest Africa. He knew little of international taxation avoidance and less of hydraulics and the properties of sea water. He could not envisage how a vessel so heavy and piled so high with containers could float.

Mox nix. Thousands and thousands of containers, carrying millions and millions of tons of cargo came into the country every year from ports far and wide. A cursory inspection of the contents made at best was all customs authorities could handle. An impossible task.

Try to bring a pair of fingernail clippers onto an airplane and security personnel had you in a room patting you down, one of them snapping on a rubber glove.

Crazy.

Robin continued watching. The ship was so slow, two or three miles per hour. Those floating behemoths did not stop and go like a sports car. If you slammed on the brakes, you'd be wise to have miles of water in front of you.

All he had to know was that it was bringing their cargo on schedule. Cargo in a container that would be winched onto a dock. Cargo that would be off-loaded onto a truck. Where the cargo in question was headed, he didn't know.

Somebody else would, though.

His job was to confirm arrival.

He phoned and did.

"Excellent."

"Thank you, sir."

"There will be seven CondorCakes aboard, four to be delivered in Seattle, three others to different cities. Disregard the latter three. You will concern yourself with the local four."

"Condor cakes?"

"CondorCakes. One word, the 'C's capitalized, but they won't be listed as that. You will continue to track and keep me posted," Mr. C the Three said. "They will be the smallest products in container five-four-three. When the time comes, I'll give you instructions pertinent to their final destination."

A new wrinkle. This was the first Robin had heard of CondorCakes and his expanded duties. Were they like gooey brownies or Bundt cakes? A Duncan Hines boxed mix? He knew not to ask.

The phone prefix for Mr. C the Three began with an out-of-country zero-one-one and through two European nations, then a ten-digit blocked number. The signal was loud and clear, so it could be from right around the corner. Mr. C the Three did say he was "pop-up."

"Yes sir."

"And, oh, Robin, kudos for the sayonara of the oldster."

"Yes sir."

He took no particular pleasure in murdering an octogenarian, nor did he feel a sliver of guilt or remorse. His quick recruitment after his defrocking spared him a subsequent profession as a homeless alcoholic. A life sacrificed, a life saved; it evened out.

He was being paid very well too, exponentially better to the only adult job he had held, preaching God's wrath, the paltry wage plus what he was able to get away with skimming the offering plates after the services. His utter lack of conscience had won the day.

"I am asking you to perform an additional duty."

"Yes sir."

"Even in a boozy haze, the widow logically suspects it wasn't natural causes. Marriages lasting that long endure partially because of full candor, a form of telepathy. Him and his plastic flowers, then coincidentally dropping dead."

"Yes sir. I agree," he lied.

How could she suspect? The woman was no doctor.

"An oldster dying and the distraught spouse doing the same soon thereafter—not uncommon. Cause of death, a broken heart. You see it in newspaper obits all the time."

"Say no more, sir."

"Do it soon. Before she spills the beans to the offspring and whomever. She is a cagy old bat, drunk or sober. They aren't the closest of families, but tragedy tends to draw one together. The son is a loser, an overage Bohemian, but that daughter of hers is formidable."

"Yes sir."

"When I say soon I mean *soon*. This project is costing me time and money, neither of which I am made."

A *project*. Robin supposed he was working with him on a project, but not the goal. He would be so informed or not. Curiosity killed cats, but not this kitty.

"You have a spare needle and contents."

"A full vial."

"Good. Having it made was a chore, you know. One step here,

the next there. So that the transactions were untraceable. It's not something you can pick up at the corner drugstore."

Not waiting for a reply, Mr. C the Three hung up.

Speaking of formidability, Robin thought, after he'd been recruited, he was flown to Portland, Oregon and put up in a motel. The next day, he was driven to a shopping mall in Salem by a smirky young guy who didn't say five words to Robin and drove harum-scarum, cutting off other drivers, weaving in and out of lanes, glancing at Robin for a reaction.

Testing him, seeing if he had a pair, Robin thought. He had tightened his sphincter and balled his fists, giving away nothing verbal.

In the mall, the kid directed him to a table by a cinnamon-roll shop, ordered him a roll and cup of coffee, and wait.

Not one minute later, a tall, well-built imposing man in his fifties sat down with him.

"My name is Mr. C the Three."

"My pleasure, Mr. C. I'm—"

Mr. C the Three waved away the extended hand and said, "You are Robin. As long as you work for me you are Robin."

Mr. C the Three's stare lowered the mall temperature by fifteen degrees.

"Yes sir. Robin. Call me Robin."

Mr. C the Three said, "I was born on November 22, 1963. It had been a difficult childbirth that rendered my mother unable to bear other children and contributed to her early death. My grandfather died suddenly and unexpectedly in December of that year, by all accounts, of a broken heart. This is confidential and all you have to know about me and my background."

Robin could not think of a response. He saw the driver and an old guy standing by a junk jewelry kiosk, watching. There was a family resemblance to the threesome. Something in the eyes.

Mr. C the Three gave him one-half of a three-by-five index card:

MISSION STATEMENT
We need to start over. And we will.

"When you read, memorize, and consume our mission statement, you become one of us," he said. "Bon appétit."

This was like a men's' lodge or Mafia initiation. These guys are mental cases, he thought, but in some regard, so was he.

"Consume?"

Mr. C the Three smacked his lips.

Robin ate the card in small, subtle bites along with a greasy, sugary roll, washing it down with a cola.

Mr. C Three gave him a napkin when he finished and said, "You were a preacher, Robin. You know all the Biblical promises of vengeance, don't you?"

"I do. I definitely do."

With a rictus of a smile, he said, "My favorite is Vengeance is mine Sayeth the Lord. What's yours?"

Robin began to stammer when Mr. C the Three stood and said, "Vengeance is mine, Robin if you fuck up or disobey me."

All this ran through his mind as he watched the *Bamsan Kiet*, thinking of tincture of aconite, the gummy non-taste of masticated paper, and of CondorCakes, a product surely not packaged by Betty Crocker.

Finishing off the old lady will be a fool's errand. He'd be placing himself at unnecessary risk. No way could Elizabeth Smith suspect anything.

Robin sneezed.

Pollen, he muttered, reaching into a pocket for a handkerchief.

Stuffed under the hankie was the tiny pistol he'd taken from Jonathon Smith.

The widow had to know that her husband carried it. Had to.

Oh my sweet Jesus H. Fucking Lord God Almighty.

* * * * *

He looked out the window at Seattle's Elliott Bay, imagining he could see the *Bamsan Kiet.*

"The payment cleared. The shipment is steaming in. All good."

"I've booked our flight, Father. It's a long one, but we can close our eyes in first class and see gold."

"Oh yeah, we can. Following the rainbow from Zurich to Ecuador."

"Last stop was Shanghai. If they were on to us, they'd be by now."

"The CondorCakes came from Iran, Pakistan or North Korea. The seller didn't specify and I could care less. So long as they work."

"All the cargo they ship out of that port, one chance in a million they'd be on top of it."

"If they do know, they're thinking ahead. No more seven-dollar sweatshirts peddled to our big box stores, but their reward's potentially a helluva lot larger."

"That Chink-in-chief, he's like old Wartface who fucked over my father. The fucking slogans. 'The people have faith.' 'The path to the dream is under your feet.' 'Fight and advocate probity and honesty.' 'Keep the alarm bells ringing.' What hypocritical bullshit. Fucking Commies."

"Capitalistic Commies or Communistic Capitalists. It's hard to tell."

"Zurich. Think Zurich."

"The terms are indelible."

"Dr. Strangelove."

"You and that old movie."

"The CondorCakes. We're okay to Minneapolis, Denver and Charlotte. Ordinary shipping by air. The suitcase units will arrive in time. We can program them remotely. The four jewel box units for here. We should have them in a couple of days."

He smiled. "Jewel boxes, cute as a button."

"Smaller than a bread box."

"One would fit in a bread box."

"Those darkies over there, they can do it all."

"Robin?"

"I was reading your body language, Father. Will he follow through, do you think?"

The old man shook his head. "The timbre in his voice."

"Not a team player?"

"No."

"We'll keep an eye on him."

"Container five-four-three. An illusion of longer-term employment."

"He has to know that he can't track everything inside."

"Particularly since we haven't given him a cargo manifest."

"Which we don't have anyway. All we care about is that they're delivered in time."

"Our back-up guy?"

"He's handy."

"May I send them the message, Grandfather?"

"You pipsqueaks and your computers."

"It'll shake things up. See who knows and does what."

"You did what I asked too?"

"At the same time, Grandfather. It goes in through the front door."

"Fucking with their heads, that's priceless, but a retainer costs us off the top. I'm not liking that."

"I promise, I can get it back before they credit it."

"All right then. Go ahead, boy. Get your rocks off. I see no harm."

11

I caught Judy when she was halfway back to her office. She answered on the second ring, sounding like she was in a cave. Meaning her phone wasn't handheld to her ear, the bad habit I shared with ninety-percent of American drivers.

When I told her what I had, the old man IDed as a KGB operative, she had said not to budge, she'd be there in ten minutes. She made it in five. I wouldn't want to have been a motorist or pedestrian in her vicinity.

I left my heap in front of Attorney Meade's and hopped into her Porsche. Her robin's egg blue 911 Carrera smelled like a shoe store and had whiplash acceleration.

I said, "The boys looked like they'd gotten lumps of coal in their stockings."

"Tough. In their envelopes were vouchers too. Scholarship money to the schools of their choice, anywhere from Ivy League to community college vocational. I've been after them to get training of some kind, learn a trade. *Anything*."

"I helped the folks set up the trusts several years ago. I was surprised. Our parents were wealthier than they let on, even though Mother gave me only limited access to their portfolio. She was crafty with money and would have been a great financial planner."

"If they don't go to school? They may be allergic to higher education."

"Then the grand total of their inheritance is the cash in the envelopes. A week or two of beer money that's likely being spent as we speak. I gave them the rest of the day off. Calm them down if you can, Theo."

I let it drop. There was enough tension in the hot little car, Judy going through the gears like we were at Le Mans.

Why can't I ever drive this beauty? I thought of asking for the umpteenth time.

I didn't. This wasn't the time to behave like the whiny kid brother.

We caught up with Mom three blocks from home, wincing as she goosed her prehistoric Impala to unsuccessfully beat a red light. We cringed as she went under it, causing cross traffic to brake and lay on their horns.

We trailed her to our childhood abode. A mansion to us then, it struck Judy and me as a cottage now. It was a twelve-hundred-square foot Cape Cod with an attached garage and a full basement that was a hostel for spiders, along with Dad's gardening tools and supplies. That and the artificial flowers he'd planted out back this spring. They were far more practical than the real plants he fussed over, complaining about pests. When he began watering the plastic pansies, though, I worried if this was a first step down into dementia. Now I knew it wasn't. Dad was on sentry duty.

Directly across the street, there had been a near-carbon copy of our home, occupied by the Weavers for ages, generations of them. Judy and I had gone to school with Weaver kids. When their parents passed away, it was scooped up from the heirs by developers who had sniffed out Columbia City's coming gentrification.

They flattened the house and threw up a four-plex box that obeyed zoning laws regarding height and adjacent property lines by a full millimeter. The homes had the charm of shipping containers. All four units sold within eleven days in bidding wars that upped the price fifty grand above the asking.

It had seemed in our childhood a bucolic everybody-knows-everybody-and everybody's- business neighborhood in a medium-sized town. Today, an urbane, upwardly-mobile stomping ground that seemed compressed due to atherosclerotic traffic in every direction, a compressed enclave in a large city that was growing faster than any city in the nation, with traffic ranked in every Ten Worst list.

Mom saw us when she got out of her car. She squinted at us and went inside, leaving the door open. When we got to her, she was standing in the breakfast nook. If she was surprised, she didn't show it.

"Well, I didn't know we were having a wake," she said, looking at us as she had when we were children who tracked dirt inside. "I'd've vacuumed and dusted. I thought we got all that out of the way yesterday."

My sibling and I didn't say a word.

"What can I get you kids? Coffee? A drink?"

"Nothing for us, thanks," Judy said, speaking for me too, an irritating habit dating from elementary school.

"Have you and your private eye learned anything?" Betty said, sitting down with us. "That's why you're here, isn't it? Not that you children aren't welcome any old time you care to drop by, even if it is once in a blue moon."

Judy ignored Mom's shot at a guilt-trip and showed her the lab report on the tincture of aconite and narrated the PI's surveillance findings.

"We apologize for doubting you, Mother."

"We do, Mom."

Mom said, "Yep. This mystery man makes sense. I knew all along that your father was murdered after he was lured to that coffee shop and brought back here in the dark alley. Didn't I tell you? I *did* tell you. I told everyone."

"Yes, you did. Why were you so certain, Mother? All the preliminary evidence indicated otherwise."

She looked at us, one at a time, as she did when we were children and didn't get her point.

"Because the police didn't find Baby on him."

"A baby?"

"No. Baby. Like I said."

"Mother?"

"Oh, forget that. I'm opening a can of worms. May we move on to the weather or the Mariners or something? I spoke out of turn."

"Mom," I said.

"They have crummy pitching when they have good hitting and crummy hitting when they have good pitching. Same old story. They'll win the World Series when your grandkids are my age."

"Mother," Judy said.

"I can put the water on for coffee. It'll take just a sec."

Judy looked at me and said to her, "My brother and I can't be with you all the time, but Aunt Leah can."

I said, "She goes to church twenty times a week so you and her will have plenty to do."

Betty fluttered a palm. "Oh, why don't you just ship me directly to the insane asylum."

"You can start with that baby of yours," I said.

Betty sighed and said, "That wasn't our nickname to begin with. It's the Browning gun company that makes it. They coined the name. To be exact, the FN Baby Browning."

"Gun company?" Judy said.

"I've already said too much."

I said, "Makes it?"

"All right. Baby is their name for their twenty-five caliber pistol. It was designed in 1927 and is so darling, wonderfully useful to this very day. Baby is semi-automatic and holds six twenty-five caliber rounds, conventional or hollow-point. Baby has no external hammer to catch on things, which is important. If you're carrying."

Carrying?

"Important to who?" I asked.

"Hollow-point rounds?" Judy said. "They're illegal in many states."

Mom continued, "With a standard powder load in the shells, its muzzle velocity is seven-hundred-and-fifty feet per second. Your father did some magic with the load to boost muzzle velocity to fifteen-hundred feet per. You could fire the whole clip without Baby blowing up in your hand. Baby is no target pistol, but at close range it can do the job. He kept it on him when he thought there might be trouble.

"Baby weighs less than ten ounces, you know. With its itty-bitty little holster, Baby is no more noticeable in a man's pocket than a wadded-up handkerchief. Lately, the last two or three weeks or so, your father was keeping it in his pocket when he was outside watering those silly plastic flowers."

Were Mom and Dad NRA faithfuls? What else didn't we know about them? I couldn't speak.

Rock-steady Judy said, "Was Father suspicious of someone or something?"

Mom rubbed an age spot on the back of a hand. "You might say."

"Why was Father suspicious?" Judy said.

"No specific reason."

"Mother," Judy said.

"Did he say anything, Mom?" I said. "Why he was carrying, uh, Baby?"

"No. It was just a feeling he had. That's what he told me, but it had to be more than that. I got after him and he just laughed it off, saying to humor his paranoia. We'd been on pins and needles for years and years, but had gradually relaxed, thinking the trail was cold or that something had happened to them."

"The trail? Them?" I said.

Mom stopped talking and her eyes glazed. It was the closest I had ever seen her to completely breaking down. She was one tough old gal. Had been for as long as I could remember.

Judy hurried to her, squeezing her hands. "Mother, we have to go to the police."

"No, no, no. We can't."

"Why not?"

"We just can't."

"Theo," Judy said. "Show and tell time."

I laid the wallet on the table and spread out the contents like a poker hand.

She examined each piece and said, "Oh dear. From your father?"

I said, "It was in the envelope I was given at Darwin Meade's office. Obviously for a reason. When did he join the KGB? Maybe I'm wrong, but I don't think they hire Americans. Spies, sure, but they don't issue them ID cards."

Mom pursed her lips as if locking them.

"This V.I. Larrionov, it's maybe their equivalent of John Doe," I said.

Mom didn't speak.

Judy took her phone out of her purse and said, "I have Aunt Leah's number stored."

"Put that thing away and promise me, no police."

"If you tell us the whole story, Mother."

I held up the KGB card. "Dad was a pup then. What little there is of the background in the picture is really blurred and he's not looking at the camera. Like he was being photographed with a long lens without his knowledge."

She stood. "You two. I give up. First step in my story. Your father's work and tool shed. You remember, he called it his hobby room."

"Not as often as he told us it was off-limits," Judy said.

She sighed and got up. "Come on along. Let's get it over with."

<h1 style="text-align:center">12</h1>

Our lot was a cozy fifty feet by sixty feet. Dad's shed abutted the wooden fence separating us from the back alley. We and the neighborhood kids had ample room in the yard to play when we were little. One of our favorite games was speculating what was in the shed.

Childhood fantasies ranged from a stairway that ran to the middle of the earth to, particularly around Halloween, various forms of witchcraft and magic potions brewed therein by resident hobgoblins. Dad was around most of the time, but seldom went into the shed to fiddle with his unnamed hobbies, raising the fantasy level to the ionosphere.

Holding a large key ring, Mom said, "Your father kept it triple-locked so you kids couldn't get into it."

Judy and I watched as she unlocked it, initially confused which key was which. We looked at each other, fairly sure now that he didn't use the hobby shed to tie flies or to whittle duck decoys.

She pulled on an overhead chain, turning on a single light, and stood back. "See for yourselves."

A workbench ran the length of the back wall, with a vice mounted on it, and a stool at the center, drawers at the sides. Hand and power tools hung on pegboard in front of the bench. There was a patina of dust throughout.

"Your father was very handy. The house came with the shed, but it was bare bones. He did all the interior finish work. It wasn't roomy enough for the old hand mower, so even before he moved other things out of here, the mower went in the basement."

"That's why I had to drag it up the steps," I said.

"Big deal. I had to do the dishes," Judy said. "I thought that was so unfair."

"It was character-building," I replied.

Judy rolled her eyes.

Mom said, "Help yourselves. Have a look around."

I slid open the drawers that contained disassembled rifles, scopes, and silencers. There were boxes of cartridges.

I picked up a box full of different-size bullets. Some of the rounds were as is, some made of lead that had been hollowed out, fine gray shavings on the drawer bottom.

Beside me, Judy said, "I am not liking this."

"Come back inside the house, kids," Mom said. "There's much more to the story. You'll like it even less."

* * * * *

Mom told all: Our father's former profession, the origin of the billfold, and his retirement on November 22, 1963.

Judy and I did not object when Mom poured herself a generous glass of merlot while speaking.

She finished and said, "Well?"

"Father was a hired killer," Judy said numbly.

"Jesus, Dad a hit man," I added.

"That was long, long ago, kids. Don't make snap judgments. Nobody's perfect," Mom said, reaching across the table to pat Judy's hand, then mine. "A wonderful man, a wonderful husband and father, who went on to become an educator, a beloved teacher of high-school history, which he came within a hair of making. His Warfare Through the Ages classes wouldn't've won all those awards unless he'd been and done where he'd been and done what he'd done."

"Still," Judy said.

I was leaning toward Mom's rationalization, but said nothing.

Mom said, "Killing bad people for bad people doesn't necessarily make you a bad person, does it? Aren't you performing a public service?"

"Mother," Judy said, arms folded tightly.

Mom thrust out her hands. "Oh, you two, if you think everything is black-and-white, go ahead and call the cops. They can slap the cuffs on me as an accessory long, long after the fact."

"Mom," I said. "No way."

"Haul me off to rot in some filthy jail, locked up with smelly, two-hundred-pound lesbian dope fiends."

"Nobody's calling anybody," I said.

"Inviting all their sicko friends into the cell to abuse a helpless old woman."

"Nobody's locking you up and you're hardly helpless, and please stop the gay bashing," Judy said. "I'm trying to process this. Seventeen people killed. Sixteen for money."

I held up a Harry's Hattery business card and said, "The fact that Dad prevented World War Three should cancel the hits out. Shouldn't it? All sixteen or seventeen. Who knows? People may be out there on the loose, thinking up schemes to give World War Three another try."

Attorney Judy glared at me, then at our mother.

"Mother, I can't believe you looked the other way."

"Not at first. The one he didn't do for money? Even if I wanted to, I couldn't see to look the other way."

"What?" I asked.

"Excuse me?" Judy said.

"To save me from the dirty, rotten, slimy, creepy, filthy bastard who had my dress up over my head, covering my face while he was beating me and trying to rape me."

13

Mom finished her wine, refilled without interference from us, and said, "May I fix you kids a drink or something to eat before I go on?"

We shook our heads no.

"Judith Ann, I worry so about your nutrition, living on sticks and twigs like you do. May I fry you a nice rib steak? I have some in the freezer. I can thaw one out in the microwave."

My vegetarian sister smiled and said, "I've never eaten a stick or a twig."

"You know what I mean."

"Stop stalling, Mother. You brought us into your confidence and we're grateful that you finally did."

Mom sipped and said, "Pandora's box. I sure did open it, didn't I? Wide open."

I raised a forearm and looked theatrically at the watch I didn't have. "Aunt Leah's in the Central Time Zone. She should be home."

"Oh, very well. When I'm done, you'll know why this isn't easy. Your father and I were in high school together, him a senior, me a junior. It was the late nineteen-fifties. Elvis and Lucy were bigger than big, and cars were just plain huge. Smoking was cool, not lethal, and seat belts would not have been worn even if cars came equipped with them."

Looking hard at Judy, she said, "None of the cars had the stupid thing I have to blow into and that seat-belt setup that tries to strangle me before I can latch it."

Judy smiled. "Same song, different verse. It's that or handing over your keys, Mother."

"Yes, well, anyhow, there were computers too, but they were as big as the tail-finned cars, used as much power as a small town, and did very little."

"Anyhow, Smith isn't our real last name. I'll take that secret to the grave, so please do not ask and do not snoop. You're wasting your breath if you try, Judy, with all your connections and secret clients who do a variety of secretive things, you'll never ever find out."

Big Sis surprised me by saying nothing.

"Your Aunt Leah is a year older than me, you know. She left home the instant after she received her high-school diploma and lived with friends while she went to business school, learning typing, steno and keypunch. She looked in on my mother—your grandmother—and I when she could, but there was only so much she could do.

"Leah's keeping the secret too, incidentally, what she knows of it, but it's almost too much for her. I'll say this for that loony cult she's in, it gives her comfort. Our childhood made her easy prey for the Bible nuts. After all, as you know, if not for your father in Dallas, that Armageddon and apocalypse they're so eager for may've already happened, and that's no exaggeration. Judy, you and I and him, long gone. If we survived, we'd be living in caves. Theo, you wouldn't even be here to be gone."

"You said Gramma died of natural causes before we were born and not much else," Judy said. "I was always curious why you had no mementos of her. No pictures or anything."

"You think I enjoy a toddy now and then? Well, it's an understatement that she enjoyed a taste too. If you can call dying of cirrhosis of the liver at age forty-five a natural cause.

"We lived in a single-wide trailer park, where every other trailer had a dead appliance on the front porch and a car up on blocks. We weren't even that wealthy. Your father's childhood wasn't a bed of roses either, with barely enough money to get by.

"He was in junior high and at school and his dad was at work when this encyclopedia salesman came to their door. His mother let him in and listened to his pitch. She didn't buy the books but sold herself to him apparently. She left a short note that your father saw first and had to show to his dad.

"She took off with the book peddler and was never seen or heard from again. His dad took it hard as you'd suspect, but didn't take to the bottle or take it out on your father. He just withdrew into himself and died young. Of what exactly? Your father didn't share other details with anyone else including me. Death by broken heart. Who knows?

"Getting back to *my* story. It was my birthday, which dear old mom, dear old barhopping mom, had forgotten all about. It slipped her mind as many things did. Your father hadn't forgotten. Stealing pansies and things out of a garden for my bouquet—but it's the thought that counts, isn't it? He came in with the flowers while one of my musical stepfathers—musical as in musical beds, not chairs—was so generously trying to teach me about the facts of life.

"Your father was a big, strong man like you, Theodore. He'd made all-league playing football. Before this creep on top of me could, you know, do it, I'd been fighting like the very devil, but was about worn out. The bastard was even bigger than your dad if you counted the beer fat.

"Your father heard me screaming, muffled kind of because my dress was up and over my head, and ran in just in the nick of time. He grabbed a lamp cord from a table lamp, lamp and all, and wrapped it around the bastard's neck. He tightened it as he dragged him off of me and outside, kicking and swinging and gagging.

"It wasn't easy. This was a big dumb-ass redneck, an unemployed laborer who was into other activities with some local goons, so it was no simple task.

"Once behind the trailer with him, your father yelled at me not to come out. There was a lot of thrashing and other god-awful noises that eventually stopped. We had a tiny shed at the rear of the park where there were shovels and other tools. I heard your father rummaging around in there.

"An hour later, he came for me and said it was over and done with. Meaning permanently. I don't remember how long he held me on his lap until I quit trembling and crying. Nobody but my mother asked about the guy. Had I seen him? Gee whiz, no. She asked only for a week or so, until she forgot and brought some other loser home.

"Your father had given me two small knives, switchblades, one to carry in my purse and one to keep under my pillow. He made sure my next stepdads knew about the knives and what he'd do if they even thought about touching me. Part of his welcoming orientation, your father called it. They probably heard or doped out what they heard through the grapevine about their missing slug.

"As I said and as you know, your daddy was a tall, strong man, so they listened. Did they ever. My new stepdaddies were as sweet as pie to me and they kept their distance. If I so much as slammed a drawer, they'd about jump out of their shoes.

"Through that same grapevine, it became known to the local gangsters what your father had done to lover boy, who they had used for more than odd jobs, which he hadn't been doing very well. A long and tangled tale I'm not getting into in any detail.

"Your father was approached, but instead of having his throat cut, he was given a roll of cash. He didn't know there was that much money in one place in the whole, miserable town. They said the dough was his if he listened to their pitch.

"As I said, my personal sex education trainer had been a wannabe member of the local mob, doing small chores, of which we had no specific knowledge. And becoming very unpopular with his superiors for reasons unknown.

"We came to the conclusion that he was suspected of being a police informant, a rat snitch or fink, I think they're known as. When the guy drank, which was more often than not, he shot off his mouth. They were happy and impressed that your father had saved them a chore. They have this warped honor code that saved your father's life and given him what you might call a career.

"Well, along with that roll of cash, they asked if he knew how to use a gun. He did. Him and his own father went hunting with thirty-ought-sixes. There were plenty of guns around their house, so he knew how to use handguns too. He was a deadeye, accurate with everything that had a barrel and a trigger.

"They said there was somebody even worse than the guy he'd eliminated that was rubbing them the wrong way. Was he interested? Why not? Gosh, it paid much, much better than a factory job.

"Yes, we talked it over and agreed that he should give it a try, providing that he was careful doing the jobs and careful of the wise guys too. It went from there. He drifted away from direct contact with them to those who our little local wise guys worked for, a good shield against treachery. So we'd thought sixteen jobs later.

"They had to be the ones who snapped that picture of him and sold it to forgers who did up the KGB card. Different organizations and chains of commands, we didn't want to know anything about, and we *really* wanted them to know nothing about us."

"When he got home after that horrible day in Dallas, we made plans for our new life. I was pretty good at investments. I got us into the ground floor of IBM and others coming along. I was no financial Nostradamus, but I always liked new gadgets. Transistor radios and electric typewriters, gizmos like those. I was mighty lucky too."

"We were very comfortable, Mom," I said.

"You invested well enough to supplement my scholarships to UW undergrad and Harvard Law, for which I'll be forever grateful," Judy said.

"Art school for me too and anything else I wanted. While I lasted, "I added. "Thanks again."

"Sixteen killings, Mother? Sixteen?"

"Don't ask for details because I'm not telling."

"Works for me," I said.

Mom said, "Yep, I was good with money, but not too shrewdly good. Ostentatious, I believe, is the word. We wanted us to be comfortable without attracting undue attention. It was a higher priority to keep our heads down than to live like maharajahs."

"It worked like a charm for a long time, Mother," Judy said, "Decades later, Father apparently proved unpopular with his former employers and those who succeeded them. Can we learn who, how and why now?"

"You tell me."

"Meaning?" Judy said.

"Let's start out with my grandsons, dear," Mom said. "It'll have to be done on computers, won't it? All youngsters know how to surf and turf and hack, whatever you call it. How to find out things people who don't want you to find out anything about them."

Making a face, Judy shook her head. "I will keep the boys on standby, Mother. For them, though, the Internet is free porn."

Both women looked at me, deference that was rather unusual.

"I did take a class in computer science once, to set up my domain and sell my paintings on my website. That didn't work out—"

"I have someone in mind," Judy offered.

"Let's keep it in the family initially, dear. A slip of the lip can sink a ship," Mom said. "When can you start, Theodore?"

"As soon as you swear on a stack of whatever's handy that you'll keep your windows and doors locked."

"And don't go out shopping or anywhere else without notifying us, Mother."

She shrugged, which could mean yes, no or maybe.

14

The old man stared out a side window, watching a ferry boat coming in to dock.

He said, "We should not have to be doing this. It should have happened long ago."

"Patience, Grandfather."

"Those Zurich Jews sitting on our gold. That fucking Chinaman is haunting us. We're spinning our wheels it seems like. Have been for years, decades."

"A little more time, Father."

"Your brokenhearted grandfather and great-grandfather gave their lives, boys. I hate those motherfuckers responsible."

"The bright side. One down, the ancient spouse to go, Father."

"Goddamn close to poetic, boy."

"Robin will handle the old lady. Killing her with her own broken heart."

"He'd damn well get it done… Before the brats know."

"My hornet's nest will distract them. Kicking over an anthill. We stir them up, get them in the open. Open and exposed."

"You and your pop-up and that which belongs to us. You put that bug in Robin's ear without asking us. I am not happy. We are not happy."

"It's like you're priming the pump, boy. I don't know. This isn't some video game of yours."

"I learned from a hacker wanted in seven countries."

"He cost us a pretty penny too."

"You want to torment them first, don't you, Grandfather?"

"I'd be a happy camper, yes, if I gave them ulcers. We're going stir crazy too. Relieve the boredom."

"Watch, Grandfather. It's what they're seeing."

* * * * *

The following appeared on Smith, Hurlbert and Kraus LLC's ultra-safe servers. It also appeared on all of their clients' servers as well as the servers of a variety of Judith Ann Smith's acquaintances.

Pop-up:
To appear suddenly and unexpectedly.
A component or device that pops up.

MISSION STATEMENT
We need to start over. And we will.

15

"A sabbatical, Kemo Sabe?"

"Or leave of absence. Take your choice of wording, my faithful Indian companion," I said.

Mr. Singh wore a white guayabera and a jittery smile. He was born and raised in Mumbai. His parents were upper caste, wealthy automobile dealers who sold the local Tata and the highly-favored Japanese brands. They were easily able to finance a college education for their eldest son, in his case at the University of Washington in Seattle.

He majored in fine arts, which they deemed as disturbingly useless, a discipline in which you studied the frivolous work of others. I knew by experience that they were more often than not correct.

In the worst way, they had wanted him to buckle down and go further, to attend medical school and become *Doctor* Singh. They could then boast endlessly about the boy to other parents whose children back home had gone on to field 1-800 help desk calls, earning thirty-cents per hour answering stupid questions posed by abusive, technology-challenged Americans. They had pleaded with him, had *insisted*.

That Mr. Singh owned three convenience stores and had an upper-middle-class income, a 7-Series BMW with all the trimmings, and a blond wife was scant consolation. They would never get over it nor forgive him, Mr. Singh had told me.

The man was a monument to self-pity, so I tried to cheer him up.

"Look, by selling primarily unhealthy fried snacks, beer and cigarettes, you're increasing the income of cardiologists, pulmonologists and pathologists, so would you not be in some context a member of the medical profession? And let's not overlook the ER physicians who treat the bullet wounds after all the robberies."

Mr. Singh was not moved, nor did he display a sense of humor.

"For a few days," I said.

"That is all?"

"Or longer. Slightly longer."

"Slightly?"

"Okay, I honestly don't know. Not exactly how long. Not to the exact day."

Mr. Singh looked at me, befuddled. His English was British-colonial-prep-school excellent and he knew the dictionary definitions of *sabbatical* and *leave of absence*—to be gone from a normal routine—but neither had ever been used in regard to Happy-Happy Convenience Store employment, a revolving door of minimum-wagers. A clashing syntax that flummoxed him.

I filled the silence. "I have to be away to research something."

"Research?"

"A crime. A death," I said, stopping there, with no intention of making it too personal.

"As like a private detective you see in the movies and television who solve the crime and shoot the criminal killer close to the end?"

I had already pocketed my .38 Saturday night special. "Kind of. Yeah."

"But are you not—how do you say—an artist, a drawer and sketcher and painter of —things? Begging your forgiveness, but is that not a sabbatical of a sort in itself?"

"This is a new duty. It has nothing to do with the fine arts profession. It has to remain confidential. A secret."

He rotated his head very slowly, as if unsure whether to nod or shake it, a strange sight.

"You are for sure to be a spy, a detective, yes?"

"Sure. That's some of it. You could say that I'm in a multitasking mode. Looking into things while looking out for loved ones."

"You will come back to me, yes? In a substantial part due to you, this is my only store at which I do not lay awake at night as a result of ongoing personnel problems."

"Yes, of course I shall return."

"But you cannot say when, so I can complete my schedule, Kemo Sabe? You are piling difficulty upon difficulty."

"Sorry, man."

Poker-faced, his teeth were clenched. Mr. Singh was silently pleading.

"I will, Sahib."

"Please, Kemo Sabe. It will be impossible to the extreme, but I will find a way to make it worthwhile for you to remain."

"Really?"

"By increasing your wage a full two dollars per hour."

"Wow. Very generous of you," I said.

"Lil has requested days off so she can attend a motorcycle rally with her terrifying friends, creating problems already for me," he went on. "Is this for truly certain you will return?"

For reasons unknown to me, Lil was his equivalent of a teacher's pet. This in spite of her intimidating him verbally and by her mannerisms. Lil may have the same effect on prospective criminals; she had never been robbed.

"Mr. Singh, I would never lie to you," I lied.

16

My humble abode was that and less, an elongated studio apartment above a Thai restaurant in an iffy neighborhood. Down the street was a dollar store and a used car lot where my '89 Corsica would be queen of the hop. I once loved Thai food, but upon being treated to cooking odors fourteen hours a day, I had nightmares about spring rolls, giant ones with tentacles.

On the other side of the ledger, I had large windows facing north, for that all-important north light, a painter's prize. For that amenity, I could ignore the comments of my wise-ass landlord who said, "North light? You could do this in the dark. If you ask my opinion, real art is a Madonna or like that Norman Rockford."

I did not ask his opinion and that he was no art lover was not a problem. He didn't care either that I had turned the floor into a drop cloth. As long as I paid my rent on time and didn't set the place on fire. So far, so good.

My former semi-fiancées and girlfriends were never short of helpful, how-to-live-your-life advice either. Katie was one of the worst, calling at all hours when she was half in the bag, reminding me that Picasso and Dalí wouldn't be caught dead in an '89 Corsica. Time warp or not, I got the idea.

The very worst were Brenda and Linda, each considering me a challenging project "who wasn't living up to his potential." If only I'd retrain and make a career change before it was too late. These ladies weren't all that different from those who developed relationships with death row inmates. Futility turned them on. The killers had no options and I wouldn't listen.

Love of my life, my resplendent Quetzal Adams, was different, but she wouldn't stay fifteen minutes in the place, after the aforementioned rutting, but otherwise voiced no criticisms. She said I had any number of problems, but reciting them to me was repetitious.

We first met at the opening of a gallery show. Perhaps the owner's faith in and loyalty to me had something to do with his business going defunct, but that's another story. I was in a joint surrealism and pointillism phase at the time. Think René Magritte's spheres floating in midair done with dots. This seemed to confuse the looky-loos who were in and out of the gallery in under ninety seconds.

Quetzal walked in, dressed in Mesoamerican primary colors and carrying an upscale shopping bag. She studied every piece while I studied every bit of her. I was instantaneously smitten.

"I'm looking for decor for my CPA office," she told me. "Nothing here quite works. Not that I don't love every picture you've painted. You do have the touch that intrigues me, though."

Normally, I'd be offended. *I am an artist, not an interior decorator, goddamnit.*

I'd thought that statement out loud a few times, very loud, killing a few sales that way by frightening them out the door.

Thinking fast, with a part of my body nowhere near my brain, I said, "I have other pieces."

Quetzal invited me to her office. She headed a bustling, eight-person firm on a fringe of downtown. It was a beehive of cubicles, outer walls a grayish-vanilla.

"What're you looking for? Which walls?" I said, speaking as an interior decorator.

"Oh, well, I don't know. Something with color to liven things up, but without going overboard with pictures of things in the pictures. You know, like the *Mona Lisa*, anything of that sort. One picture will do. I want some dazzle without being distracting."

Meaning none of my pointillist Magrittes. No worm-pitted apples floating in the sky. So she was a fine-arts Philistine? I was gaga like never before.

"Let's see what I can do."

I dashed out a couple of pieces, mostly color fields with a contrasting line. My first plunge into Minimalism, blue bisecting orange, though careful that they weren't Denver Bronco blue and orange. We were in Seattle Seahawk land.

When the paint was barely dry, I brought them to her office.

She studied them long and hard. "I love them both, Theo. I can't decide."

"Take them both. Two for the price of one."

"That's so generous."

"One for here, one for home?" I said, angling.

"That's a super idea, but I don't know where to hang it. My condo has a vaulted ceiling and all sorts of angles."

Aha. "If you like, I can help you decide."

"I hate to take up your valuable time."

"Not a problem."

"Are you available for dinner tonight? I'm a numbers gal, no good at things like this and I can nuke TV dinners, the limit of my culinary skills."

As a matter of fact, I was available for dinner. I arrived fashionably late (ninety seconds), bearing flowers and wine.

Her peek-a-view condo was just north of downtown Seattle, halfway up Queen Anne Hill. It could fit inside Judy's, but would nevertheless go for the high six digits in today's white-hot market. The interior architecture was genius, with nary a right angle. Establishing the perfect spot to hang the painting, requiring me to stare upward, evaluating the ceiling and the adjacent bare walls.

"Hmm. Obtuse, acute and right angles. The geometric possibilities are daunting."

She lay beside me. "Did you take geometry in school?"

"In plane geometry class, I was a star."

"Any ideas?"

"Well, over there to the upper left above your sideboard. Or the right, where you'll capture afternoon light."

That was bat guano, but it served my purpose of getting our bodies and faces moving. As I hoped, we softly collided.

Neither of us left her home for three days.

Quetzal called in sick. I had nobody to call in to, so I didn't.

As I fired up my aging laptop, I thought of the relationship between math and computers and the angularity of Quetzal's condo. How we had studied every facet, wrapped up together, me on top, her on top, and in every other possible configuration.

Euclid and Archimedes, those guys would have been proud.

In high school, I'd done badly in trigonometry. I didn't lack aptitude, but could not for the life of me comprehend why it was important to be so intimate with a right triangle. Sine, cosine, tangent, cotangent, secant, cosecant, so what? It seemed voyeuristic and useless. Same with algebra. I mean, who ever used algebra for *anything*? Those were among classrooms in which I did not belong. My grades verified that.

Plane geometry was different than tortuous math. It was more like a logic class than a math class—hard lines and angles that conjured Piet Mondrian, sans primary colors. I received a rare A.

Fortified by strong black coffee, I first checked conspiracy theories, anything to shoehorn the old man into, regardless how peripherally. Things Mom didn't know or was concealing. The sheer numbers were eye-poppers. Before I read on, in lieu of cream and sugar, I flavored the next cup of java with bourbon.

In recent surveys, fifty-plus years after the assassination, over half of those polled believed that Oswald *didn't* act alone. Pro-conspiracy organizations and blogs flourished. It was estimated that between a thousand and two thousand books had been written on the subject, the vast majority supporting conspiracy theories, many still on sale. Some had been near-best-sellers.

Conspirators abounded, hundreds of them—individuals and groups, an alphabet soup of fiends: FBI, CIA, KGB, NSA, NRA, KKK, LBJ, PTA, and even RFK. Not to mention the military-industrial complex, Freemasons, Castro, Khrushchev, Nixon, Ike, J. Edgar Hoover, and space aliens from inside and outside the solar system, little green men responsible for crop circles and cattle mutilations, and those who were not, the Trilateral Commission (not formed until 1973, but this was where space-alien time travel came in), the NAACP, DAR, League of Women Voters, Rosicrucian Movement, Christian Scientists, Druids, Knights of Columbus, the San Diego Zoo, Proctor & Gamble, and a rogues' gallery of Mafioso.

On Amazon, I sampled opening chapters of the conspiracy books. Many read like science fiction for seventh graders, written by seventh graders.

Lee Harvey Oswald had above-average intelligence, but was unstable to the extreme. A dyslexic dropout who'd been more or less raised by a wildly-hysterical mother, he had received a less-than-honorable discharge from the Marine Corps.

He'd gone to the Soviet Union, was assigned a flunky job assembling radios in Minsk, married a Russian woman named Marina Nikolayevna, soon became disenchanted with the Bolsheviks' socialist paradise, came back home, where he abused Marina, batting her around out of frustration for his myriad failures, and held and lost a variety of nothing jobs.

He'd been in Mexico in October 1963, trying to get to Cuba, to join in The Revolution. He'd made a nuisance of himself at the Soviet and Cuban embassies, demanding a visa. Each embassy read Oswald as a nut job when he walked in the door and wanted nothing to do with him, ping-ponging him off to the other.

Oswald came home to Dallas, broke, with nothing on the agenda, argumentative and unlikable as ever. Thanks to the help of a friend of Marina's, he was hired as a picker by the Texas Schoolbook Depository. Lee Harvey Oswald was in the wrong place at the wrong time, a pathetic little man who for reasons unknown sought to be in history books for centuries to come. He succeeded.

Was he part of a conspiracy, manipulated by a sinister puppeteer? C'mon.

Common sense dictated that nobody with more than a room-temperature IQ would conspire with a mercurial loser like Lee Harvey Oswald to break into a parking meter.

If Oswald was motivated by anything, I guessed it was how he'd be received in Havana, as a hero of The Revolution. A couple of things were wrong with that.

First, Oswald had no way of getting to Cuba. Second, even if he did, Fidel Castro would ship him back to us in ten seconds flat. Castro was a royal pain in our ass, but no fool. He didn't survive ten U.S. presidents by being recklessly stupid. He knew that we'd come to town for Oswald in extreme force, an invasion not at all like the Bay of Pigs fiasco.

Same with Jack Ruby as a conspiracy pard, a sleazebag nightclub owner and mafia groupie who plugged Oswald. Chalk that one up to unbelievable carelessness by the Dallas Police Department. Nothing else.

All common knowledge and common sense if you wanted to face facts.

The Dallas Trade Mart, now known as the Dallas Market Center, was still going strong today, much expanded since 1963. Even so, I had no trouble picturing it as it was then.

I reported to Judy that there wasn't anything new I could report. "That's it?"

"If there's a seating chart to the Dallas Trade Mart on that day or a police report on the two nudes, it's long gone. Harry's Hattery too."

I could see her eyebrows raise, even though I couldn't. I could hear her sigh, even though she wasn't.

"Look, Sis, whatever this is about, a grudge held for over half a century, there's some serious money behind it, piles and piles of money. Aconite Man was no lone killer like Lee Harvey."

"You're probably right."

"No 'probably' about it, girl. Dad's visitors at the Dallas Trade Mart. Now this. Call me a conspiracy nut, but I'm not talking grassy knoll or any of that bullshit. Here's a man liked and loved by everyone. No known enemies. Unless it's one of his students he flunked on a test about the Spanish American War."

After a pause, she said, "Okay. Don't go away, Theo. I appreciate you trying, but I'm sending you an expert."

17

As soon as I hung up, Ty and Chris rapped on my unlocked door and came in, making themselves at home as usual.

"That was quick. You're the experts?"

"Us experts?" Ty said. "Is that a trick question? We're not experts on nothing."

I said, "Your double negative ought to be a triple negative."

"Last dude who called me an expert was that judge, the motherfucker," Chris said.

Splayed on my thrift-store couch alongside his brother, Ty said, "What the fuck did Gramps have against us, Uncle T?"

"What do you mean?" I said, knowing exactly what he meant.

"He gave us shit. Like he wrote us out of his will is what it came down to."

"Stop whining. He loved you louts. He gave you the means to better yourselves. He wanted you to become productive citizens and make positive contributions to society in general," I said insincerely.

Ty replied with a shovel-scooping motion.

Chris snorted. "Like that's gonna happen and he fuckin' knew it."

"The vouchers," I said. "They're worth thousands and thousands."

"They're hand-written," Ty said. "I thought you had to print them."

I groaned. "What else did he bequeath you besides a fortune in educational opportunities you're too dumb to use? Like I was."

"Did he be who?"

"Bequeath. Bequest. Stick inside your envelopes."

"Right. A big herkin' two-fifty in cash," Ty said.

Chris said, "Last of the big fuckin' spenders."

"Fine. Ignore me and act like three-year-olds. Your grandfather believed in miracles, boys. The tooth fairy and others," I said. "Get your lazy asses off my couch and go to the fridge for beers. A few cold ones may settle you down."

They immediately obeyed as they did when I dispensed this sort of advice.

Chris said, "What're you doing on the laptop, Uncle T?"

"Research."

"Yeah, really, what?"

"Ancient history."

"Mind if I have a turn while you take a break?"

"I'm taking a break?"

"Somebody your age, you sit too long, you get blood clots in your legs, which is some bad shit."

"Help yourself."

He sat down and searched RED-HOT PUS—

I slapped his index fingers off the keyboard, jerked him back, and swiveled him to a one-eighty. "Shoo. Go finish your beer like a good boy."

I was good-natured, but firm. They'd never admit it, but they craved the familial discipline they didn't have growing up with Judy and her hundred-hour workweeks and their worthless fathers. So long as it was light-hearted, unlike the type they received from law enforcement, they generally played ball.

I said, "If you boys want porn, get it up close and personal and three-dimensional with those skanks you date. While you have some money left, take them out to dinner and dancing or a movie and whatnot."

Ty said, "We'll settle for the whatnot."

I answered a knock on the door. A gangly kid with stringy hair and thick glasses wore a black T-shirt and black jeans that rode high, exposing white socks. A pocket protector stuffed with pens sealed the deal.

"Mr. Expert, I presume."

"Mike," he said in introduction as I let him in. "I was sent here by my dad's lawyer, Ms. Smith."

"I'm Theo," I said, shaking his hand and standing aside. "Mike, this is Ty and Chris. Chris, Ty. Mike."

"Yo."

"Yo."

"Yo."

Mike looked around and sniffed. "Dude. You really live here?"

"Laptop's on the table. Help yourself."

"I'm smelling what?"

"Linseed oil, exotic Oriental spices, and beer. Care for a cold one?"

"Maybe later. Is that Thai I smell?"

"Do you like Thai?"

"Not so much. I dig Mexican."

"Mexican chicks rock," Ty said, doing an awkward hip swivel.

Mike said, "You're a painter, huh? Mr. Smith said you were. What do you paint?"

"Things and non-things."

"I'm seeing non-thing things on these pictures of yours. And things in these leaning up, parts of things."

"Paintings of mine, not pictures. You take pictures with a camera."

"That one there parked up on the, uh."

"Easel."

"Right. These people, they're at the airport staring at the big board, all those flights cancelled. There are some spots you haven't filled in."

"I call it *Weather Delay 2013*. How Edward Hopper would do it."

"That's like five years ago."

"It's not done yet and their flights are still delayed," I said. I'd been after Quetzal to let me paint her in, like Hopper often did with his wife Jo. She said she'd think about it every time I asked.

He pointed at my triptych that was in the shape of a stretched-out H.

"You dig baseball? That guy on the left, swinging. He's built like a fireplug."

I said, "Hack Wilson. I've never been a baseball fan but something about this guy intrigued me. See the stumpy build. They're saying now that he had fetal alcohol syndrome. In 1930, he set the record for RBIs in a season that still stands. One hundred and ninety-one."

"Cool."

"I don't understand how the hell could you have fetal alcohol syndrome or any other birth detect if you set the longest-standing major baseball record," I said.

I doubt if anybody else in the family made the connection, but I'd worried early on that Mom drank during her pregnancies. If she had, I wondered if it affected us in the womb. Not Judy for sure. Me? I lacked the physical symptoms, but whenever I screwed up, well—.

I had not uttered an FAS word to a soul and never would. The triptych and my lifelong fondness for the tragic Mr. Wilson was my voice.

"That section in the middle, baseballs whizzing. After this Hack dude blasted the ball."

"There's an art critic buried in your nerdish exterior, Mike."

"That thing on the right, in that part of the picture, it looks real but I can't place it."

"The iris of a camera lens. The viewer decides."

"Cool. What happened to your boy Hack?"

"He was a boozer and barroom brawler who died young. Age forty-eight."

"These other pictures—"

"*Paintings.*"

"Right. Looks like they're street scenes and stuff, parts of things that are, you know, some finished, most not."

"Also inspired by Edward Hopper."

"That artist, huh?"

"The greatest American artist ever."

"Cool."

"Who's your favorite artist, Mike?"

"The guy who draws Spiderman. In the comic books."

Chris said, "You got taste, dude."

"Yeah, thanks," Mike said, "You really do live here?"

"It's a self-fulfilling rumor that I do."

"Huh?"

I gestured to the card table, folding chair and laptop.

"Enough niceties, gentlemen. May we please get to work?"

"Dude, this computer of yours, did it come over on the *Mayflower?*"

"Please. Get. To. Work."

"It'll do. I guess," Mike said, sitting down carefully, on the lookout for foreign substances.

I'd tread gently with him. Judy's clients might be oily, but none were paupers and many were (I believed) dangerous.

"Before you get started, I'm unclear, Mike. Are you a client of my sister's too or just your father?"

"Only the old man is."

"What does he do? What did he do?"

Mike rocked a hand. "This, that and the other thing, you know. I gave up trying to get a handle on it. He's not much of a father, but he's one smart dude where money's concerned. He's in Belize now. Or the Caymans. He, like, moves around and shit. My mom, if she knows where he is, she won't tell me, like I'm a baby or something."

"Offshore," Chris said. "I can dig it."

Mike said, "What he's doing, I gotta believe, he's down there soaking up the rays and visiting while he's keeping his head down. I heard my mom once on the phone say to a friend that he's fooling around with the native girls. She's hoping and praying he's catching diseases from them, and she doesn't even go to church. I heard her one time on the phone with him, she was yelling, if your dick rots off, it serves you right."

"Gross," Ty said, squeezing his crotch.

Big Sister's clients. I'd have to put on a full-court press, see if they were somehow a link to this nightmare of ours. Tell her where she could shove her client confidentiality.

"You must be pretty good with computers, Mike," I said.

"I'm okay."

"At hacking?"

"You might say. Hack. It's a four-letter word these days, you know. I prefer research and development. R and D."

"Can you hack into the Pentagon?"

Mike affected a yawn. "Bor-ing. They write these dumb-ass emails to each other all day long. You know what the biggest issue is?"

"Stopping North Korean missiles?"

"Where to have lunch."

"Yeah? Not tariffs or Congress or Russian spies?"

"Not."

"Gerrymandering?"

"What's on the menus, and how they can charge it to their expense accounts. Then there's gossip, all kinds of gossip. Who's fucking who and who's fucking who over. The titles some of these dudes have. Assistant deputy undersecretary to the deputy assistant to the undersecretary. The second biggest topic is how they hope they won't screw up."

"The biggest?"

"How they hope so-and-so will screw up and get busted down a pay grade or busted by the law."

"My sister told you what we need?"

"Kind of. The events of that day way back when, when that president was shot, up the street from that Dallas Trade Mart building. More details on specifics wouldn't hurt, Mr. Theo. Ms. Smith used the word 'hypothetical' like ten times."

"Curiosity killed the nerd, Mike. Let's begin with the Dallas Trade

Mart on that day. Everything you can ferret out. And call me just plain Theo."

"Okay, here. A seating chart when that old president from way back in the last century was gonna speak. That's one thing. What's his name again?"

"John F. Kennedy. His friends and everyone else who liked him called him Jack."

"Yeah, him. Right. It's all coming back. We studied it in high-school history class. Where he was to speak before, you know—"

"I know," I said impatiently.

"Okay. Here we are."

"Wow. That fast."

"It's about patterns and overlays. On the regular Web and the Dark Web. The Dark Web, it cuts through the red tape."

"The Dark Web. I've heard of it, but I'm not sure what it is," I said.

"To begin with, think of a jagged sine curve that's vertical, not horizontal, made up of overlays you gotta peel off by opening up encryptions, kind of like bitcoin bandits do, busting off links of the blockchains to get at the digital bread, but moving through the layers, which is less easy."

"Sure," I said.

"And think of a tunnel that spirals to, like, you know, the core of the earth. You got goblins and gremlins and Bulgarians and other nasty, bad-ass shit down there, but it's not all spooky. There's halfway normal stuff you can't find on the regular Internet."

Ty said, "Hey, what's dark web beaver like?"

Mike looked up at him. "Scary."

I looked at Mike, who looked at me, blushed and said, "I went there one time, you know, out of curiosity is all."

"Let's check it out, man," Chris said. "I like mean and nasty chicks."

"I don't know, dude," Mike said, "You know what the girl praying mantis does to the boy praying mantis while they're getting it on?"

Chris said, "Talks dirty bug talk to him?"

"She eats his head off. Scarfs it right down."

"Fuckin' gross."

"Dark web porno broads are even worse than that, I kid you not."

"That's enough technical info for me, boys," I said. "For openers, Mike, I want the name of the person at the Dallas Trade Mart who was seated at the second row from the rear, fourth seat from the right."

Mike hunted-and-pecked. Screens scrolled, an electronic smear.

"Here we go. Dave Bob Hoopsma. Is that a Texas name or what?"

"See what you can find on Mr. Hoopsma, why he was there."

Mike typed and muttered for a good five minutes. "Zee-row on any Hoopsma. That name, Polish or Uzbek?"

"Fort Worthian," I said.

"Yo, here's our boy. Found him in the Dallas and Fort Worth obits. Been dead for like fifty years is Hoopsma's problem, why he was hiding out from me. Let's see. He owned five service stations in Texas and Oklahoma. Dave Bob is whipping it on us from that big gas pump in the sky. Wife and four kids, six grandkids. Dave Bob died of lung cancer."

"Did he have a criminal record or anything else that stands out?"

"Zip. He was a deacon or archbishop or some shit in his local Baptist church. As far as crime goes, clean as a whistle."

"Any organizations or clubs."

"Here's one that has to do with Southwest gas stations. He was sergeant at arms for three years. Aside from that, he didn't belong to the Elks or Chamber of Commerce or any of those. He was a gas station lifer, period."

Dave Bob Hoopsma, a gas station magnate back when they checked your oil, cleaned your windshield, and had free road maps. Picked at random, seated conveniently enough to be a believable target, to plunk Dad down where they wanted him.

"Harry's Hattery?"

"Easier. It went out of business in 1971 when the owner, Harry Hanson, retired. He died in 1977 of natural causes."

"The two young gentlemen at Harry's Hattery when President Kennedy was due to visit?"

"Yeah, them. How come they're important? I mean, with the President and those bigwigs down in the atrium—"

"Remember what I said about curiosity and nerds, Mike."

"Man, this thing is getting weirder and weirder."

"You wouldn't be here if it wasn't."

"You're thinking police records?"

"Unless they brought a change of clothes we don't know about and split. I don't know where else to look."

"The records, they gotta be old and dusty, in the police archives. Whoa. It came right up. How goofy is that? The dynamic duo made the papers three days later. A big deal. Can you be arrested for sodomy and crimes against decency?"

"There and then."

"Well, they were hauled in, running for it bare-ass naked. Busted before they got out of the building. Lots of ladies screaming. Guards and cops piled on them like they were recovering a fumble. After Kennedy was offed, the whole town was swarming with cop activity. This was kind of a sidebar, though, being there where they were, doing what the law thought they were doing."

"Cornhole City," Ty said.

I said, "Or were they going to step out when the president arrived and do a dance revue or something? A protest kind of situation? I don't think the dots were ever connected. The Texas School Book Depository and Lee Harvey Oswald, they were the center of attention."

Mike said, "Yeah. Oswald clipped a cop named J.D. Tippit too, tried to hide out in a theatre. *War is Hell* was playing."

"That's common knowledge. Who were they?"

"They?"

"The two nude gentlemen in Harry's Hattery."

"Right. Well, that's the funny thing. They had no fingerprints on file. Guys who do that kind of shit, you'd think, jaywalking at the minimum. One gave his name as Blaine Johnson, the other Jerry Davis. They said they were brothers-in-law, Blaine from out-of-town, Jerry a customer of Harry's Hattery, doing him a favor by letting them look out onto the Kennedy thing from his shop. Seeing the sights, hoping to see the president when this dude with a ski mask and a gun shoved them in the hat shop just as they were arriving and putting a key in the door, and took their clothes and everything else. Watches, wallets, everything. They were victims, not criminals against nature."

"Faggots," Chris said, offering his opinion.

"The cops must've been shaking their heads, watching their noses grow."

"For certain, but on that day, who could be sure about anything? They could have stashed their clothes somewhere in case they got caught violating nature. They were held pending charges, bail posted at ten thousand."

"A tidy sum now, a huge wad of cash then."

"Yeah. Their stories maybe stunk to high heaven, but the law was what you'd call preoccupied. Oswald assassinating JFK. Fifty dozen eggs on their face for letting that Jack Ruby dude plug Oswald right under their noses. They thought a high bail would keep those boys under their thumbs for the time being, until they could concentrate on them and figure it out. But you know what?"

"They made bail?"

"They did. The next Monday. A lady by the name of Delilah Henn Condor, a resident of Dallas, older sister of the pair, sprung them. Her story is they were retards who got in a bad crowd of degenerates and were taken advantage of because of their low IQs. She apologized up and down and sideways for them. Said they'd learned their lesson, and she'd keep leashes on them."

"How did she explain all the different names?"

"Husbands, broken marriages, like that. The police notes were choppy and scribbled. Mrs. Condor and the boys were due back in a week, the following Monday, to face the music at a hearing or arraignment. Guess what happened."

"Nothing happened," I said.

"Uh huh. They checked out Mrs. Condor's residence and phone number. No such phone number then. Address was a vacant lot. An eighteen-story office building's there now. Search of names of all three took longer then, without computers. Guess what finally happened."

"Nothing finally happened."

"Yeah. We got a huge shitload of zip and zilch. They disappeared into thin air when they were thin air to begin with."

"This Condor surname, it's unusual."

"It is. I've been coming up blank, but I'll keep after it."

I laid out the contents of the wallet.

"You know all this is confidential," I said.

"I know, I know, man. Hypothetical too. I was told by Ms. Smith. A slip of a lip will sink my ship. She's kinda scary when she talks to you that way."

"Tell me about it," Ty said.

Mike sniffed the contents. "Where'd you get this moldy, antique stuff?"

"Flea market."

"Yeah, right. The KGB card. It's so cool. I got a video game about them. Them against us. Spies and counterspies, and nukes flying back and forth, vaporized by the coolest military hardware. Are they still in business for real?"

"Different initials, same line of work," I said. "Comrade Larrionov?"

Mike searched screen after screen. "Nope. There are Larionovs with one 'r', but not this dude."

Confirming beyond a shadow of a doubt that dear old dad was slated to become Comrade V.I. Larrionov when he was discovered upon JFK's assassination and his own suicide.

"What the hell's this?" Mike said.

"Must I remind you, curiosity and the nerd."

"No, I mean this."

Pop-up:
To appear suddenly and unexpectedly.
A component or device that pops up.

And.

MISSION STATEMENT
We need to start over. And we will.

"Beats me," I said. "I get spam all the time. Do me a favor and delete it."

Mike pounded the keys so hard I thought they'd break.

"I'm trying ten different varieties of 'delete' and it won't."

I had a disturbing thought.

"Never mind that and hold on."

I went into the hallway. Through vents, I heard yelling in Thai, as well as pots and pans banging.

I called Judy, giving her what Mike gave me.

"I'll check that pop-up thing later. Father's story is confirmed. This was a powerful and well-moneyed organization. Was and is. Then and now," she said.

"It seems so. Mike would like to complete the jigsaw puzzle. The Condor name bugs me too."

"I don't think that's wise, not at the moment. There's a limit I want to his involvement."

"Who else do you have?"

"Good point. We'll let him proceed."

"What about Mike's daddy in the Caribbean, who's chasing native girls around palapa bars, catching exotic VD?"

"Sorry, Theo. Attorney-client confidentiality, so please stop prying."

"A hint?"

"All right. One snippet. Without the proper documentation, he claims he's stranded. His Learjet has been impounded too. He is not happy."

"Allegedly unhappy."

"I'm protesting to the Feds, so far to no avail. Several alphabet agencies are interested in him too. Give Mike a glass of milk and freshly-baked cookies, then send him on his way."

"Chris and Ty are still here. They don't do milk and cookies."

"God, Theo. Keep them away from Mike. He may be a computer genius, but he's an innocent, if you know what I mean."

"Too late. They're hitting it off, so lost innocence is guaranteed."

"Please do your best. His mother is a friend and—"

Was and is. Then and now.

Interrupting her and talking a mile a minute, I ran downstairs, two steps at a time.

18

S oon. A nebulous, imprecise word.

Mr. C the Three had ordered Robin to eliminate the old lady soon.

He interpreted the earliest practical *soon* as nightfall. Darkness was an ally, a common sense approach Mr. C could understand.

However, the presence of the miniature pistol in his pocket was roiling his stomach. The pickled old woman certainly hadn't—

Robin tried to banish his worries. After he had reported what he observed on Seattle's Harbor Island, the Very UnReverend Robin presumed that all details of the widow-elimination project were left up to him, so long as he acted quickly. Essentially, he was ordered to be proactive. Mr. C the Three's trust elated him. Details on the mysterious CondorCakes would be the next to come as he tracked Container five-four-three. His efficiency, his competence, his results. He would be one of *them.*

He went to a uniform supply store, bought appropriate clothes, drove to a car rental agency street near the Seattle-Tacoma Airport, and rented a small parcel van. He left his rental car in a twenty-four-hour parking lot and drove the van home to the small apartment Mr. C the Three had provided him.

The south Seattle complex was not remotely upscale. The newest vehicle in the lot was seven years old and Robin's minimal furnishings were shabby, but everybody minded their own business.

He went inside and dressed as a generic delivery employee, in matching brown shorts and shirt. He was in business. Ready to rock and roll. So proud of his ingenuity, he kicked back and channel-surfed until the beginning of twilight.

On his way out, Robin found a small cardboard box in the recycle Dumpster, straightened it out, tossed it in the van, and drove to Columbia City, to the widow lady's house, initially to drive past, to reconnoiter.

He cruised her street. No neighbors out and about. This was good.

A light drizzle was starting, that and darkness an assurance that those at home, potential nosy parkers were staying indoors.

One more lap around the opposite block in the van—Robin had done a double figure eight so nobody might discern a pattern—and he'd stop. He felt silly in the outfit, like an overaged Boy Scout. Long-sleeved and made of material too heavy for the season, it itched.

But when dear old Elizabeth (Betty) Smith, recently widowed, answered the door, she'd receive instead of her order, a tincture of aconite injection.

Robin would then helpfully support the old dear as she began to tumble and carefully back her toward the first available chair. Then tsk-tsk as her legs went out from under her and she succumbed of a broken heart.

If you believe in God, I'm so sorry, God doesn't love you. If you believe in Jesus, Jesus is in step with his mythical father. Nonetheless, Armageddon be on the horizon, though not the Biblical version. Give thanks that you won't be around to see it.

All trite, yes. But her death would not be a rare occurrence, not a coincidence at any level. Just read the obits. One long-married octogenarian spouse checks out. The survivor, distraught, helpless, grieving, disoriented, cannot cope, has lost his/her will to live, and that's all she wrote. The bodily vitals kept running by companionship, joint projects, daily chores, and small pleasures screech to a quiet halt. A week later, dead as a doornail.

It will require ninety seconds tops, Robin guesstimated, depending on how long it would take the old lady to hobble over to the door. He'd be out of the vicinity posthaste, bound for the rental agency, then get back to business tracking the mysterious CondorCakes. Stressful multitasking, yes. Mr. C the Three was asking a lot from him, but he was up to it.

Robin made his last around-the-block circuit and slowed, adjusting the syringe inside his sleeve.

Behind him, barreling along the street like gangbusters, discharging a rooster tail of blue smoke, came a rolling wreck, an obsolete model of Chevrolet. It swerved into the Smith driveway so hard that the centrifugal force should have jettisoned a half dozen rusting body parts. Theodore Cleaver Smith, the marginal son ran out of it, barely slowing as he unlocked the front door and went inside.

Robin drove on by, eyes forward. Thinking, thinking, thinking.

At the first intersection, he passed a baby-blue Porsche. It took the corner as if in the Indianapolis 500. Into the widow Smith's driveway it went and into the house Attorney Judith Ann Smith went, wearing two grand worth of female business apparel.

If he and his employers were lucky, Robin thought, the old gal had an episode without his help, thus the panicky visit by the children. If that blessed event occurred, he would of course take credit.

He headed out of the neighborhood in the direction of the closest thoroughfare, dubious of good luck in general. For one thing, there were no emergency aid vehicles en route.

Robin tried to remain calm.

Per Mr. C the Three, the books needed to be cleared.

And cleared soon. Robin thought it wasn't just money. It simply had to be done before a deadline unknown to him.

As insinuated, the old woman was an impediment to the implementation of his inscrutable CondorCakes and all else on his unknown docket.

Robin knew that Mr. C the Three had zero tolerance for failure.

Telling him that if he had been a mere ten minutes earlier, the situation would be hunky-dory. A fantasy. A fairy tale.

Soon.

The adult children barging in like a SWAT team, something had galvanized them to sense an emergency and take charge. The child-parent role frequently flip-flopped when the parent became in the children's view too elderly and frail to live on his/her own again.

Robin knew he'd lost his last chance to get the biddy alone.

A mile from the old woman's house, he pulled over at a strip mall, scratched his numerous itches, and made a call he wished he didn't have to make.

Praying a prayer he expected to be unanswered that the children would leave without their mother.

19

Exceedingly annoyed at us, Mom said, "Oh, stop looking at me that way, you two. For your information and every other blue nose, red wine is packed with those flavonoids you read about that helps your ticker keep on ticking."

Judy took Mom's glass of wine from her, poured it down the sink, and said, "Dark chocolate accomplishes the same thing, Mother. Without destroying your liver and numerous other things."

"Thank you, Carrie Nation. My eighty-some-year-old liver is fine and dandy. Just my luck, at my age I'll get acne from the chocolate you're dying to shove down my throat for my flavonoids."

I said, "We're not here about your boozing. We have some new info. You can't stay here, Mom. Not for the time being"

"What new info?"

"Long story. It's computer data we didn't have before."

"Computers are a fad. They're full of nothing but garbage and nonsense."

"That they are, but a computer expert—"

"Who? One of those nerd kids you read about who hack into other people's computers instead of dating girls like normal boys do?"

"That's close, Mom, but someone we believe who's mixed up with whoever killed Dad is playing computer games with us. Why and how is a mystery, but it's obvious to us that you aren't safe by yourself."

"If you want to make it a permanent move where you'll be safe, we can help, Mother."

"Permanent?"

"At least until we know you're out of danger."

Mom wiped her eyes before they teared up.

Judy hurried to sit beside her. "Mother?"

Judy was in courtroom cross-examination mode, gentle though persistent. Mom didn't stand a chance.

"Oh, the memories."

"We'll put your things in one of those self-storage places," I said. "It'll be safe and nearby. We'll run you there any time you want something."

"I see that look in your eyes, both of you. You think you're sticking me somewhere? An old folks home where they all sit around gossiping and drooling, or crocheting or knitting or some other stupid thing. Ugh. Or to Leah's... Well, you have another think coming."

"Mother, we're not bluffing about Aunt Leah."

I said, "You'll be in the nick of time to help with the alfalfa harvest and the Rapture."

"For all I know, she keeps snakes in the house to practice on."

"Excuse me?"

"So she can handle them at church without getting bit and all those other crazy things they do."

"Mom."

She shuddered. "Slithering all over the place."

Judy said, "Bottom line, once and for all. We are of a mind that whoever wanted Father out of the way won't stop with him. Theo and I are in total agreement on this. It is linked directly to 1963 Dallas and to you, Mother, the last living link to him and that."

"Bosh."

"Not bosh, Mom. They know or they think they know that you know what he knew or think he knew."

The women looked at me.

"You know what I mean."

"We're not sticking you anywhere. I have oodles of room, Mother. You'll even have your own bathroom."

Big Sis did have oodles of room. Her downtown condo suite was on the top-floor, nearly as high as her office, with floor-to-ceiling windows on two sides, the glass two inches thick, as there was no visible support on the corner. If anyone in Seattle had a better view of the cityscape, Elliot Bay, and the Olympic Mountains, I don't know who it'd be. Real estate ads for similar unhumble-abodes were listed as 'by appointment only', no price given. If you have to ask—. I did see an ad in the Sunday paper for a comparable one: $12,500,000.

Judy's office building was visible, an easy three-block walk from there to there. A nice commute. Easy to stay in touch. And keep an eye on Mom. An ideal solution.

"A swanky prison for me is all it is. Like those towers in England those old kings like Henry the Eighth had, where he kept his ladies he fooled around with before he got tired of them and had their heads chopped off."

"I have a private elevator and there's shopping and a nice restaurant on the ground floor," Judy said impatiently.

"Oh sure. Like you'd give me the freedom to come and go as I please. I'd have to grow out my hair and lower it like Rapunzel's to have any visitors."

"Mom, you can have all the visitors you want. You can screen them in the lobby before letting them up. We have twenty-four hour security."

"My lady friends, your security boys, they'll frisk them, free and easy with their hands. I know how that goes."

"Mother."

"How about if I want to head out for a daily constitutional? Is that a no-no too?"

Judy didn't answer.

I didn't either, assuming that her constitutional was to the nearest bar.

Mom stared off into some middle distance like I remembered her doing when she didn't want to respond to her children's questions and demands.

"Theo will move in too. Temporarily until this situation is cleared up. Okay, Theo?"

To babysit and/or to be babysat. "I will?"

"You will. He will."

"I will, Mom," I said.

Arms folded tightly, Mom said, "I can take care of myself right here, thank you very much."

Judy sighed. "Fine, Mother. You win. I'll hire round-the-clock security for you. I know a firm that is the absolute best. All their agents are authorized to carry firearms, so anyone who wishes to do you harm had better think again. They wear uniforms too so there's no mistake."

I smiled and got up. "Your neighbors are gonna love having the neighborhood infested with rent-a-cops who're armed to the teeth. Secret Service wannabees. Anybody gets out of line, like mowing their lawn too early, it'll be OK Corral."

There was a good thirty seconds of dead air.

"I can bring what I want to your high-altitude jailhouse?"

"Anything and everything," Judy said. "What there isn't room for, if you want it really handy, I have storage space in the basement. If we run out of space, I can rent more."

Mom silently fumed, fresh out of rebuttals.

Judy said, "Let's get you an overnight bag or two for now. We'll make a list once you're settled."

I said, "Except what's out in the triple-locked shed."

20

The Very UnReverend Robin hadn't long to wait to confirm that God had snubbed him, got even for his blasphemy, whether He existed or not. Away went the Porsche, the junker, and the old lady's vintage Chevy Impala. Guessing where they were headed, he trailed the hurriedly-packed Smith family at a discreet distance. Sure enough, the strange three-car caravan went to downtown Seattle and into the parking garage of an office building-luxury condo tower.

Robin entered a general parking garage directly across the street and nosed the van into the first slot he found, on the fourth floor, then walked to the landing and watched the gate to the condo garage open and close for tenants, hoping for an ongoing malfunction that could grant him entry, a miracle he knew would not occur. He'd have to possess cartoonish super powers to get to the old bat now, zooming up the outer wall.

He made the next call that he dreaded, describing where he was, where they were.

"I was seconds away, mere seconds, sir," he said, then related the Smith sibling blitzkrieg, fabricating complications that were out of his control. Traffic. Nosy block-watch neighbors. Police activity less than a block away. A burglary? Who knows? The timing, the situation, it couldn't been worse.

"These snags occur," Mr. C the Three replied evenly. "Life is imperfect. Stay with them, monitor them, trail them if it is as you hypothesize, a transfer of the old woman. You are a good man, Robin, a problem solver."

Robin's first call to Mr. C the Three had been met with monosyllables and silence. This one did not go as he had so greatly feared, a tremendous relief. The man listened to reason.

"The daughter's made of money. She lives on the top floor," he said, sighing.

"We know that, Robin. This was included in your orientation."

"Yes sir. Her and I, so close, yet presently so, so far. However, I see ways, possibilities, a solution, but it'll take time to analyze their individual schedules and—"

"You're being repetitious and annoying, Robin. Let me place this predicament of ours in perspective with an analogy. The conjunction of Earth and Mars. When the two planets are at their closest, an event that occurs once every two years, a satellite launched will reach the Red Planet in eight months. That must seem interminable to those involved in the program, but at any other time, the distance between their orbits is nigh impossible. Do you see what I'm saying?"

"Yes sir," Robin lied.

"The planets are now all out of conjunction. Two other planets, the adult children, have joined in orbits of their own. If we are speaking of the solar system, it'd be a nightmare for NASA."

"Well, uh, sir, if I gather what you're saying, the kids aren't necessarily up to speed. The mother wouldn't necessarily confide in them, I mean any wild paranoid theories are in her head."

"Wild paranoid theories such as?"

"That, you know, he didn't die of old age."

"Would she have just cause to think that, Robin?"

"Oh no, no way. I'm just saying, sir, how her old pickled mind might work. It's possible."

"Judith Ann Smith and Theodore Cleaver Smith bought her wild, paranoid theory, so they're moving her out of harm's way? Is that possible too?"

"A faint possibility. Yes sir."

After several seconds of silence, Mr. C the Three said, "They brought the old woman's luggage?"

"Well, there was what appeared to be a suitcase or two and other belongings tossed into their vehicles. Not too much luggage. Not much at all. It might not be a permanent visit. The convenience of her there. Temporarily. Giving her time to settle down. So she doesn't have to mourn alone. It's really too soon to say."

Robin's voice trailed off.

"There you are, Robin. It logically follows that the threesome has circled wagons, either for the short- or the long-term. An enormous complication and we're running out of time."

Running out of time for what? Stupidly, Robin replied with a nod.

"Robin, are you there?"

"Yes. Yes sir."

"The daughter is a prominent attorney."

A question? "Yes, yes she is."

"This is her residence?"

"It is," Robin said.

"The top floor of the condominium tower, high in the sky."

"I'll check out which unit. Which unit on the very top floor. The lawyer girl, she's made out of money."

"And do what? There will be security in the lobby."

Robin could see uniforms in the lobby.

"There will be, yes. There is, actually. Not an insurmountable problem. Those guys, they make as much as they'd make flipping burgers. They aren't FBI or anybody at that level."

"If they cannot be purchased or interdicted, you'll be a human fly and scale the wall?"

A joke? He had discerned no sense of humor in the man. Robin said nothing.

"Robin? Are you there?"

"I will take care of all three. It may take a little longer. This development. It's only a small hiccup."

"See that you do. Time, it is a'wasting. We're working on the problem at this end too. Stand by exactly where you are, keep your eyes peeled, and await further instructions."

"It's late in the day."

"Indeed it is. The relevance of that observation?"

"Uh. I'll be here."

Stand by exactly where you are, keep your eyes peeled, and await further instructions. He obeyed, standing there until morning. His feet and legs were numb. He was hungry and thirsty, and desperately had to find a bathroom.

In the throngs exiting the building were Smith's adult children. For all the good it did him.

The security guards were fat and bored. Later, with Judith and Theodore gone for the day, he'd breech them with smooth talk or a distraction. Find the old lady's unit, get inside, and do her. No aconite, no subtlety. Wait for the son and daughter, do them too. Choreograph it as a murder-suicide. Or a slaughter by a madman. A burglar surprised as he rummaged for loot. Let the authorities sort it out.

A crazed fantasy, he knew. That Earth-Mars thing. Robin's planets were orbiting Jupiter.

If he had been a short ten minutes sooner in the delivery van.

It was eight-thirty in the morning and the garage was filling. The exhaust fumes were making him nauseous.

"Excuse me. Sorry," said a man in a suit, carrying a briefcase, in a hurry as he brushed by Robin.

Robin felt a slight sting in one leg, but thought nothing of it, probably a cramp from stress. But he was fast becoming dizzy and had to cling to the wall.

The man was back, examining Robin with concern.

"Are you all right, sir?"

"I'm cold," Robin rasped. "So cold."

"It's perfectly normal to feel cold," the man known to some as Hawk said as he half-backpedaled and half-dragged Robin, and sat him down between a Chrysler minivan and a Mercedes SUV. Hawk was compact and muscular, and did so easily.

"So cold. Who are you?"

"You were inefficient, Robin. You know the penalty. You know what Mr. C the Three expects. He pays very, very well and expects performance commensurate to pay. You wolfed down the mission statement, didn't you?"

Robin tried to focus on the man.

"You did. I know you did. We all do."

Robin tried to nod, but couldn't.

"Not to worry. Relax," Hawk said. "It'll be over soon."

And it was, twenty seconds later.

Robin's last thought: *Religion, this religion, and most others, exist simply because we cannot accept the finality of death. Your God, his earthly son, the rest of it, they're no more bona fide than the security blankets we cuddled with as children.*

The man known to some as Hawk wiped off his weapon with a tissue. He worked with a 3.5 inch, spear point paring knife, one-piece, fully forged, cambered and finely-balanced, with a riveted handle. A favorite of chefs such as himself. Hawk could break down a side of beef in no time at all.

Creative carving in the kitchen and on humans, and his love of Millicent. This represented all he had, all he needed and all he cared for.

The sting and the leg cramp Robin had felt was a quick horizontal motion into a thigh, slicing a femoral artery and withdrawal of the knife. In and out, virtually no pain. Prison executioners should consider the technique.

So preferable to a carotid, albeit the same marvelous result. No visible flash of blade, no neck-spurting for everyone to see, Hawk firmly believed. A severed femoral artery spread onto trousers, in the darkness of the garage, at initial inspection an act of involuntary urination.

Hawk went to the elevator and took it to sixth and top level. There were few cars, no squealing of tires up and down the ramps.

Mr. C the Three craved anonymity, so Hawk attempted to control his temper. At times he was successful.

He had taken Robin's baby pistol and his cell phone. He redialed the last number on the screen.

"Done," he said, hung up, stomped on the phone as if it were a dung beetle, and distributed the pieces in several trash receptacles.

He rode the elevator down to Level Three. A slender, attractive woman got on. She was half a head taller than him. Aroused, Hawk smiled at her. She looked through him as if he were invisible.

As the elevator door closed, he heard either a scream or squealing tires.

Hawk preferred the company of tall, younger women, the primary attraction being the reaction of others. He enjoyed asking younger taller males who looked askance if they wanted to make something of it. When some were foolish enough to take him up on it, the end result made his day.

This woman's obvious contempt infuriated him. When she stepped at the ground level, Hawk applauded himself for not giving her what she truly deserved.

21

"Is it my imagination, Judith Ann, or is it only males of the species who bring your coffee?"

"Nobody's ever accused you of lacking imagination, Theodore Cleaver."

Seated by her desk, I sipped my hot coffee. I needed warming after Inge's subarctic response to my smile and her return to whatever she wasn't doing.

Chris and Ty were working as Correspondence Supervisors. I had to wonder if they had made crude advances toward her, poisoning the Smith family well.

"This one, Brendon—"

"Brandon."

"Isn't Brandon young to be a lawyer? He looks like he's in high school."

"You're seeing him from the vantage point of your advanced age. Brandon is entering his last year of law school. He's an intern. As you age, people you knew when you were younger become younger in your eyes. The elementary school teachers that you regarded then as ancient were—"

I cut off her lecture. "Young Brandon, a victim of sexism and anti-ageism too. The whole package."

"Quit being your witty and charming self for a minute and pay attention to business."

She handed me a sheet of paper. "Read this."

I said, "That pop-up and mission statement thing that wouldn't go away on my laptop. Mike was finally able to delete it."

"Mike eventually got it out of our system too, but not before I had twenty calls from clients wondering why I'd sent them that. Mother needs to accept the seriousness of all this."

"Which twenty clients?"

She ignored me, swiveled, and swung the sports-bar-sized monitor around and closer. As I leaned forward, I saw behind it that my Minimalist masterpiece hung five or ten degrees cockeyed. It had been straight up and down in my last visit.

Did Judy bring it out strictly for my visits or was the janitorial staff careless when dusting it? If the latter, nobody but me noticed.

Which reminded me, where would I paint in Judy's condo? Answer: nowhere. Except possibly in the basement storage room, which had no north light or any other light. I'd be a commuter to my studio-tenement.

"Read this and tell me what you think," she said.

As she slowly scrolled, I read a terse report from the security personnel who were monitoring Mom's home. They hadn't seen anything out of the ordinary, but in canvassing neighbors learned that there was an unmarked delivery van that had been driving by earlier, as if searching for an address. The number of trips up and down the street made it unusual in this era of GPS.

They presumed that it was a delivery van because it was windowless and the guy behind the wheel that they couldn't describe beyond being a white male wearing a brown UPS-like uniform. A woman right across the street who been out front weeding around her roses recalled the last four numbers of its license number—1943—because it was the year her recently-deceased father was born.

Judy had ordered her private eye (Richard/Richie/Rich/Dick?) to check out the van, giving it their highest priority, damn the expense. He did, learning that it belonged to a car and commercial vehicle rental company, and had been rented to a man named J.K. Robinson whose only distinguishing feature was that he'd paid in cash.

The ID presented at the agency proved to be a counterfeit driver's license. The investigator's search divulged that the renter was not in the state's DMV and that his address of residence was, if it had existed, in the south end zone seats of Century Link Stadium, where the Seahawks and Sounders played.

Present whereabouts of the van: unknown.

She swiveled her monitor back around, sipped her coffee, and said, "If I were paranoid, and I am, a requisite in my profession, I'd say it was Aconite Man."

"Why him now? Again? That enduring question. I have a sound answer you won't like hearing."

"Try me."

"A new or recent client of yours connected dots or saw the family resemblance in you, that and your first name being beyond a coincidence."

"Good, Theo. There are less than ten million Smiths in the world. Let's examine your public exposure and fifteen minutes of fame."

"At the Happy-Happy Convenience Store. Ringing up a guy's six-pack and chips. Less likely, Sis."

Kemo Sabe.

"Don't forget your fifteen minutes, little brother."

The .38 revolver, the Saturday night special was under my mattress. Might be a good idea to start carrying it, legally or not. Packing heat.

"Fifteen minutes compared to one of your black-hole clients."

"Sorry. My clients are—"

"Confidential. I know. And you don't chase ambulances, but you may represent a fleet of ambulances run by the Mob."

She stuck her tongue out at me. "Don't be a snot."

I stuck my tongue out at her, a repartee going on as long as I could remember.

Judy scrolled her computer screen.

"Show us the money," I said. "Money is at the root of Aconite Man. Let's say he didn't blow town after he —did what he did."

"I'm taking that approach too."

I said, "This thing is going north in a hurry."

"Isn't the expression 'going south'?"

"That's all wrong. South is warm and Technicolor north is cold and monochromatic. You freeze your ass."

She replied with a sighing groan.

"Let's not forget Mom's DUI trial. It was theatrical and strange, like *Perry Mason* and *Boston Legal* combined. It did make the news."

"One time. A sidebar. Years ago too."

"One time is enough and we know they're patient. Fifty-some years of patience."

"'Theatrical' is less flamboyant than a shoot-'em-up at a convenience store."

"That was months ago."

"Social media has a long memory."

"Social media has the attention span of any oyster."

Her fingers came off the keyboard as if it were electrified.

She looked at me, cheeks flushed.

"What?"

She pushed a button and said, "I need Monte. Now."

22

Elizabeth (Betty) Smith was trying her utmost to get settled in her new home, her daughter's stratospheric condominium. Good Lord, ten feet higher and you'd have to wear an oxygen mask.

Not for an instant believing their "temporarily." Oh, the kids meant well, but this was reverse parental abuse, pure and simple.

Judy's condominium was like one of those ultra-modern model homes you see advertised or featured in the Sunday paper. They weren't really real homes for real people. Hers and theirs were three times the size of those la-di-da hotel rooms in New York or somewhere for celebrities and crooked politicians and shady financiers that cost two thousand dollars per night.

She'd furnished with leather and brass and glass, expensive and hard and cold. Why, just look at that kitchen too. All the stone and stainless steel and newfangled buttons and readouts and blinking lights and a remote control to do who knows what. It was like a restaurant kitchen on a spaceship.

Betty couldn't remember when she last saw her little girl cook either. In high school she said no to home ec, so she could take all advanced placement classes, the hardest ones they taught. Here, up in the sky, Judy kept froufrou prepared meals in the fridge and freezer too, so all you had to do to clean the kitchen was dust it.

By herself here, it was as silent as a tomb. All these closets and drawers were out of place, nothing like her *home* of fifty-some years.

And where did Judy keep her liquor? She must have some, being who she is with highfaluting party guests(nary a one she'd seen yet) who drank the best champagne and hundred-year-old single malt Scotch.

She looked everywhere, thinking that her child was hiding it as if her mother was a child or a drunk. She remembered Judy and Theo as teens, watering down her merlot with grape juice siphoning off some for him and his rowdy friends, and for her National Honor Society friends who were, to be perfectly honest, every bit as naughty as his long-haired goof-off jocks.

Betty heard a ruckus down on the street. Sirens? So much for quiet. That daughter of hers had bragged about how soundproof it was, how you'd never be bothered by outside noise.

She looked out and down, across the street. Ambulances and police cars were making a hellacious racket. They were all going into that big ugly parking garage, hanging their yellow crime-scene tape at the entrance like confetti. She had seen enough TV cop shows to know this was serious business. There were dead bodies on the ground or fleeing bank robbers holed up somewhere in that thing.

Betty shook her head. What kind of neighborhood was this, anyway? Paying a small fortune for this sky-high palace and out there it was Dodge City, killers and dope fiends and rapists and who-knows-what running loose with their drive-by shootings and muggings, bushwhacking innocent citizens. An old bird like herself, she'd be risking life and limb out there. Not that she couldn't take care of herself.

She went to the door, thinking what was the harm if she went downstairs and checked it out? There were police all over the place, so she'd be safe.

No, the rent-a-cop Nazis in the lobby would turn her around and herd her back in the elevator, like one of those home-detention prisoners you read about, those sex perverts who shouldn't've been let out of jail in the first place.

Betty returned to her search for suitable beverages, thinking that a small taste would sure hit the spot. Besides, she was going stir-crazy and had to stretch her legs, if only on her tiptoes seeing what Judy kept where.

As she positioned a stepstool to reach to the rear of cabinets, she thought, this was hopeless. Judy kept it locked up in one of those hidden wall safes.

As far as the outside world went, by God, nothing ventured, nothing gained.

All those overweight fascists in the lobby could do was turn her around and escort her back up the elevator like a kid caught playing hooky.

Betty checked her makeup, fluffed her hair, and down Judy's private elevator she went.

On the ground floor, she realized she had nothing to worry about after all. All eyes were on the furor across the street, the storm troopers too, standing by the front doors, craning their neckless necks to see a stretcher being loaded into the meat wagon, a sheet covering all. A dead body, not an injured one. Oh dear.

Head held high, gaze straight ahead, out Betty Smith went. She turned right and was gone.

She'd play sightseer, a tourist. It was summer, the tourism season. She'd do some window-shopping, and locate a store that sold fine wine. She'd buy a bottle or two or even more if they were running a sale on merlot. For an occasional nip. Strictly to maintain her sanity.

And find a hiding place for it of her very own.

23

"Tell me why you flipped out and did a calling-all-cars about Monte, whoever the hell Monte is,"I said."I didn't know you were dating again."

"I did not flip out."

"You did. I've seen you do it every ten or twenty years, and I know flip-out when I see flip-out."

"You can be a royal pain in the ass, Theo."

"So?"

"It may be nothing,"Judy said, "But considering the circumstances, the power of suggestion."

"It isn't nothing. Tell me."

"Have you ever met Monte?"

"The name's familiar. One of your horde of lawyers. One of two hundred at last count."

"Save it, Theo. Monte is my most elderly employee and the first attorney I met when I joined the firm. I don't know how old he is. I could check his personnel file, but that'd spoil the fun. Monte gets teased about being a Watergate burglar, the one who got away. He runs our pro bono program and is the first face the majority of our boutiquey clients see. He screens dubious requests for representation too."

"Your gatekeeper."

"Yes."

"Dubious requests, as in?"

"For instance, a few months ago a prospective client saw an image of the Virgin Mary on his smart phone."

"Not on a tortilla? What did the guy want from you?"

"To sue the phone maker. At times around here, *Boston Legal* doesn't seem all that farfetched."

"Sue the phone maker for what?"

"Irreverence. It was made in China, he said. Two-billion atheistic communists trying to bring down our way of life. Monte declined on our behalf. He let the guy down easily. He's good at that. He's soft-spoken, kind, avuncular."

"Monte referred him to an electronics exorcist or a microchip whisperer?"

"He didn't elaborate, but if there is such an animal, Monte knows him. He brings those type of experiences up at staff meetings to lighten the atmosphere when it's tense."

I feigned surprise. "When is it tense?"

"Always."

"So Monte is Smith, Hurlbert and Kraus LLC, Attorneys-at-Law's smiley face too?"

"You have a way with words, but yes."

"Whip another Monte goody on me."

"Theo, you may have all day but I don't."

"One more. That's all. C'mon, c'mon. Scout's honor, just one more."

"Will you ever grow up?"

"What fun is that?"

She sighed and said, "You know that pink dye banks put in packs of money they give to robbers? A robber wanted us to sue the bank."

"No. Can't be."

"Yes. He said that since it was all over the news, he'd be endangered in prison."

"Pretty in pink?"

"Yes. As he stated it to Monte, he'd be labeled, and I quote, a 'faggot' and become a 'fuck boy' and the 'old lady' in the most dangerous cell block. Needless to say, Monte couldn't help him."

"How did you find this sterling client?" I asked.

"Not a client. The firm was doing a favor for a client. The gentleman in pink was a distant relation of a client."

"How distant?"

"Let's move on," Judy said.

"Moving on, I'm all ears."

"Monte has a recent client."

"Ah."

She looked at me and tapped her nails on her priceless desk.

"Your Monte and the new client?"

"I shouldn't've even brought it up with you in the room."

"The wallet," I said. "Dad enlisted me."

She looked out at her magnificent view and said, "I was preoccupied or I would've spotted his note earlier. Monte alerts me in red ink. This time he boldfaced it in caps, with a request to meet me."

"Wait a second. Doesn't he screen the red-ink types out the door?"

"He does."

"C'mon, Sis. Let's light that candle, regardless how dim," I said. "It's maybe a chicken or egg thing. Did Monte's new client bring Aconite Man in or did your new client come after Aconite Man, if the chicken actually laid that egg or the egg hatched that chicken or even if the chicken crossed the road? What do you have to lose? You've already lost billable minutes, sitting here debating with your kid brother."

"I desperately need Quetzal back to babysit you."

"No argument there."

Judy phone buzzed. "Thanks, Monte, for getting back to me so fast. Come right on in."

24

As previously stated, ninety minutes before the Smith siblings sat in Judy's office waiting for the venerable Monte, the man known to some as Hawk had taken the parking garage elevator down from the fourth level.

When it stopped at Level Three. A slender, attractive woman had gotten on. She was half a head taller than him. Aroused, Hawk smiled at her. She looked through him as if he were invisible.

As the elevator door closed, he heard either a scream or squealing tires. In fact, the sound the man known to some as Hawk heard was not squealing tires, but a scream.

A woman had taken the stairs up to the fourth floor of the parking garage, in too much of a hurry to wait for the elevator. She was going for paperwork she'd forgotten in her Mercedes SUV, which was parked next to a Chrysler minivan. The woman worked as a city-planning consultant and had been in her office since six-thirty. She was early to rise, late to leave.

Thinking of many things, downtown bicycle lanes among others, but not murder and mayhem, blood and gore, she saw Robin just as she lost her footing on his blood puddle and fell on the goo.

Leaving her one-hundred decibel scream in his wake, Hawk moved about the surrounding sidewalks as if on a fitness walk. Polite and law-abiding, he shared the sidewalk with passersby, waiting at intersections, not WALK-ing as many did on WAIT signals.

Hawk had been briefed on the Smiths by Mr. C the Three, intel as current as could be under the rapidly changing circumstances, that and "contingency orientation" over the past several days as he'd termed it. The word "Armageddon" had been mentioned, though not explained. Bizarre, Hawk had thought, but this detour in his life had been more than bizarre.

For the time being, Mother and Daughter would have to wait their Maker. The ladies lived way, way up in the condominium tower, like medieval royalty. Thanks to Robin botching the job, access to Queen and Crown Princess was problematical.

Per his orientation, the daughter power-walked to work. She was known to many who said hello, some of those greetings deferential. There was lobby security at each end of her home-work route. The mother had not left her aerie; he did not expect her to unless she was somehow lured out.

Today, though, an anomaly. The siblings had stayed at Judith Ann's and had gone to her law office together. So there we were and there Hawk was: Dissolute Son was doable, vulnerable, an irritant, thus *numero uno*. Theodore Cleaver Smith. Starving artist and his workplace, a pitiful excuse for a studio and abode.

He reported this to Mr. C the Three and gave his bird-in-hand recommendation.

"You know what to do, Hawk."

Click.

Hawk did know what to do.

He went to a parking garage five blocks away from all the police furor and retrieved his rental car. It was an unobtrusive dirty-white tin can of Korean manufacture, but it did have GPS. He'd paid extra for it. If expense money was any object to Mr. C the Three, Hawk had not been so informed. The urgency to complete the "project" gave it an open-ended budget, he thought.

Hawk drove to Theodore's Cleaver Smith's neighborhood, disappointed though unsurprised by the semi-squalor. It jibed with what he had been told.

The Thai restaurant that floored the ramshackle building did look prosperous, though. They weren't open for lunch yet, but all tables had been set.

From there he stayed on highway southbound, and took a room at the first motel he came to that hopefully wasn't infested with cockroaches and pimps.

Hawk had time to kill, too much time. Prone on the bed, eyes on the fly-specked ceiling, he considered the inaccuracy of actuarial tables. Why, just look at Robin, taken in the prime of life, a victim of his own bungling. Two strikes and you're out. Mr. C the Three could not have made it clearer.

Hawk trusted nobody but Millicent, so he operated under the assumption that it was one strike and you're out, not two. This kept him sharp, alert, careful.

Mr. C the Three had discovered Hawk in a two-star Michelin eatery in LA. The only night there wasn't a celebrity sighting would be a Tuesday during a blizzard. Expect to be vetted if you made a reservation. Unless you were a *People* magazine cover child, expect not to be asked which hour or day you would prefer, but which week. Or if a true nobody, which month.

Mr. C the Three was no celebrity—for obvious reasons, that's how he wanted it—but he knew which palms to grease and how generously. A subtle projection of menace did not hurt his chances either.

Dining alone, Mr. C the Three had been enjoying llama osso buco accompanied by polenta made of hand-ground, multi-hued Andean corn. The price was high-altitude also: eighty-nine dollars. As he remarked to his waiter that his meal was divine, he heard a commotion. Four cooks tumbled out of the kitchen, fists flying and their chef's hats tumbling like oversized mushrooms.

It took an impressively-long time for three large, red-faced guys to sit on one man a fifth of their combined weight. Mr. C the Three locked eyes with the man and had an epiphany, so he'd later explained to Hawk.

Diners at the closest tables jumped ship. Those out of range watched, fascinated.

Mr. C the Three plunged into the scene and compensated the manager to the extent that he sent the police away as soon as they arrived, dismissing it as a situation that had been cleared up.

"We may lose a Michelin star over this," he'd whined.

"Nonsense," Mr. C the Three said as he pressed another roll of currency into the man's hand. "This is notoriety. Excitement. You're the *in*-place now, yes, but you were dull too."

"Dull?"

He swept a hand. "You have elevator music and snobbish waiters. This and your outrageous prices will become tiresome. One day you're chic, the next day you're out. With a rep for a swashbuckling kitchen flair, the trash tabloids will swoon. You can raise your ludicrous prices ten percent."

Fascinated and puzzled, the man who would be known to some as Hawk calmly stood aside. When business was concluded, Mr. C the Three led Hawk into to his 7-series BMW. When they were two blocks away, without preamble, he offered the unemployed chef a job.

"I need a man like you."

"I have news for you, whoever the hell you are. This is a mighty expensive blow job you're not getting."

"No, no. You misunderstand."

Remaining suspicious that it was an ornate homosexual advance, the man who would be designated as Hawk asked, "Hire me to do what?"

Giving fair warning too, he added, "The last guy who tried to queer me, when I finished with the homo, he was eligible to try out for the Vienna Boys' Choir."

Mr. C the Three laughed and said not to worry, that he'd looked into Hawk's eyes while he was flattened by a third of a ton of beer fat and "had a perception of mutual interest."

"If I want the sky to fall on someone, and I surely will, from the skirmish I saw, you'd be the man for the job. The position requires detective work too and the acceptance of a code name. Hawk," he said. "Interested?"

"Call me Chicken Little if you want, sir."

"For my agenda., fisticuffs alone will be inadequate. Your opponent will *not* get off the canvas after the count ten. You must realize this. Object now or object never."

The guy had a weird way of talking, but Hawk caught the meaning. He had never taken a human life, but any number of guys who offended him had wished they were dead.

"I know," he said, seeing behind Mr. C the Three's unsettling eyes, aware that his knife skills might be utilized. "I know."

"When can you start. I gather you're unemployed."

"Where?"

"Seattle."

Within thirty miles of his permanent home. Millicent would approve of the move.

Hawk extended a hand. "Now if not sooner."

Centered on the stated two-strikes-and-you-re out policy, Mr. C the Three and his organization had reasons for their philosophy relating to retirement and longevity and Hawk had his. If there was a misstep on his part or a fib in his orientation, he'd keep it under his hat.

Hawk pledged devotion to Mr. C the Three and Mr. C the Three alone and the deal was done after he had eaten a piece of paper that was not any shape or form a fine dining experience.

Hawk planned to reach age-eighty, the published estimate of longevity in his present age range. That he had maintained and lived in a domicile of his choosing was his own business. They were pop-up, Mr. C the Three explained, so *he* was pop-up. He was to stay in the crackerbox apartment they provided on a northern fringe of downtown Seattle, suitcases open and ready to pack at a moment's notice.

His permanent home was his secret, an anchor thirty miles from Seattle, passed along by his late parents. Hawk was devoted to Millicent also, who loyally went where he went. He also kept that relationship to himself.

There was a limit to blind loyalty, for Mr. C the Three was not telling all either, hinting at his further obligation. For example, what on earth were CondorCakes? That arrived on a ship, container number five-four-three. Sounded like a mystery basket ingredient on *Chopped*. He did not like the mention of Armageddon, although it did sound abstract. Hawk made notes on his calendar.

Eyes on the grimy ceiling, Hawk reminded himself to stay on the alert. Otherwise he might never know until it was too late that he'd swung and missed the second strike.

If the second strike was actually the first strike.

25

Monte was of a certain age and then some. He was lean, pale, and pinkish around his watery eyes. He looked to me as if he'd missed his sunrise trip back into the coffin.

Monte's movements were stiff, verging on arthritic. He wore a Nixonian dark blue-suit and white shirt that matched his complexion. He kept a toe into a long-past decade, wearing a paisley tie and thinning white hair with sideburns. How Elvis's hair would look now, I thought.

"Go ahead, Monte," Judy said.

"This recent client you pointed out is a real head-scratcher. PUP and Associates, the PUP in caps" he said. "They bypassed my screening process, so I couldn't initially decline representation."

"How did they bypass it?"

"A good question, so far unanswered."

"Who are they, what do they do?"

"They identify themselves as a lobbying firm."

The wise-ass gene in me couldn't resist. "I had a hunch they were lobbyists."

"Theodore, please dismount your high horse," my sister said.

I smiled at her.

"Go ahead, Monte. Never mind him."

Never mind him was unnecessary, I thought. Monte was paying no attention whatsoever to me.

"Well, PUP and Associates identifies themselves as simply that.

Lobbyists. No details."

"You have no idea who PUP's clients are?" Judy asked.

"I haven't an inkling," Monte said. "PUP and Associates voluntarily paid a retainer that exceeded our minimum. I researched them as I do every prospective client."

"Voluntarily?" Judy said.

"By exactly ten percent, like they knew our scale even before I explained our fee schedule. Per standard policy, confidentially by both parties is guaranteed for thirty days so long as they don't request any legal activity by us. The thirty days expire on June twelfth. It's a feeling-out period, where each side can delve into the other."

"I don't imagine you'd tell me what the retainer is," I said.

Judy smiled at me, her annoying little brother, and said, "Please go on, Monte. What did you learn about PUP and Associates? Surely *something*."

"Absolutely nothing. They have a one-page website that looks like an introductory page, but it leads nowhere. There are links, but they are inoperative. I handed it off to our IT kids. And whatshisname, that other boy who's the son of, I forget the client. A bright, computer savvy youngster."

"Mike."

"Yes, Mike. He's stumped too, but Mike refuses to quit. He told me he takes it personally when he can't break through, as he terms it. That young man is resolute."

Judy said, "Unless I hear otherwise from these mystery lobbyists by the deadline, We're dropping them like a hot potato."

"Prudent," Monte said.

Judy sat up straighter. "Do you think they learned anything about us they shouldn't have?"

Thinking of Mike at my laptop: *What happened to the two would-be killers and the woman who bailed them out? Blaine Johnson, the other Jerry Davis, and a lady by the name of Debra Davis Johnson, a resident of Dallas, wife and sister of the pair, sprung them. They were due back a week from the following Monday to face the music, and didn't.*

If Mike couldn't solve this enigma, who could?

Monte shook his head. His Nashville hair didn't move.

"We found no indication they have."

Judy said, "Fine, but you're never completely sure in this day and age, are you?"

Monte answered, "No. Not with those Russians and Romanians over there and their malware and bitcoin ransoms, they have their methods. Technology changes in a blur, day by day. Every ten minutes, even. It's hard to stay ahead of the curve."

"How did PUP and Associates contact the firm?" I asked.

"By email. Payment was made through a third-party site. No personal or voice contact. They said they'd received glowing recommendations about the firm, but gave no specifics."

"No names? "I said.

"No names."

The complicated phone-laptop-whatever thing on Judy's desk that I'd often teased her as being the Red Phone buzzed.

"Excuse me. I have to take this."

Judy scribbled notes, hung up, and said, "Monte, thank you. If they contact you again, please let me know immediately. Me and nobody else."

"Can do," he said, standing.

"If they don't by tomorrow, email them, offering to extend."

"I can't."

"Why not?"

"I diary retainer reminders a week before they expire. I've tried, but it bounces back. Like the old song. Return to sender."

"An Elvis hit from way back when," I said.

Monte looked at me and smiled.

"That digital door opens both ways," I said, totally uninformed. "Representation of PUP gave them the opportunity to peer deeply into your system."

"No, no," Monte said. "We have safeguards."

"That's what the Trojans said."

Monte's eyes were on me on his way out.

Judy said, "That call was from Richard, my investigator. I've had him keeping an eye out in case Mother tries to stray and slip by building security. There was a murder in the parking garage directly across from my building. The police found a suspicious rental van parked beside the victim."

"Is Mom aware of any of this?"

Judy punched in a number.

"Mother doesn't answer."

"Maybe she's taking a nap."

She keyboarded furiously.

"Can you check inside your place?"

"What the hell do you think I'm doing?"

I got up and stood behind her. She moved the screen from camera to camera, room to room.

"Shit," she screamed. "Mother's gone."

I hadn't heard her screech like that since she was a teen. Something to do with a high school prom, her date cancelling at the last minute. I was never clear on that and Judy refused to clarify.

* * * * *

Our only consensus was that our mother was missing, that she had slipped through the lobby probably while security was distracted by the activity across the street in the parking garage. Soon to be unemployed security employees, Judy said.

Judy suspected that she'd been kidnapped five minutes after she slipped out of the building. I wasn't so sure.

We split up in the lobby, Judy leading a group of rent-a-cops, so many and menacing it looked like a mercenary army set to invade an African nation. Believing that I'd only be in the way, she didn't object to me splitting off on my own to pursue an unexplained hunch.

My unexplained hunch being barhopping.

I started at the closest watering hole, working my way outward in a spiral, stepping inside the bars until my eyes adjusted, then leaving before anybody could give me a menu or a dirty look.

At the seventh, a froufrou wine bar, there she was, by herself, perched on a stool at a small round table, watching a big-screen television, her big floppy purse hanging over another stool.

"Hey, lady, may I join you?" I said.

"Theo, what a surprise."

"Not a pleasant surprise. Everyone's worried sick about you, Mom. There was a murder in that garage across from Judy's building, you know."

"Well, I knew it was something big like that. All that hoopla and police tape and the stiff being rolled out of there, sheet covering it like they do on the TV shows."

"They're saying a suspicious rental van was found in there too."

She pointed at the TV. "A hockey game. A Stanley Cup tournament, I think it's called. One of the final rounds. Grown men bashing each other. When they fight, did you know that they take their gloves and helmets off? That is so stupid. If you had an ounce of sense, you'd keep them on, wouldn't you?"

"Mom."

"If you ask me, this isn't the kind of establishment for televised hockey. The prices they charge in here, it should be genteel and boring, like golf or baseball."

"What's this you're drinking? "I asked, pointing at a wooden tray with six small glasses of red wine, three of the glasses empty.

"It's a flight, Dear," she said, lifting one…"A varietal sampling. This flight is called Merry Merlot, my favorite flavor."

"Don't we all know."

"I've tried three and they've been quite good."

"I can count."

"You've never had a flight?"

I said, "I drink whiskey and beer in dangerous bars. They don't do flights."

She touched an empty spot on the tray. "That one was from Eastern Washington. It was exceptional."

"Right. Hints of toffee and cinnamon and all that," I said, phone to ear.

"Oh, after you tattle, Judy will raid us with a small army."

"It's a medium-sized army."

"Don't be so impatient."

"I'll just tell her you're safe," I said, lifting a glass from the tray. "We'll drink to that before we go. One for me, *only* one for you."

"That leaves one."

"Jesus H. Christ, Mom. I can count."

"Please don't take the Lord's name in vain."

"Since when were you born again?"

"Theodore, may I tell you something?"

"Uh oh," I said, putting down my phone before I sent Judy's number.

"How very proud we've been of you, your father and I."

"That's the merlot talking, Mom."

"It is *not*. You are your own man, our family Bohemian. Your sister, I love her equally, but you, you've been your own man since you were a tiny, little boy. Like that Sinatra song, you do it your way. Judith Ann, well, how she became so driven—I don't know where that came from. It's as if failure or mediocrity or—I don't know—is nipping at her heels.

"But you, Theodore Cleaver. You've danced to no drummer but the one in your handsome head and your art. The rest of the world can go to hell and I love you for your independence. That's why, I think, your father entrusted you with the wallet."

"I've been trying to figure that one out."

"He knew you'd take the challenge and solve that dirty puzzle, come hell or high water. You wouldn't let him down, wherever he is if he's anywhere except in the ground."

"Jeez, Mom," I said, wiping my eyes on a sleeve.

"You, not making a fortune with your art, but staying on the straight and narrow, unlike those adorable grandsons you have on a leash."

I shrugged.

"Your name. Why we named you what we named you."

"Mom, let's not start on that, okay?"

"Theodore Cleaver. On the show, he was so adorable."

"I'm not adorable, never was adorable."

"Yes you were."

"Was not."

She clung to my arm. "We meant no harm. We felt terrible when you were teased and picked on."

"Let's drop it, Mom."

"That class bully with you in the fourth grade, what was his name?"

"Wally, just like the Beaver's older brother on the show."

She grinned. "We dared not say it then, but we were so proud of you when you knocked out two of his teeth."

"You were?"

"We didn't even mind paying the dental bills."

A new flight arrived and I knocked one down, savoring the moment, her revelation. It didn't taste bad.

"If there is an afterlife, I'm gonna get my scrawny butt kicked along with your father. For what we did way back then. The sanctity of human life and all that crapola."

I put an arm around her as she looked up at the TV. Her eyes were puddling too.

She sniffled and said, "Where is it they're playing? I forget."

"According to the box in the corner, Las Vegas."

"*The* Las Vegas?"

"Yeah. I see on the sports page that Vegas has a very good team."

"Better than the teams in the frozen cities up in Canada."

"They are."

She shook her head and finished her glass. "That is so stupid. It's two-hundred degrees there this time of the year. How on Earth do they keep the ice from melting?"

The wine was getting to me. I had no answer, wise-ass or halfway informed. I drank and watched.

26

Hawk tried, for the most part successfully, to avoid the full-frontal Hawk in a mirror, especially avoiding the eyes. Eyes that had troubled people since he was an infant, himself included.

When he shaved, he concentrated on cheeks and chin and bare scalp. Brushing teeth zeroed in on teeth and gums. It was an odd superstition of his that if he couldn't describe himself, neither could an assault victim or a witness.

Having graduated to the ultimate form of assault, Hawk's superstition intensified as he spruced up for his date with Theodore Cleaver Smith. Theodore now lived in the sister's condo tower, but he retained his workplace. He'd turn up, for the last time in his life a bad penny.

Late, after the Thai restaurant closed, Hawk parked several blocks from it. Seeing no lights inside Smith's hovel, he went into the building and crept up the steps, taking them two at a time to minimize creaking on the worn stairs.

It was child's play to enter Smith's unit. The lock wasn't a deadbolt, so the old credit card into the loose jamb did the trick in six seconds flat.

He walked onto a spattered floor that resembled a Jackson Pollock drip painting. He took in the stench of various oils. When his eyes adjusted to the dim light cast through the windows, he saw canvases leaning against walls covered with paint depicting partially-finished city and rural scenes, discombobulated from the real world. A starving artist who in a short time would starve no more. The art critic in Hawk determined that the canvases required improvement.

He improved two of the leaning canvases with Zorro-like knife slashes. The one on the easel, depicted airport frustration. Not too terribly bad if finished properly. A sticky note taped to an easel leg: *WEATHER DELAY 2013*.

Swipe, swipe, swipe with his trusty blade. The Mark of Zorro, Zorro playing an artistic genius and censor.

And up there on a wall, dominating the non-decor, a framed three-painting collection of an old baseball player swinging a bat, a speeding baseball, and a camera lens. Mighty strange.

Hawk's druthers were to stage a burglary gone bad when surprised by the owner, an innocent victim paying with his life. What to steal? To wit, since there was little of value here, it was a logical presumption that items of value had been taken, should they ever have existed. In this part of town, the cops would write it up as that in five minutes, or a drug prowl gone sour. A scene they had investigated hundreds of times.

No, wait. Hawk had to grab something in case friends or relatives knew what was there and what wasn't. Bingo: On a rickety card table, a laptop three times the size of current models.

First, though, a peek under the mattress, finding only the box springs. In the toilet tank, the freezer compartment of the fridge. No controlled substances, no valuables, no nothing in spots where clueless homeowners hid things.

A bookcase and beside it, books piled helter-skelter. Ten bucks worth of credit at a used bookstore. What a fucking loser the guy was.

The laptop it'd have to be. The obvious scenario: A junkie swapping it for a dime bag.

Hawk unplugged the computer. He stood at a corner of the room by the door, listening for footsteps and looking at the stumpy old baseball player.

Motionless, barely breathing, purloined laptop on the floor behind him, Hawk clutched his three-point-five inch, spear point paring knife, one-piece, fully forged, cambered and finely-balanced, with a riveted handle. A favorite of chefs.

*   *   *   *   *

If you ask me, same-day hangovers were the worst. The absolute pits. You didn't have fitful sleep, night sweats and masochistic nightmares to process the toxins out of your system. This one was ten times worse than my worst ever, because I'd been drunk under the table by my eighty-two-year-old mother.

It was mortifying, enough to make me swear off drinking. Almost enough.

I'd finally had to give up and call Judy before I toppled off my stool. When Big Sis and her mercenaries rushed in, she eyed us with mixed emotions—disgust and relief. Mom wasn't ready to go as the hockey game was in overtime and she was rooting loudly for the Vegas Golden Knights.

Judy pulled our latest flights out of reach and ordered coffee for Mom, who promptly lost all interest in hockey. Back at the condo, Big Sister ordered me to stay put until I sobered up. I didn't argue. I obeyed, sitting for hours like a misbehaving child.

Head splitting, half groggy, I opened my door.

My flat was as dark as the hallway, no need for eyeball adjustment. The card table was on the far side of the room. My laptop was gone, a couple of my Edward Hopper knockoffs slashed. Hack Wilson remained up on the wall, swinging for the fences.

If the burglar was still there, I sure could use Hack too, him and his one-hundred-and-ninety-one-RBI bat. If my surprise guest was on the premises, he could hide in two places, the bathroom and behind the front door.

With both hands, I shoved the door hard, slamming it against something just as hard, too soon to be the wall. I charged in and turned around to face a short, husky man who swiped at me with a small knife.

"Take my laptop," I said. "Be my guest."

The intruder didn't answer. He moved slowly toward me in a crouch, knife in his hand, holding it low, tossing it from hand to hand, how it was done in the movies.

Shaved head, eyes that even in the near dark were eerie, like those of a rabid cat.

No, not a movie. He was out of a fucking comic book.

I was thinking that I sure could use the Saturday night special, the.38 way under my mattress. Between here and there, if I ran for it, I'd have time to bleed to death.

Kemo Sabe.

I backed slowly, no plan in mind but survival. I had the advantage of knowing the lay of the land, which, realistically, was no advantage at all since there was very little land.

At the card table, I flung a folding chair at the guy, who brushed it aside as if a fly.

He lunged and I fell against the table, allowing him to slice through my shirt and graze my midsection. Going for my family jewels? This was scarier than the chest or carotid. If I was to be sliced and diced, please, death before castration.

I kept the guy at bay by pressing the card table against him. He was strong, though, moving the table forward with one hand, dagger in the other.

I had nothing behind me but the bathroom. If I was quick I could lock myself inside and call nine-one-one, hoping the cavalry would arrive before he kicked the door in.

Trouble was, my phone had fallen out of my pocket when I fell against the table. And even if I barricaded myself inside the bathroom, my deadliest weapon was a disposable razor.

I heard a loud rolling noise, then *thump*. The legs went out from under my would-be killer as the knife flew upward and out of his hand.

Head down, legs churning, Quetzal Adams had accelerated her suitcase at speed into his calves and the back of his knees.

Right behind her, Chris and Ty joined in, stomping on him when he landed on his back.

"Forty yard field goal straight through the uprights, motherfucker," Ty said proudly as my attacker scrambled into the hall on all fours.

"If he ain't pissing blood for a week, we lost our magic touch," Chris said.

""go away and you can't stay out of trouble," she told me in the midst of a long, smoochy hug.

"You're early. A nice surprise. A very nice surprise."

"I missed you terribly."

"Really?"

"Sort of. I'll explain later. To keep it a surprise, I had the boys pick me up at the airport."

"I'm bleeding. And, hey, love of my life, thanks."

She kissed my cheek and inspected the damage. "Theo, you look like you were in a turkeyshit shovel without a turkeyshit shovel, but you're not bleeding to death and you don't need Florence Nightingale. I can patch you up. And you're welcome."

Quetzal wedged a chair against the door after I said not to call the cops, that I'd explain later.

Chris was rummaging in my fridge.

"Uncle T, man, your beer's warm."

A circuit breaker must have shut the fridge off again. Warm beer versus an electrical fire that wiped out the neighborhood, a small sacrifice.

I said, "Pretend you're in England."

He squinted at the can he'd harvested. "Huh? This ain't Guinness."

"Who was your friend?" Quetzal asked.

"A door-to-door knife salesman? Your guess is as good as mine."

She made repairs with Band-Aids, gauze, disinfectant and tape, as she observed, "This place of yours, what you have in your dump and bathroom, it's like an ER in North Korea."

"Ouch."

"Did mama hurt her little boy? I'll kissy kiss you and make you well."

I made a face, but I was lapping it up. Her and her perfume and her close proximity.

"So how's things where the corn's higher than an elephant's eye?"

"With any luck it'll be harvested and turned into ethanol before the Rapture."

Ty said, "Rapture?"

"That's where the good folk are whisked up to Heaven and rest of us are left down here for famine and global warming."

Ty said, "Me and Chris, we'd be royally fucked."

"The old man went on and on how it's coming any second. My mother said he was off the sauce, but I'm skeptical. His breath smelled like Saturday night at last call."

"Him and Aunt Leah should meet. Ouch."

"Hold still, you big baby, or I'll call for an ambulance."

Melodramatically, I clutched the sides of the chair.

The boys complained further about the warm beer, but managed to suffer with it. When we were done and getting ready to leave, they were wrapping up a belching contest.

I called Judy, who agreed with me that it was good not to involve the law.

She'd notify security, and said to bring Quetzal with me. Unpacking, CPA duties, and anything else could wait.

On the floor beneath Hack Wilson, I saw the intruder's weapon, a small chef's knife.

I told Judy.

"Bring it along, but don't touch it."

Quetzal found a baggie. With a kitchen fork, she flicked the knife into it.

"DNA City," Ty said. "Cool."

*****

Hawk drove straight to the Greyhound station, the best incognito mode of travel when one desired to flee town. He knew he was done with Mr. C the Three and that Mr. C the Three was done with him, in the most permanent way.

He had left behind his chef's knife, his baby. And his fingerprints on it. One strike of this magnitude and he was *out*. His exit interview would be akin to the one he'd given Robin.

Millicent was home waiting for him, keeping his bed warm. Abandoned. He felt terrible leaving her. But you did what you had to do, looking out for *numero uno*.

Hawk left the car at the curb and got out carefully. He breathed in and out slowly, minimizing the sting of what he believed was cracked ribs. The little gal who plowed into him from behind, he could handle. But not with the two goons she brought along, kicking him while he was down, the cowards.

Hawk bought a ticket for the bus leaving the soonest, a southbound coach to Portland and beyond. He'd switch there to the next bus south or eastbound.

If his final destination was a surprise to him, it will be for them too.

Won't it?

He remembered his well-read mission statement, how he swallowed it in Mr. C the Three's presence:

MISSION STATEMENT
We need to start over. And we will.

He could cook anywhere under any name. It was an itinerant profession, a good thing for him.

The CondorCake and the rest of Mr. C the Three's agenda was not his problem. So he told himself.

But the thought of Mr. C the Three and the awful taste and texture of the mission statement. He thought of Millicent.

Hawk ran into the restroom and threw up.

27

Judy's sleek steel-and-glass mountaintop nest was like a childhood home to me. Kinda, sorta. Not because of altitude and architecture. Because of family.

Dad was gone and Mom's Beaver Cleaver home was hundreds of feet lower and miles away. It was a three-way hen party too: Mom, Judy and my resplendent Quetzal. Thanks to their life-saving heroism, Ty and Chris were welcome after their mother confiscated and hid their car keys.

Quetzal and Judy were tight. The latter needlessly reminded her—within earshot—that she was too good for me. I had to agree, and not just to keep the peace. Ms. Adams and I shared a nonmarital bed without anybody's protest, and thanks to top-of-the-line soundproofing, did what we pleased, which was plenty, making up for time lost when she was in corn country.

It was like home in other ways too. In the morning, Mom giving me the stink-eye until I went back in and made our bed. After breakfast too, until completing my assigned chore—rinsing off plates and silverware and getting them into the dishwasher.

I behaved like a good boy and didn't even gloat about using common sense to find Mom while Big Sis had put out an APB and a dragnet. What the burglar had done to my Edward Hopper-esque paintings in progress festered, though. My airport canvas on the easel that was damn close to completion (so I convinced myself). That especially grated.

Judy worked at home the next two days, unusual for her, running a law firm that size. She went into her bedroom to make some calls. I knew not to snoop.

She had sent off the knife to an unnamed party for fingerprints. We were pessimistic about DNA testing as the only blood on it was mine. Her and I maintained that none of this was police business, not yet anyway. Judy definitely had a gift for sidestepping officialdom and getting results in a fraction of the time they would.

After Quetzal had consulted her laptop, she'd said, "I'm laying money that he was a chef before he became a mad slasher. That knife is a topnotch chef's paring knife. This brand sells for seventy-five bucks. It's versatile, used for paring, slicing, trimming and chopping."

"And disemboweling," I added.

Quetzal pinched my cheek and said, "You were busy while out of my supervision, weren't you?"

"Who else does fingerprints if not the authorities?" I said, probing my sister.

"Others," Judy said. "And five times as fast."

"Aren't they backed up too, Little Miss Cryptic?"

"Not if you elbow in at the head of the line."

"Even with your sinister clients bullying whomever, he'll be long gone."

"Speaking of fingerprints. Here we are," Judy said, sticking out her tongue at me as she printed out five pages.

Quetzal hugged me from behind and said, "I'd give you a big, slobbery kiss, but your size-ten is already in your mouth."

Mom watched Judy's printer and said, "Nothing in this newfangled world surprises me anymore."

Judy said, "Nor am I after reading this."

"Go ahead, young lady," Mom said. "Keep us in suspense."

Judy said, "Leroy John Hopperd. He *is* a chef. Him the former owner of a topnotch chef's paring knife. Culinary-school trained, said to be Michelin caliber, but unable to control his temper and hold a job for long. Several arrests for assault, one at a bar and grill in Wichita where he mopped up every drunk in the place after one complained about his cooking, but charges dropped in every arrest when the victims got cold feet. I can quote others."

I asked. "Any idea where Chef Hopperd lives and where he might be going, now that he's worn out his welcome?"

"Last address given is, hmm, well, well, Tacoma, Washington. A single-family house. Previous owners named Hopperd too. They bought it in 1959.Leroy inherited it from his late parents."

"Tacoma is thirty miles south of here," I said. "An easy drive."

"Theodore," Mom said, looking at me.

"I'll take no reckless chances," I said.

Mom said, "That's a load of hooey."

Quetzal said, "I'm guessing Mr. Hopperd is elsewhere, Betty."

"He's taking a sabbatical," I said. "Leave of absence."

"Mr. Hopperd's fingerprints should be all over that van, shouldn't they?" Mom said.

"I wish they were, Mother, but there are prints all over it, though none his."

"Let's forget Hopperd and make ice cream sundaes like we used to," Judy said. "Loaded with chocolate and sugar, we'll be better able to figure out our next step."

"I'll run out for maraschino cherries," I said.

"If that's necessary," Mom said.

"It is. There's a specialty store in Tacoma," I said. "They have the best. Made on the premises by artisans from the old country"

Judy walked me to the door."Be careful, Theo."

"I will."

"Remember when we were kids and we'd play Mother's and Father's vinyl on their record player?"

"I do."

Lowering her voice, she said, "There was a singer named Peggy

Lee. She had a sultry voice and had a message in some of her tunes. *Is That All There Is?* has stuck in my mind. Remember it?"

"No."

"You might if you heard it. I hear it often in my head. Theo, I am filthy rich, worth a fortune. I am highly respected. Feared too—don't ask further. I have power and influence. I could run for office. I have a loving family that has held together stronger than ever after Father was murdered. My personal life is nonexistent, exactly how I want it now. But I keep asking myself, like Peggy Lee did after stanzas of notable moments in her life, *is that all there is?*"

I couldn't think of anything to say, so I didn't.

"I am doing a clumsy job of saying that my career *isn't* all there is. You, Mother, Quetzal, my incorrigible sons, you guys are. Okay?"

"Okay."

She gave me a great big hug. The first since—I can't remember when.

28

Quetzal told me to take her car, a newer C-Class Mercedes. "If your horseless carriage makes it that far, it won't make it back, so I'd have to come for you."

Harsh, but true. I accepted without argument.

First stop was a hardware store. I bought a clipboard, tape measure, and a note pad. If asked by neighbors at Mr. Hopperd's, I was a home-value appraiser hired by a realtor.

I drove south on I-5 to Tacoma, thinking of Quetzal's pickled old man, his imminent Rapture, and the rest. Judy and I had been forced by our non-believing parents to attend Sunday school until age twelve, at which time we could choose yea or nay. Their thinking (I think) was to expose us to Christianity just in case there was something to it, and to imbibe us with The Ten Commandments and other interpretations of right and wrong. On our twelfth birthdays, we bailed, and the subject didn't come up again.

My view on God, if there is one, was that He's one sadistic, game-playing asshole. A supreme deity who when bored fiddles with His joysticks and comes up with the black plague, Adolf Hitler, coral snakes, gang rape, prostate cancer, religious wars (which the majority of wars have been), hurricanes, and other sick forms of Heavenly entertainment. The planet Earth, all we are to Him is one big fucking video game. I'll have to run that by Quetzal's dad if I see him again, which I sure hope I don't.

Jesus nuts hated Jews, even though He was one, but often depicted as a brown-haired, blue-eyed hippie, like a guy you'd find in a Stockholm gay bar. It was all too confusing.

Leroy lived in a less than prosperous neighborhood east of downtown Tacoma in an area where the C-Class stood out as a realtor's car, in a way protective coloration. Three homes on the block had for-sale signs.

Leroy J. Hopperd's house was a small, prewar box, showing its age and indifferent care. The paint was oxidized and peeling. A yard with overgrown grass was losing out to a bumper crop of dandelions. There was no garage, just an unpaved driveway by a side door into the house.

The home next door was the same, a twin to the Hopperd's when built, but not the same now. The difference was an emerald-green lawn, fresh paint, and an add-on in the rear. A fiftyish man was in front, watering bona fide flowers, not plastic, one eye on his pansies, the other on me.

A block-watch kind of guy, great to have around unless you were a strangely-behaving stranger. I knew his suspicions would be easily aroused if I didn't state my intentions. I walked over with the clipboard and introduced myself.

"Hi, I'm Larry Hayes. I was sent out to do an appraisal."

"It's going on the market?"

I shrugged. "As far as I know. This realtor I work for has them appraised first. Then they look at the numbers and decide."

"If you don't have a key, good luck getting in," said the man who introduced himself as Ed.

"Unfortunately, I don't, Ed. The realtor couldn't find one. The owner isn't around?"

Ed carefully worked the spray around a section of blossoms and said, "Hardly ever is for long. He was an only child and inherited it from his folks, nice friendly people. They had health problems and passed away not long apart, oh, five or six years ago.

"I'd talk to Leroy maybe twice a year. He's an odd duck, not real friendly. Always has been. A high school dropout, suspended a lot for fighting and truancy. Once, when he was older, he said he'd gone off to culinary school and became a chef. They work long, funny hours, so if that was for real or a story he gave out to explain why he was gone at all hours, who knows."

"Well, I'll have a look-see anyway," I said. "I can take measurements and peek inside and try to get a handle on what prospective buyers need."

"If you can get a good look through a window," Ed said. "See if you can spot a cat. Maybe it's my imagination, but I think I've heard meowing. Leroy hasn't been around for a few days and I know he liked cats when he was a kid. If he has one now, he might've let it out at night late. There's been some digging around my flowers."

I said if I saw a cat, I'd call the pound, see what they could do.

I went around back, onto a small, cracked-concrete patio, the natural gray turned a moldy-green. I peeked into a small kitchen. Like my apartment's door, Leroy's back door was a sloppy fit. I slipped my credit card in there, jamming it hard, scraping the chip, not a problem since it was maxxed out anyway.

I took a deep breath and went inside, hoping for no gory, decomposing surprises.

Is that all there is?

No bad surprises, but an odor of well-used kitty litter pervaded. By the sink were near-empty food and water bowls.

I called out "kitty, kitty," but received no response.

I went from room to room, finding a few items of clothing and nothing of value. It was like a suite in a hot-sheet motel without maid service. Mr. Hopperd wasn't in contention for homemaker of the month.

Strange that the few articles of clothing were fairly clean, but nothing else was. Mandatory for anybody in the restaurant industry, I supposed.

My search of the bathroom was brief. A few towels and a medicine cabinet with the bare basics: disposable razors, toothbrush and paste, and a bottle of aspirin. I had to admit that this dump wasn't a whole helluva lot worse than mine.

Next, the kitchen. Dishes by the sink done, a few pots and pans in cabinets. I checked the fridge, first pawing around in the freezer compartment. In the TV cop shows, the scofflaws hid their drugs and contraband behind the frozen corn. There was a bag of corn and nothing else but frost.

I opened the lower compartment, a sound that neutralized the cat's shyness. From wherever it was hiding, a beautiful gray shorthair tabby came meowing and rubbing against my legs. She had a collar and a tag that identified her as MILLICENT.

"Well, Millicent," I said, bending down and petting her. "You're the kitty I've been waiting for all these years while my father was falsely allergic. Mom admitted it after his funeral."

Millicent, uninterested in my petty personal problems, rubbed harder and meowed louder.

"You must be starving."

Millicent meowed a reply that yes, she was starving.

The fridge didn't hold much for man or beast, but there was half a quart of milk that hadn't turned and half a can of cat food, which I dumped into the bowls.

While Millicent chowed down, I resumed my search, taking my time, looking closer. I pulled out a drawer and found a set of chef's knives, minus a small one.

Pinned to a corkboard by the wall leading into the living room was a piece out of a local maritime journal, announcing the recent arrival of a container ship, the *Bamsan Kiet,* and a calendar, with Container 543 and CondorCakes hand-scribbled at the bottom of this month, June. Handwritten directly above it: ARMAGEDDON???

Pinned below the calendar, a photocopy of:

MISSION STATEMENT
We need to start over. And we will.

I reread everything, making no sense of any of it, in particular the CondorCakes. He didn't seem the sort for charity bake sales. I removed calendar and all, clipped it on my clipboard, and called Judy, telling her what I found.

"Mission statement?"

"Yeah. If we're trying to put two and two together, that's a good start."

"Bring it all with you, Theo. Every scrap."

I said, "Why don't you invite Mike over for our ice cream social?"

"Why?" Judy said.

"The woman in 1963, Delilah Henn Condor, who bail-skipped off into the sunset. Now CondorCake and Armageddon. Let's have Mike dig into it and the rest of this."

"Good idea. I'll get him and you get the hell out of there."

"I'm bringing a surprise too."

"What?"

"Then it wouldn't be a surprise, would it?"

I hung up and said, "Bon appétit and hurry up, Millicent. We're going for a drive. You have a new home."

29

I never did stop off for maraschino cherries. Millicent was a loud, antsy passenger, and I was afraid she'd run for it if I opened a door.

Nobody cared about cherries or ice cream either. Everyone flipped over Millicent. It was love at first sight as it had been for me, a cat-deprived child.

Millicent was no fool. She knew adoration when she saw it. Playing the aloof courtesan, she took over Judy's home immediately. Competition for her affection was fierce. An anonymous member of our merry band had T-shirts made and delivered later in the day— ASK NOT WHAT YOUR CAT CAN DO FOR YOU. ASK WHAT YOU CAN DO FOR YOUR CAT—superimposed on an aristocratic portrait of Millicent.

Judy brought in a veterinarian who gave Millicent a complete physical. I had no idea vets made house calls, but this was Judy and her myriad connections.

Quetzal made points with Millicent by going out for the kind of cat food on TV commercials that was wolfed down by exotic breeds, stuff that cost more per pound than prime rib.

I'd watch Millicent promiscuously move from lap to lap unable to reconcile such a beauty being owned (or the other way around) by a maniacal knife slasher and lifelong loser. Mike was already there. Ty and Chris had wanted him to hack into video game programs, getting them as freebies, but their mother shooed them away, as if into a corner wearing dunce caps.

I gave Mike the material I'd brought from Tacoma. He began with the calendar.

"This container ship, the 'Bamsan Kiet' was named after a Laotian god or somebody like that. That's all the search engines gave me. I can check further, but I don't think it's relevant. Its cargo is unloaded and its being refueled. It's just a tub that carried all kinds of things," Mike said, clicking the keyboard so hard and fast it sounded like popcorn popping.

"CondorCake?" I said.

"It's not on the manifest, so it could've been shipped as anything," he said.

"Where did the 'Bamsan Kiet' come from?"

"Well, let's see. The ship. Liberian registry, address a Panama City P.O. box that I bet receives no mail, not even junk. The tub came from China, the Port of Shanghai, one of the world's biggest port if not the biggest, with stops beforehand at Bangkok and Sihanoukville, Cambodia's main port. Where it was before, your guess is as good as mine, dude."

"The cargo? Can you pin it down?"

"The manifest is kind of sketchy, but I'm laying another bet that most came from China. Clothes and shi—stuff, like seven-buck T-shirts. Some other commodities, you know, like tungsten, hardwood, and here, something sort of weird, two hundred pounds of lead, listed as lead billets. China has a bunch more lead than anywhere else, but there's no lead shortfall in this country that I can find."

Everyone took a moment to digest that, a moment that was a moment of uncomfortable silence. Left unsaid was the general knowledge of what lead shielded. We all learned that in high-school science class.

I said, "See what you can find on this. Even without the Biblical goofiness pertaining to 'Armageddon', this is scary."

MISSION STATEMENT
We need to start over. And we will.

Mike read it and said, "Is this weird or what? How many of these are there out there?"

I said. "We agree on weird. You find out the what and how many and who and why."

Mike tried, working faster and faster, perspiring.

He leaned back and sighed.

"Harder than the Pentagon, huh?" I said.

"Man, I've tried every combo, tried to bust in from every direction, but zilch. It's just some dopey mission statement companies have."

"An inspirational slogan," I said.

Quetzal said, "Yeah. Instead of salary increases."

Judy said, "Let's work with PUP and Associates. PUP for pop-up, possibly?"

I said, "This is a job for Monte. But let's hold off. Mike, let's work further on the mission statement."

"I have. Brick Wall City, man."

"How about mixing it in a goulash," I said.

"Huh?"

"Goulash isn't a technical term?"

"I'd know if it was, man."

"Condor."

"A high-flying bird in the vulture family with an insane wingspan. It can soar around all day up there catching thermals."

Judy said, "In the vulture family, so everything is edible, dead or alive."

"Including us," I said.

Mom said, "These Condors, they're the skunks we're after."

I said, "Okay, Mike, parachute into your dark web, do a mulligan stew by mixing it in with JFK, his assassination, Larrionov, everything in the wallet. That and a surname of Condor. Emphasize Condor."

"Whatever," he said, dismissively.

I backed off as he brutalized the keyboard.

"Shazam," he cried less than five minutes later.

"What?"

"Step into my office, man. It's an obit out of an old Dallas, Texas newspaper."

We gathered behind Mike and read:

On December 11, 1919, Jerome Condor was born in Enterprise, Alabama, the fifth of nine children. It was the day the city erected a statue honoring the boll weevil in the town square.

The way of life in Enterprise came under threat in 1915. An infestation of boll weevils had found its way into the region's cotton crops, resulting in the destruction of most of the cotton in Coffee County. Facing economic ruin, the nearly bankrupt area farmers were forced to diversify, planting peanuts and other crops in an effort to lessen the damage and recoup some of the losses inflicted upon them by the invading insect.

Two years later, that area was the leading producer of peanuts in the United States. Enterprise was able not only to stave off disaster, but its economy was renewed by the thriving new crop base. In appreciation, the people of Enterprise erected a monument in the city center to what the monument describes as their "herald of prosperity"; the boll weevil.

The Boll Weevil Monument was dedicated on December 11, 1919, as a reminder of how the city adjusted in the face of adversity. It is the only monument to an agricultural pest in the world.

When young Jerome was old enough to

understand the significance of the monument, he took the coincidence of its erection and his birth to be no coincidence at all.

How something so unlikely became a salvation. It was an omen, a sign, he often told close friends.

He attached no religious significance to it, however, to the doing of any God.

His father, who owned a dry goods store, supported his theories, reminding him of the significance of his name: Condor, a very large bird that could fly four miles high.

Jerome grew up to be a dynamic young businessman who owned a successful recycling business during World War Two, finding and selling scarce metals vital to the war effort was a mission that drove him.

He was instrumental in supplying these vital metals to China and spent much time there in dangerous conditions with the forces of both Chiang Kai-shek and Mao Tse-tung, aiding their fight against the Japanese and their evil Greater East-Asia Co-Prosperity Sphere.

The War ended as wars eventually do, and with the denouement came even loftier thinking. This should have been The War to End All Wars, as the one that ended in 1918 promised.

Instead, the most dangerous of scenarios developed: US vs. USSR. One had The Bomb, the other thanks to spies would soon have it too. Then what?

Jerome had adroitly invested profits from wartime enterprises into corporations riding the postwar boom. By the late-1950s, in addition to his altruism, he was wealthy.

It was time to organize his take on philanthropy, to

spearhead his passion to abolish warfare once and for all.

Alas, his dream never came to fruition. On Saturday, November 30, 1963, he passed away unexpectedly, all too soon of an undisclosed illness.

He left behind his son, Jerome Condor II and his wife Sharon. Alas, he would never know his namesake grandson, Jerome Condor III, born on November 22, 1963.

"Good call, man," Mike told me, reaching up for a palm slap. "It was the date that made the connection."

Judy said. "Kind words, but undeserved. No mention of what actually killed him?"

"Let's take a longer and deeper trip into DarkWebVille. Dude," I said.

Mike swiveled his chair and looked at Judy.

She sighed and said, "Go ahead. If need be, I know where to find a good lawyer."

30

“She’d called out her own personal National Guard. Liked to have pushed me into the street when they went marching by.”

“You and your cabin fever, boy.”

“I kept a discreet distance, Grandfather.”

“National Fucking Guard, huh?”

“You’d think so by the looks of it, Brownshirts in 1932 Germany.”

“The old lady helping her son get off the barstool and stay upright. I wasn’t ten feet away. It was hilarious.”

“Hilarious if we hadn’t blown our best chance.”

“We didn’t know. We couldn’t mobilize. It was wham bam.”

“Doing them both, like a gangbanger drive-by.”

“It’d take out innocents too.”

“Spilt milk. Collateral damage. We don’t have a time machine, so let’s move along. Your sophomoric pop-up-mission-statement nonsense? Give me an update.”

“*Nada.*”

“No harm?”

“No nothing.”

“You swing, you can miss. I haven’t told you the second most sickening swing I have personally missed. Second only to that botched day in Dallas.”

“No, Father.”

“No, Grandfather.”

“I hadn’t even told my late wife.”

"Grandmother's car accident. Father and I are unclear—"

"Don't veer off the subject, boys. Keep your eyes on the ball. I'm sorry I mentioned the woman. You were a pup and you, boy, you weren't even born on Saturday night, June 17, 1972. You remember what that is."

"The Watergate break-in."

"Yes, good. Watergate. An old lawyer at the Smith law firm, people say he was the burglar who got away. He ran before the guard came or he hid in a closet."

"True?"

"Not precisely. Per my information, reliable information, he had a urinary infection and was on diuretics. They make you piss like a racehorse. He was down the hall in the can when they were busted.

"But that matters not for what I am going to tell you. The break-in at the Democratic National Committee Headquarters was unnecessarily paranoiac. Nixon and his gang of dirty tricksters feared and loathed the Kennedys and were terrified that Dick would have to face Ted Kennedy in 1972.

"That was asinine. When Teddy drove off the Chappaquiddick bridge in 1969 and left that girl in the car with him to drown, his career outside of the State of Massachusetts was dead in the water too. He couldn't've been elected dogcatcher.

"The stupidity didn't end there. The botching burglars were traced back to the Committee for the Re-Election of the President, CRP. Unfortunately for them, the acronym was known as Creep. There was a cover-up that was covered up, in due course uncovered and bringing them all down.

"With that history lesson, I'm taking my eye off the ball too. *My* story concerns Saturday night, June 10, 1972, when I first made a major contribution in the family effort to connect with Zurich for our gold. I led a small team, all, mm, deceased, that broke into the DNC.

"We cared not for DNC secrets or Republican interest in them. We were redecorating the DNC as if we were secret agents out of the Kremlin. We made a fucking mess in there, stole documents at random, and left behind a Zenit 35-millimeter, single-lens-reflex camera manufactured in the Soviet Union, stage-managing as if we'd heard footsteps and fled in panic. A full roll of film had been shot and was in the camera. On this model of Zenit, all lettering was in Cyrillic, so there could be no mistake.

"Talk about your smoking gun. There should've been an uproarious uproar, fingers jabbing at the Russkis, who naturally would deny all, us calling them liars, them accusing us of a set-up, red buttons set to be pushed. Tricky Dick and his itchy trigger finger, Brezhnev and his gang slapping leather too.

"It didn't happen. Know why?"

"No."

"No."

"No smoking fucking gun is why not. Somebody got in there and snatched the camera. Straightened up the paperwork too. All before Monday morning."

"Common thieves, Grandfather?"

"I think so or janitors or the guards. They pawned the camera and used the proceeds for a dime bag or two, or to buy groceries. See what I mean about a swing and a miss."

"Bad luck, Father."

"This is our third swing for Armageddon and a billion in gold. We won't miss this time. Cannot miss…"

"No sir."

"No sir."

"Grandson, use your computer skills before we move in on them. Pucker their bungholes with a dash of misdirection and confusion. Do a chunk of the one that got away, that we couldn't have claimed credit for. Too early. Fuck up their minds before the bell lap. Stir them up."

"Yes sir. Realrealityresearch is there for us."

"Attaboy. World wars are far too important to be left to the public sector."

31

Ty whispered in my ear, reminding me that Mike said that the hottest porn was in the Dark Web, no comparison to any other, unlike the weenie stuff anybody can download.

I reminded him of the praying mantis analogy.

"Yo, we'll take our chances."

"It may be illegal. I'm making a mental note to organize your anklet jewelry line. In five designer colors."

That shut Ty up momentarily, no small feat. I steered him in the direction of his brother, who had moved into the rec room, on a sofa beside Millicent. Chris was playing a video game on one of those machines with the buttons that wirelessly hook up to the TV. Me, who thought Pong was the end-all.

On a screen the size of a soccer goalmouth, aliens were destroying cars to get to the humans. Or destroying humans to get to the cars. Or destroying cars just to destroy cars, and humans just to destroy humans. The sound physically pulsed and the wallpaper seemed to flutter.

That disciplinary chore done, I shut the door on them and got back to Mike, who said, "This Condor offed himself. Shotgun in the mouth. That's a bitch of an undisclosed illness."

"Like Hemingway," I said. "Pulled the trigger with a toe?"

"Whoever, whatever," Mike said. "Anyway, the Dallas PD kept a lid on it."

"Why?"

"'The why is long gone."

"About when the pseudonymous Delilah Henn Condor bailed out her slow-witted boys."

"Yeah, nobody connected those dots either."

"What else, Mike? Even if his death was exaggerated, Jerome the Eldest couldn't've killed my father or done much of anything else. Not at age ninety-eight."

"Not even running him over with his wheelchair or clubbing him with his walker. Let's hunt for a next of kin."

We all huddled behind Mike and read:

Jerome Condor II, his only child, was born on December 7, 1941.

Once again, fate, an omen, a sign somewhat more pretentious than hungry boll weevils. If you believed in that sort of thing. I didn't, but maybe the Condor clan did.

Mike said. "Gerry the Deuce, he'd be like deep into geezerhood, you know, age seventy-six. Might be ready and willing, but not able to do a whole lot of killing unless he had a wheelchair-mounted bazooka."

"I beg your pardon," Mom said.

"Careful, dude," I said.

"Was Jerome Two as deeply involved in the Dallas Trade Mart project since his father, architect of the plan, was largely incapable of orchestrating the details? He'd brought in his father's sixth ex-wife and two unemployed stepsons, sons of her Bulgarian fourth husband," Mike said.

"Where do you see that?"

"Inside my head."

"Could well be," I conceded.

"Yo, another tidbit. Jerome Condor the Third was born on that same November day, a caesarian performed on his wife."

"What time of day did they slice her open?"

"Half past eleven at night."

"Her life would or would not be in danger, hers and the baby's, if it went on that long. There's no way of knowing now," Mom said.

"These people are truly sick if they hurried the poor woman so the kid can be born on a historic date."

"Truly sick is a given, Mother," Judy said, "As the presidential motorcade passed the Grassy Knoll. If you're motivated by omens, some cockeyed portent, I estimate her water broke. How much more of a sign could one ask—"

> There was the beginning of hope again, the most promising since the cruel disappointment of October 16-28, 1962. Films taken by U-2 spy planes of Soviet SS-4 and R-14 ballistic missiles on Cuban soil, lined up like Cohiba cigars (Fidel's favorite brand) in a box.
>
> On the edge of a glorious cataclysm. Then came the unthinkable— diplomacy that actually worked. A secret agreement was reached whereupon the U.S. pledged to dismantle all missiles deployed in Turkey and Italy again. In return, the USSR removed their missiles and Ilyushin Il-28 bombers from Cuba. Crisis defused.

"¡Ay *caramba!*" Mike said.

"Where the hell did that come from?" I said.

Mike said, "A Dark Web rabbit hole. Hey, it vanished."

"Where did it go?"

"Monte," I said. "Time to bring in Monte."

"He's working on PUP and Associates," Judy said. "Monte's a digger."

I said, "Let's get him over here to excavate with Mike."

32

Monte sat in an easy chair made of brushed metal and buttery beige leather, one of the few people I'd ever seen use a laptop on their lap. He was pivoting slowly, looking around like a kid at the circus for the first time. As if taking in the elephants, the bearded lady, the idiot shot out of a cannon.

Millicent had gown bored with Ty and Chris, resenting the noise and their preoccupation with video games. She sat on the carpet in front of Monte, licking her privates, before yawning and walking to her food bowl.

It was next to a price-is-no-object, special-delivery combination cat climbing toy, scratching post, multiple playhouse and bed. She had no interest whatsoever in it, but on occasion napped in the box it came in that nobody dared recycle.

"You offended her," I said. "Disrespected her."

"Theodore," Judy said.

Monte blinked and looked at me.

I ignored Judy. I was trying to loosen him up. "You didn't bring a present. A dead mouse or anything."

"You can take the kid out of the wise-ass, but you can't take the wise-ass out of the kid, Monte," Quetzal said. "Or is it the other way around?"

"Children, children," Mom said.

"Down to business. Monte, anything new on PUP and Associates?" Judy said.

"Nothing but silence, which may be something. I tend to think that PUP is a play on Pop-up. They're trifling with us. Why? I haven't the foggiest."

She handed Monte what I'd brought back from Hawk's:

MISSION STATEMENT
We need to start over. And we will.

"A connection?" Judy said.

He studied it thoughtfully again and said, "Both PUP and Associates and this are puzzling. And a powerful common denominator I cannot decipher."

"Why?" I asked.

"Their brusque appearance in our system."

"CondorCakes and lead as shielding and the Cuban Missile Crisis," I said. "I'm not liking any of this."

The ensuing silence spoke that nobody else liked it.

Mike finally said, "Yellowcake. I remember from science class. It's stuff you get from uranium ore they do stuff to. It's yellow, uranium oxide or something of that nature. You don't want to make spice cake out of it or anything."

"Swell," I said, "Let's talk about PUP and Associates' retainer."

"What about it?" Judy said.

"How much is it, Big Sis, and don't give any confidentiality crap. Inquiring minds need to know."

She gave me a hard glare before saying, "Thirty-five thousand."

Ten percent of three-hundred-and-fifty grand. I suppressed a strong urge to react loudly and immaturely.

I said, "Monte, your email to PUP and Associates ricochets. Why don't we try this? Send the retainer back to them, saying thanks but no thanks."

He looked at the boss, who nodded.

He worked until his face turned the color of his Elvis hair.

"What's wrong?" Judy said.

"I can't send it back."

"It locked up?

"No. It's already gone."

33

Quetzal said, "That stupid mission statement business, missionaries who came to Yucatán said to repent before it's too late. I know I'm off the subject, but I am not liking the word similarity. They give me a headache, and they are too damn similar when you consider all this."

Mom said, "As far as I'm concerned, the whole thing is poppycock, nothing to lose sleep over."

I said, "Mom, CondorCake shielded by lead can mean we're dead."

Mom plugged her ears.

Judy said, "May we please focus?"

Millicent grew tired of the nonsensical human drama and retired down the hallway to nap on the bed of her choice.

Monte and Judy took turns on the laptop. Same conclusion— the thirty-five grand was long gone, to parts unknown.

I said, "Long gone like that pop-up thing."

"Yes."

"So it wasn't a simple hack and grab," I said, "May I offer a suggestion?"

Before anyone could say I couldn't, I said, "Judy, let's cut the confidentiality guano. I promise not to rat you out to the bar association. We need to find the mole, and he's burrowed under your lawn."

Mom said, "For once your brother's right, dear."

"For once?"

"Ariadne's thread," Mom said.

We all looked at her.

"Jonathon taught it in one of his advanced-placement classes. Logic or history or something. It comes from Ariadne, a gal in Greek mythology who fooled around with mazes and things like that. Her thread is a thread in a maze that goes from a beginning to the end solution."

"Trial and error?" Judy said.

"No. It doesn't look for one end. It looks at all possibles. I used that approach for our investments. Sudoku is given as a common example on Ariadne's threat. Beyond that, I'm fuzzy."

She looked at Judy. "Dear, if we can't take a peek at your clients, Ariadne's thread is snipped and we're screwed."

Judy took the laptop from Monte and obeyed Mom, punching in a password and entry code with angry index-finger jabs.

She handed it to me and said, "You have ten minutes. *One* smart-ass comment and your ten minutes are up."

"Sis, I only care about your recent clients, not Lucky Luciano."

She yanked the machine out of my hands. "How recent?"

"Let's say six months."

She tapped in some adjustments, said that the newer clients were bold-faced, and sidearmed it back. If my hand hadn't been right there, it would have sailed like a brick Frisbee.

With Mike looking over my shoulder, I scrolled through seven double-spaced pages, client name only, some with links, some not.

A smattering of the linked clients were Fortune 500 companies and others recognizable that'd be on the Fortune 1000 and 2000. If I had any doubts that my sis's firm was Big Time, I did no longer.

I counted sixteen recent clients without links or much activity. They had catchy names, This-or-that International Bank in tropical countries. One I recognized, a company that owned supermarket tabloids. I recalled a headline while standing in line with a loaf of bread and a six-pack. It placed Elvis on the Grassy Knoll.

I looked at my sister, smiled, and said, making it up, "Bermuda Triangle Offshore International Bank."

She grabbed for the laptop, but I pulled it out of reach in time. "Sorry, couldn't resist."

Judy said, "Read the Constitution, Little Brother. Every citizen is entitled to legal representation."

I smiled.

"You behave yourself, young man," Mom said, wagging a finger at me.

"Please listen to me," I said. "Somebody has motives below and beyond tax evasion. Like Mike's daddy. Here's one or two that don't look strictly slippery-financial. In the same ball park with PUP and Chums."

"Pretty please," said a grim Judy.

She took the laptop from me and gave it to Monte.

He scrolled up and down and said, "Well, we don't have many. This one came in very recently and does strike me as a head-scratcher. Realrealityresearch. One word. They came on a couple of months ago."

"I vaguely remember them," Judy said. "Marketing and investigative services. Small retainer. We assigned it to a junior associate."

"Investigative services sounds like private-eye, not how many rotten apples can you sell Johnny," I said.

Monte said, looking at Realrealityresearch's file, "They have two offices, one in Seattle and one in Portland. We've done low-level work for them."

"Like what?" Judy said.

My control-freak sister *didn't* know, I thought? Smith, Hurlbert and Kraus LLC, Attorneys-at-law was too big for its britches.

Monte said, "I see only three requests for our services, complaints about rival firms encroaching against clients with which they had clients."

"Is that illegal?" Quetzal asked. "Whatever it means."

Monte said, "I'm not familiar with their profession, but it may have been unethical. I just don't know. Our people sent letters to the alleged miscreants and the problems went away."

I said, "Do you have a website and any contact information for Realrealityresearch?"

Monte said, after a frowning, tie-loosening pause, "Oddly, a one-page website with no links. Phone numbers for their Seattle and Portland offices, yes."

I looked at the screen as he dialed Realrealityresearch in Seattle and then Portland. No answer at either.

"Street addresses?"

"No."

"When did they last request your services? "I said.

"Oh my. The day before yesterday."

"What did they want?"

"Not stated."

Judy said, "Did a letter go out?"

"Not yet, but it will be soon. Faster service, faster billing. We're running a little bit behind."

Mom said to Judy, "Oh, dear, I'm afraid that you have a barn door that opens both ways. If they have that sort of thing in computers."

Quetzal said, "This is a job for your house nerd. Where did he go?"

I looked down the hall. "He's saving the universe or destroying it."

"If somebody can tear Mike away from the video games with my boys," Judy said."If it's pornographic, I'll skin them alive."

I broke up their party and ordered Chris and Ty to stay where they were as Judy was setting up at the breakfast nook table.

At the laptop, Mike said, "Dark Web, here we come."

Judy said, "I didn't hear that."

Mike muttered and fiddled, finally saying, "Realrealityresearch is a dead end, the mother of all cul-de-sacs. You drive round and round. That's it."

I said, "That name. It's as if they're being playful, teasing us, flipping us the middle digit, saying catch me if you can."

"What next?" Mike said. "Me and the dudes, we're taking on SUVs from Alpha Centauri."

"The Alpha Centaurians will keep. Think factory recall," I said. "This tub that sailed in, the 'Bamsan Kiet', let's dig deeper into its cargo."

"Easier and harder," Mike said. "Easier, on account of it offloaded on Harbor Island a couple of days ago. Harder cuz they carry everything but the kitchen sink, unless it's kitchen sinks. If it is, they'd carry five thousand of them. Made in China, of course."

"Thanks for the editorial. I'm curious about the two hundred pounds of lead," I said. "That piece on the Cuban Missile Crisis, that was before my time, but it was a big hairy deal."

Mom said, "Oh, it was. The most dangerous time in our history. If President Kennedy hadn't stared that awful Khrushchev down, that ugly little toad, and the Soviets hadn't backed off, who knows what may have been?"

"The missiles were nukes," Judy said.

Mom said, "That is correct. Your father and I were considering having a bomb shelter dug."

"Lead does a lot of bad things, but it shields radioactivity, a good or bad thing, depending on if you're pitching or catching," I said.

Everyone looked at me.

"Okay, let's make a queasy assumption it's shielding nukes of some sort," I went on. "Can we track that two hundred pounds of it?"

Mike said, "I think I can. Guess who took possession?"

I said, "Realrealityresearch?"

"Shazam," Mike said. "No date given. No address, which they don't have, given. These are some tricky dudes."

Mom stood up. "Stop the music. This isn't a grand scheme where we can connect the dots and follow the thread. It's a fish market full of red herrings."

"Except CondorCake," I said.

"Except CondorCake," Mom said.

Judy raised a finger and said, "Let me handle this."

34

"The CondorCakes are in, packaged, and in shipment?"

"They are, Father. Our jewel boxes are here. Denver, Minneapolis and Charlotte. Packages are en route too."

"The upcoming holiday will be a glorious one to celebrate. "Yes, yes it will."

"We'll pop corks elsewhere. How's the weather in Ecuador?"

"Equatorial."

"Zurich?"

"On alert."

"The new execs are in step? No delays, no fucking around?"

"Their ancestors speak gold and money from that great numbered account in the sky."

"The Chinamen are hot to trot?"

"By saying nothing, they presumably are."

"But do they know? Did Chairman Mao alert the next bosses, who alerted the next bosses?"

"Impossible to say. Mao was a kinky fuck. If this gang knows, they're seeing no evil and cannot wait to see the evil. The old Red should've put that in his Little Red Book."

"Works for me."

"That fat chink with the wart, he said that a journey of a thousand miles begins with a single step. We're nine-hundred-and-ninety-nine miles into it. We can see the finish line."

"I have new information on our troublemaker, Father. We can't wait on him. I don't think we can."

"Is he still there?"

"Hold it a minute. I have to refocus the binocs. Yeah The number of silhouettes is unchanged, so he's in his sister's condo with the rest. I know that lawyers can make gobs of money, but she is off the charts."

"The fucking bitch, a lot of good that'll do her in a few days."

"There's movement."

"When he leaves, we can't let him out of our sight. He is a loser, but he's capable of gumming up the works even if by accident. We don't know what they learned from Hawk. What he passed along to them."

"Any news on Hawk?"

"Sorry. I neglected to tell you. He transferred in Portland and got off a bus in Redmond, Oregon. Stupid, stupid man. He thinks that if he doesn't get into a rental car or on an airplane, he can elude us."

"Do we have anyone handy?"

"A freelancer in Portland, an hour from there by commuter air."

"Call him."

"In the meantime, I'll stick with Theodore Cleaver Smith and release the Gull when the place and time are right. Smith is erratic, impulsive. We'll get a break."

"It has to be done. We take them out when we can. All of them. Have to."

"Our Gull has the wallet?"

"He does. He's on stand-by."

"Wherever we send him, he's in?"

"He's cowardly, but he knows we own him and he needs the money."

"Here we go. Something came up just now at the convenience store, Grandfather. I'm looking at that raghead East Injun's email. The timing couldn't be better for us."

"Good job, boy."

"If he agrees."

"Smith needs the money too."

"It will be attributed to an occupational hazard."

"Happens every day. So sad in this violent land we live in."

35

"I implore you, Kemo Sabe. I appeal to you with all my heart," Mr. Singh said.

I had stopped by the Happy-Happy Convenience Store to reply to his urgent message, as if I didn't know what it was. Stupidity and/or loyalty on my part.

"I remain on sabbatical, my faithful Indian companion. Leave of absence. I'll return as soon as I can. Can't Lil work extra hours? On the rare occasion when she's speaking to me, she bitches about money problems. Money she owes her abortion doctor for one. Her tattoo parlor too. I didn't know they financed."

"Therein lies my quandary, as I was so notified," Mr. Singh said. "At her motorcycle rally, accompanied by a band of ruffians I steadfastly advised her to refrain from keeping company with, she participated in a barroom fight, in all practicality a riot, in which she bested an equally-drunken off-duty police officer, breaking his jaw and four teeth with a beer bottle, then driving off quickly and erratically, and subsequently pulled over after a high-speed chase and ticketed for a DUI, among an assortment of felony charges."

His long sentences dazzled me. They were done without taking a breath, unless you counted the heavy sighs.

"That's easy, man. Just bail her out, and deduct the cost from her pay."

"From the jailhouse, she pleaded with me in her demanding way to do exactly that, Kemo Sabe. I then made the calculations. The

214

authorities are behaving vindictively as the wounded police officer is a beloved member of their precinct. Her bail is outrageously unfair, not unlike an amount set for a serial killer. Even if I deduct only one half of her pay, we will break even in the year 2344.In mid-February of that year, to be accurate."

"So?"

"Please, sir. One infinitesimal shift."

"One shift, only one shift at double pay, No, *triple* pay," I told Mr. Singh, telling him that my family pleaded with me not to do stop by here at all.

"They're out there, I was warned by my mother."

"Who is this they out where, please?"

"Gun-toting bandits. Lurking everywhere."

"A low-percentage risk is my Happy-Happy, Kemo Sabe," Mr. Singh said. "There are tens of thousands of convenience stores waiting to be robbed in this great land."

"Triple pay, Sahib."

He gasped, but averted fainting by hanging onto the counter.

"Yes. Triple. Pay. For. One. Shift."

I fastened my apron, admitting only to myself that I needed ten or twenty triple-pay shifts at the Happy-Happy to pay for damages done to my home and canvases by that son of a bitch with the chef's knife.

* * * * *

All the talk about robbery made me extra alert to danger (i.e. paranoid). Good thing I was. The fourth customer in the store wasn't carrying a shopping list, but rather a squarish, automatic pistol. Also a red kerchief over his face like a Wild West outlaw.

I sensed that he wasn't in for a pack of smokes when he aimed the thing at me without a word.

Oh, dear, I'm afraid that you have a barn door that opens both ways. If they have that sort of thing in computers.

For a crucial two seconds, the guy had trouble releasing his safety. I drew my Saturday night special before he could get off a shot. Crouching, pistol above my head, I fired blindly.

He popped off at least fifteen shots in my general direction as I fired all six rounds in his general direction. The majority of the damage either of us did was to the cigarette cartons to my rear and the beer cooler on the opposite wall. The fusillade also shook loose dust and asbestos particles from the ceiling.

One lucky shot struck the guy in the hand. His pistol flew out of it. A pistol that held a helluva lot of rounds. It was like the Lone Ranger and other shoot-'em-up shows where they just kept firing and firing their six-shooters."

He yelped and ran out the door, me in hot pursuit. He tripped on the door's loose step plate that Mr. Singh had been meaning to repair for months, stumbled across the sidewalk, and slammed against a lamppost headfirst before hitting the ground.

Barely conscious, he grasped the lamppost and rose to his hands and knees. Whereupon I administered the *coup de grace*, a kick to the ribs, which flattened him again, groaning, bleeding from both nostrils, and emitting foamy spittle.

I heard approaching sirens.

I tore off his cowboy-robber kerchief, revealing a pinched rat face made even more attractive by pain.

I yelled, "You don't have the right to remain silent, asshole. Talk to me before the cops make the scene."

He remained silent. I took a sample of his blood with a corner of my hanky that was clean.

I patted him down and felt two wallets, one plump, the other thin. I thought of Dad and multiple wallets as I took the skinny one and stuffed it into a pocket.

36

Mr. Singh arrived soon after the police.

"I monitor the store cameras regularly, Kemo Sabe. You were magnificent. You shot the gun out of the criminal's hand remarkably once more."

"Don't get mushy, Tonto. I drew blood this time."

"A mere scrape on the webbing of his despicable fingers. The Lone Ranger would be so proud of you," he said before hurrying into his store.

I'd called Quetzal too. She and Mom showed up soon with Judy, behind the wheel of her supersonic Porsche, Quetzal cramped in the rear.

"He kept shooting and shooting like he had a pocketful of pistols," I said. "Like they do on TV when nobody reloads."

Mom looked at the guy's gun as the police were bagging it.

"Dear, it's a Glock 19 that fires nine-millimeter Parabellums, nineteen of them in a single magazine. The recoil is short so it was able to be fired quickly."

"Of course," I said.

In the presence of my family, Mr. Singh came back with a notepad and made the mistake of asking my help with recording his losses on insurance forms. Quetzal shot him a look that could kill. Mom took him aside by a sleeve and told him what he could do with his ungrateful insurance-cheating itemization while her son was still in shock, having just cheated death, adverbs and adjectives I had never

217

heard her utter.

Thus their conversation ended.

I went through it and gave it to Judy who looked at it, used words Mom had, and got on the phone, summoning Mike.

He did everything but sniff the lone piece of ID in the gunslinger's wallet (which I concealed from the police who were gone with the mute perp). It was plastic-embossed, the property of V. I. Larrionov, member of the SVR RF (CBP P), Russia's Federal Intelligence Service, its external agency, successor to the KGB, with a recent photo of one Theodore Cleaver Smith.

"Dude," Mike said, looking at me.

"Déjà déjà vu," I said. "I'm found with this and riddled like a colander. FBI and CIA agents will be my pallbearers."

Mom flapped a hand. "I don't know, son. The cops would have treated it like just another armed robbery. There are Russians all over the place these days. Those babushka ladies and their gangster husbands. Oh, don't get me started."

Mike had his laptop with him. He typed and scrolled, then shrugged. "Same-old-same-old dead end."

"The same pattern leading up to——," my resplendent Quetzal said, her voice trailing off.

Hugging her and looking over her shoulder, I said, "How about it, Big Sis?"

"How about what?"

"You were going to handle something."

"Before you went off half-cocked."

"Handling it by calling in the cavalry?"

"I wish I could."

"So?"

"Selectively," she said. "Everybody, head back at my office."

Which we did after I evaded police questioning, convincing them without much effort that it was a random convenience-store stick-up. One of the cops knew a cop who had been on the scene of my infamous Kemo Sabe event.

He closed his notebook and said, "Man, you oughta change jobs. The next one might know how to shoot straight."

* * * * *

"Grandfather, they're going into her office building. Smith too. He's alive and uninjured."

"Motherfucker."

"The wallet?"

"The police band summarizes the incident, Father. As far as the wallet is concerned, Gull still has it."

"Is he talking?"

"No, not according to the chatter."

"Will he talk?"

"Gull has to be stand-up, Father. He has a lot to lose."

"We'll play him by ear."

"No."

"No?"

"We have to move. Jump the gun."

"I don't know."

"What you don't know is irrelevant, boy. Get the process underway."

37

I was careful to avoid eyeing Inge as we got off the elevator, not that she cared or noticed. Inge in black skirt and gauzy white blouse, grayish lipstick, mile-high cheekbones.

My resplendent one had once caught me ogling her and said there'd be an ancient Maya sacrifice in my near future if I didn't cease and desist, my living and beating heart removed with an obsidian knife. If I didn't believe that she knew the old ways, just try her. Judy would help her hold me down too. Saying it like Big Sis would be more pissed than her.

Because of Judy's influence, her "handling things", I imagined her capable of notifying everything and everybody including close assistants of POTUS. Ten alphabet agencies and ten people familiar to anyone who kept up on the news?

"No," she said.

"No?"

The problem was, she explained, for reasons of our own personal security, we had to conceal Dad's former profession and the KGB business. Mom was an accessory after the fact, and when we're talking sixteen murders, a crime for which there was no statute of limitations, "after the fact" was indefinite. She'd attempted to use her contacts to go through a side door for help, but came up empty. Bottom line was that we had to circle our wagons and clean up this mess on our own. However, she was not without resources.

She left the room, made twenty minutes worth of private calls, and told us, "I have people standing by."

I didn't waste my breath probing for details.

Mike studied the mission statement again.

MISSION STATEMENT
We need to start over. And we will.

We had to act fast, but where, against who, and to do what?

I said. "The shipment of lead. The rest of it. They're gonna obliterate us and Russia, whoever they are."

"Not a chance. You watch too many dystopian video games," Judy said.

"Not a sure thing, I'll concede, but a strong possibility," I said.

"I find the word 'obliterate' distasteful," Quetzal said.

Mike said, "It's like a synonym, you know, for 'delete'. Both sides hit the delete button at the same time."

"Three words," I said. "Dallas Trade Mart. No, make that six words. Nineteen-sixty-three."

Nobody replied.

"Look, Sis, I've said this before and I'll say it again. Whatever this is about, a grudge held for over half a century, there's some serious money behind it, piles and piles of money. Aconite Man was no lone killer like Lee Harvey."

Monte had been brought in for this powwow.

He said, "Going back to when the USSR first perfected the atomic bomb, 1949 or thereabouts, it is not, in my view, required that explosions be simultaneous. Providing that this dreadful theory became a fact."

I said, "Mushroom cloud over Moscow, Russkis pissed, mushroom cloud over DC."

"Conceivably true," Judy said. "But Seattle?"

"Our fair city isn't all," I said. "Think insanity and a grievance settled against multigenerational Smiths."

"Possibly," Judy said, nodding.

I said, "Sinister as all hell and *probable*. Seattle goes and, let's see, Vladivostok. Then mushroom clouds right up the population rankings, one after the other. Works for them so long as the Smith clan is turned into a pile of radioactive dust too."

"Using your logic, New York or Washington and Moscow," Judy said.

"Hitler and Stalin slaughtered people in stages. These madmen don't have their patience."

Judy said nothing.

"So we have to save the world," I said. "Not what I had in mind for a career choice."

"We're spinning the doomsday scenario based on our imaginations," Judy said.

Mom said, "Children, I have an idea."

38

Business hours were ending and traffic below quickly became a spidery parking lot. It was just us three Smiths and Quetzal, an honorary Smith herself. Becoming a legally-married Smith if Mom and Judy had their way.

After scolding us young people for being impatient, Mom said her idea might take awhile to explain with her throat so parched. Not to mention the life-saving flavonoids that would be depleted from the effort. So of course if you wanted her to survive long enough to present her brainstorm—

My sister shook her head disapprovingly, but took Mom's leaden hint and went into another room. She brought back a tray and glasses of red wine from an undisclosed location.

It didn't click until my teens that Mom had passed along her lecturing gene to Judy because she didn't employ it often. But when Mom did, you might as well kick back and relax.

Mom's idea was based on Ockham's Razor. She asked us if we knew what it was. We did, but Mom told us anyway.

"Try the simplest things first, in this case the only thing we can do is what we can do. Your father taught this in his classes. William of Ockham, who lived around eight hundred years ago taught that too."

Like obedient children, we nodded.

"This gun-toting criminal who tried to kill my son at that dreadful little store, he continues to be uncooperative with the police?"

"I just checked, Mother," Judy said. "He hasn't said a word, not even giving his name."

"His Constitutional right to remain silent," I said. "He's abusing it."

Judy said, "He had four sets of false ID in his wallet. The police are attempting to discern which one, if any, is correct."

"That is totally unacceptable," Mom said. "William of Ockham asserted that among competing hypotheses, the one with the fewest assumptions should be selected. Furthermore, his preference for simplicity—"

Judy's phone rang. She listened, made notes, thanked the caller and said, "The DNA search has identified our gunman as Terry Ray Gull of Reno, Nevada. No fingerprints on file. His last known address was a vacant house occupied by squatters until they were tossed out. We've made an anonymous call to the Reno police. They're are going through it now."

"Is bail for this Seagull creep set yet?" Mom said.

Judy checked her screen and said, "The alleged Mr. Gull's bail is a quarter million."

"Has he lawyered up?" Quetzal said.

"No," Judy said.

"He's not represented and he's not talking, so shall we do what William of Ockham would do?"

Judy smiled indulgently and said, "Which is, Mother?"

Mom sighed and beseeched the ceiling.

"Apparently we didn't raise you kids in the ways of the world. Make his bail, bring him here, and torture him until he talks. This way, we bypass all that silly courthouse nonsense, the Miranda thing, and the rest of the do-gooder impediments."

Judy reached for her phone. "In principle a fine idea, Mother, though I'll have to edit the barbaric portion."

"Oh, poo."

*　*　*　*　*

A long day was becoming longer, but Judy got things done in a fraction of the time a mere mortal could, if at all.

In under two hours, ex-cop Richard and a guy twice his size and half his age came in with Mr. Terry Ray Gull. They seated him in the conference room, one holding a shoulder, plunking him down hard.

Richard, who didn't introduce his colleague, said, "He's not what you'd call a motormouth. 'Ouch' and 'ow' is all he said on the way over. Don't hesitate if you need us, ma'am. To, you know, soften him up."

This was my first really good look at Gull, sans kerchief and pain: average height and weight with a nice start on a pot gut, a thirty-five-year-old white man whose pinched, acne-scarred face was made for mug shots.

"How's your ribs, Terry Ray?" I said.

He gave me a look that said nothing and stared at a wall as blank as his expression.

"That's too bad," I said.

"Theo, please lay everything out for Mr. Gull," Judy said.

I spread out the wallet and the Russian ID in front of him and said, "There's a history to this that will get you in a world of hurt, Comrade Terry Ray. The cops don't have it. You're a Reno boy, so you know what a wild card is. If we accidentally find it and hand it over to them, we're talking espionage."

"That is much, much more serious than you playing Billy the Kid in that awful little market," Quetzal said.

No reaction, not even a sidelong peek at it.

"Dear, can you waterboard people in the bathrooms on this floor? I think that's what they call it, what we do to those Arabs down there in Cuba," Mom asked Judy.

"Mother."

Quetzal said, "We can improvise. Holding him by the ankles and dunking him in a toilet."

Feigning amusement, Gull's eyes darted between the women.

I leaned across the table and held the mission statement in front of him.

"Is this funny too, Terry Ray."

MISSION STATEMENT
We need to start over. And we will.

I thought I detected a gulp. Otherwise, nothing. This was one cool cat. For us good guys, it was half psychological gamesmanship, half not knowing what the hell to do next. For Terry Ray Gull, it was time out of jail, enjoying the evening.

Mom said, "I have an idea, young man."

He studied the table top. We studied Mom.

"Well, you know, if you buy a toaster from a store and it's defective, what do you do? You return it and get your money back. That's what you do."

I grinned. Brilliant.

Quetzal got it too. She clapped her hands. "*Muy bueno*. Can we do that with defective humanoids?"

Mom said, "With a bum toaster, you can complain at the top of your lungs too."

Judy smiled, pen poised at notepad.

Mom said, "On the other hand, if the toaster *isn't* defective, you can return it *without* a reason. The store will ask why it's coming back. Oh, say you had a big brunch for your bridge club and you needed a second toaster. The store won't like it, but they'll take it back rather than have the customer raise a big stink."

Terry Ray Gull said, "Please, no. You can't."

Mom said, "Why the hell can't we, Mr. Gull? You and your mouth are on the fritz, like a toaster that won't toast."

"Hey, c'mon, they'll think I talked."

"They?" we chorused.

Terry Ray said nothing.

Judy picked up her phone and said, "I'll call a press conference, Mother. To announce that he gave us vital information, hoping we'd let our guard down, then tried to run for it before we could vet his info. We had no choice to remand the suspect. He's a flight risk."

"Shit, they'll believe it for sure," Gull said.

Mom said, smiling sweetly, said, "On dear, I've heard those ghastly stories about what's done to stool pigeons in jail. Yuck, the shower room. Are they true?"

"They are true," I said. "They make those shanks out of toothbrushes and razor blades."

"Okay," Gull said. "Shit, okay."

39

Judy said, "Terry Ray Gull is not your real name, is it? Otherwise you wouldn't be so easy to trace."

He said, "Yeah, Terry Ray Gull isn't my real name. Mr. C the Three made me take it."

"Mister C as in Condor?"

"I don't know. He said Mr. C the Three is all. He's not, you know, the kind of guy you ask personal questions of."

"The other IDs?"

"He gave them to me. I don't know where they came from. He said it was none of my business. I was supposed to show one if I got stopped for something. He ain't gonna like me losing the wallet to the cops."

"Who are you?"

"Terry Ray."

"No last name."

"Ray's my last name. TJ's my first name, the one my mother gave me. I got no middle name. I go by TJ."

"Where did you live? And don't say Reno."

"Nowhere. On the street. Homeless shelters. They offered me this job off the street here in town. I came up from Reno, where I was last."

"Where and when?"

"A few days ago. You can almost see where from this building. In the fall when the rain comes, I head south. LA, Phoenix, like that."

"Why aren't your fingerprints on record?"

"I've done stuff I'm not too proud of, but I never got caught and locked up for nothing. That's the first thing Mr. C the Three asked, have I ever been fingerprinted? I said no."

"Your DNA?"

"I heard of it, Like it's HIV? I'm not sure what that is."

"A foolproof, scientific way of identifying you," I said.

"Oh yeah. They once made me spit into this tube. At this drug rehab place, not that I ever had a dope problem."

"The gun?"

"They gave me that and taught me how to fire it, Mr. C the Three did."

"The Glock 19 retails for between five-hundred and seven-fifty," Mom said. "It's the very dickens getting a permit for a handgun in this state."

"I don't know from permits."

I said, "Pretend we're NRA and you're among friends."

"Mr. C the Three made it seem like an accidental meeting, but I know now it wasn't."

He looked at his fingernails, then at Mom.

"The old broad there, I don't like how she's staring at me."

I got up. Fast.

"That's our mother, asshole. Be respectful or I'll take you out to your friends. See how you like the way they're looking at you."

He smirked at me.

"We're voiding your warrantee," I said, lifting him by the scruff of his shirt.

Ray cringed and hung on to the sides of his chair.

"Ow, my fucking ribs."

Judy said, "Please sit down, Theo. Mr. Ray, my brother's right. You insulted our mother and you're wasting our time. Open up or my colleagues are returning you."

"Okay, okay. Like I said, Mr. C recruited me. There was an older guy along too, mean-looking dude, who stood behind him, watching.

They had this SUV. They stopped someplace, got me some new clothes, then through a drive-through line for burgers, and out in the sticks to teach me how to fire the gun at targets they'd pinned up on trees. I didn't shoot for shit and was lucky to put one hole in the target."

"Mr. Jerome Condor the Second and Third?"

"I can't say for sure, but yeah, maybe. There was a family resemblance."

"The old one, isn't he fairly old to be involved in hired killings?"

"Yes and no. The older one is older and the younger one is younger."

"Wow," Mom said. "Such insight."

"Like I said, there were two of them, plus this younger guy who stayed in the SUV, who did the driving and set up the targets. He didn't say two words."

"We know damn near everything," I said. "Fill in the few remaining blanks, like what's up their sleeves."

"They said that after I offed you, I was supposed to toss the wallet on top of you."

"The skinny wallet."

"Yeah, the plump one was gonna be mine. They showed me this cash they said they'd stuff it with. All hundreds. More money I ever saw in my life… they said they'd be waiting outside. Before I went and tripped in the doorway, I saw that they were gone. They were hanging me out to dry, is what they done."

"Isn't murder out of your job description?" Judy said.

"Lady, if you saw all that money and all they promised too."

"Promised what too?"

"They were gonna give me enough to fill ten wallets, all hundreds, and let me work with them with their Condor Cakes. Those two words, they're one word. That's what the old guy said. CondorCakes."

"What are they, those CondorCakes?"

He looked at me and shrugged.

"Since I didn't off you, we didn't get to that part."

Judy said, "You aren't here to treat us to your sarcasm. These CondorCakes, did they hint at what they planned to do with them?"

"Once, Mr. C the Three said they'd be served up on a special day and the old guy said to shut the fuck up, his language, not mine."

"Do you have an opinion at all what they are?"

"None, but how they said it, it's like the chow they serve us in this slammer is how I pictured it in my mind."

40

He stared out the window; the view of the water never got old. Watching a ferry boat, laptop on the sill, he said, "The Smith lawyer made bail for him, Grandfather."

"That fucking bitch, what's she up to?"

"Don't know. Our boy *does* know what we'll do to him if he talks."

"Are you sure?"

"Two big guys picked him up and took him into her building. Her lights are on, so that's where he is."

"He doesn't know the whole story, Father."

"He knows more than we want them to know."

"Can we begin?"

"Hold your horses, boy. We have a timeline."

"But they'll go with everyone else."

"Have you seen what a loved one looks like after he's eaten a shotgun barrel?"

"With all due respect, Grandfather, you've described—"

"The lower jaw and ganglia, that's our loved one."

"The one who did it. Robin made sure *he* knew, Father."

"So you know why it's personal, why they have to pay first. See what's to come."

"We can see your point—"

"Her other offices, Father. Minneapolis, Charlotte, Denver. If she's alive, she'll know."

"Think of Zurich, Grandfather. Gold. Ecuador."

"Please, Father, Armageddon or bust."

"Yeah, Grandfather. Our very own gold rush."

"You boys."

"Please. Now they've got him."

"For sure?"

"I'm looking right at them. All three."

"You win, boys."

Mr. C the Three opened the garage door under them.

41

We apologized profusely and insincerely to TJ Ray aka Terry Ray Gull for insinuating that we bailed him out to cut him loose if he cooperated. This as we handed him over to Richard and Godzilla to return to the pokey.

There was no further need for him, and even Judy could use the refunded bail money, a hefty chunk of change. There wasn't anything else we could do until (if/when?) Mike dug up something new on CondorCakes or anything else pertinent.

Mr. Ray-Gull had taken it badly, firing off a string of four-letter words as he accused Judy of violating legal ethics.

Sis told him to complain to the bar association.

"You are a defective toaster, young man," Mom said. "As defective as a toaster can be."

We reached a consensus that a good night's sleep was the best next move since no others came to mind.

* * * * *

In the morning, while Quetzal and I spoon-nestled, my phone rang.

"What were you thinking, Theodore Cleaver?" Judy said.

Theodore Cleaver.

"Thinking about what? What the hell did I do now?"

"You're supposed to be supervising Tyler and Christopher. Yes, we've all been under stress and preoccupied, but right under your nose."

"*My* nose? Please. Explain."

"They fixed Mike up."

"June is a romantic month," I said lamely, aware that I was in some manner of deep doo-doo even if I didn't cause it. Not directly. I had a hunch that this was not a match made in anybody's heaven.

"He wants to marry her. Evidently, thanks to her, Mike—how do I put thus?"

"Had his cherry popped?"

"I couldn't have put it better myself."

"Who's the lucky popper?"

"Look at the attachment on your phone."

I did. The girl of Mike's dreams had a pink mullet, earrings the size of pizza pans, no bra, unshaven pits, and more tattoos than the Sixth Fleet. Because of the adornment, I couldn't tell if she was attractive or not, nor how old. A dead ringer for Lil's kid sister or love child, if she had one. A Real Housewife of Transylvania. I almost said something recklessly inane like: *you can't judge a book by its cover.*

Quetzal was awake, peering over my shoulder.

"Um," I said. "She's my fault?"

"You're their babysitter."

"C'mon, Big Sis. They're adults. Sort of."

"Mike's mother is beside herself."

So that's what was driving her outrage. An attorney-client temblor.

"Understandable. His dad?"

"A 'more power to him' comment, the asshole."

I wasn't touching that one with a ten-mile pole.

"Mike's still working on our problem. Thanks only to a stern lecture about responsibility from his mother."

"Oh, good."

"He said he'll do as much as he can before the wedding and honeymoon."

I wasn't stepping into that minefield either.

Again I said, "Um."

"Any brilliant ideas how to postpone the nuptials?"

"Well, as long as he keeps working, he can't do something stupid we can't easily undo. Can he?"

She said she was holding me to that and hung up.

I buried my head under the blanket.

One elbow on my back, Quetzal was holding my phone, evaluating Mike's intended.

"In the past, my father tried to convert fallen women such as this, to pull them away from the jaws of Satan."

"How did it work out for him?"

"I asked for specifics. He clammed up on the subject."

"The painted hussies turned the tables?"

I watched closely as she sat up and stretched.

She said, "I didn't rule that out."

"What's a special day to serve CondorCake, do you think?" I said. "Today's June eleventh."

"The Fourth of July's coming up soon. You could make a statement then if you were a political terrorist."

"Soon but not too soon," I said.

Quetzal said, "But aren't they moving along faster than that?"

I thought of Millicent's former home and TJ Ray, and said, "Um."

"I think they are."

42

Paramilitary inspection time in the sparsely-furnished living room above the garage in the pop-up accommodations on a steep hill:

Mr. C the Two and Mr. C the Three had their recruits stand in military formation in their parcel delivery uniforms. That disguise hadn't worked out earlier, but Robin's mistakes would not be repeated, not with this foursome under very close supervision.

The four men had been showered and shaved. They gargled with mouthwash too, also with limited effect.

"Very good, gentlemen, upright, albeit raggedy. Let me ask you boys a question. Are you being adequately paid? Even generously?"

All mumbled to the affirmative.

"I must be frank. Alcohol damages the memory, short- and long-term. Reach into your left-hand shirt pockets, please, and withdraw the card I have given you," Mr. C the Two said.

They obeyed.

"They are as we promised, gift cards to a big-box beer and wine chain store. Their stores are numerous. One is stumbling distance from here."

"How much?" one said.

"Unlimited," Mr. C the Three lied. The cards had twenty-five dollar limits.

"The cash in your pockets too."

No lie there. Each was issued four-hundred dollars in ten-dollar bills, a bonanza to the foursome who were accustomed to pocket change and rumpled small bills, gleanings from panhandling used to buy fortified wine.

"My people and I shall drive you to your locations in the van. I'll accompany each of you on your deliveries until you reach your assigned floors. You know what to do then."

They looked at him and at each other.

"No problem. I'll remind you at the time."

43

Saturday at Smith, Hurlbert and Kraus LLC was a normal workday for the one-hundred-and-twenty-five or so attorneys in the head office, most making an ass-kissing appearance for Judy's benefit, Big Sis who was always there, as were others putting a wrap on their ninety-hour work weeks, praying on their knees to make partner before dying of a nervous breakdown or exhaustion.

Today, but for Judy's private office, the place was vacant. Like it was occasionally on Christmas and Thanksgiving. She had ordered the minions to take the day off or telecommute. No exceptions and no explanation given. I imagined that those on medication for paranoia were doubling their dosage.

Having been ordered by his mother, Mike slept in the office, shielded from his fiancée, as it were, a figurative Victorian board between them. He was hard at work, Ty and Chris stood by, unnaturally pale. They had gotten the word from *their* mother that they were in the biggest of big trouble.

Quetzal and I said hello to the boys and sat down with Mike, wisely making no mention of his whirlwind romance.

Judy said, "Theo, we've been talking about holidays. The Fourth of July in particular."

I said, "That's a long way off, Sis. First, let's concentrate on Russian holidays. Anything like our Fourth coming up?"

She was looking at her screen. "In the old Soviet Union, May Day was their biggie."

"I remember," I said. "The parades with the tanks and missiles. Like they do in Pyongyang twice a week."

"Here, stop, Mike. Since the break-up, it's Russia Day, June twelfth. As a matter of fact, that's today. A big deal there."

I looked at the site. No missiles or tanks. It looked closer to our Independence Day. Russia Day had been around since the Soviet break-up in different forms and officially named Russia Day in 2002.

Still, I thought.

MISSION STATEMENT
We need to start over. And we will.

"Mike, how small can nuclear bombs be, the smallest ones?"

He pulled up pieces on suitcase nukes. They looked like small barrels with backpacks and wires, like you'd throw together after cleaning out your garage and leave at the curb for recycle pick-up, hoping they would.

"Bigger than a breadbox," I said.

"Dude, they'd be a bitch to carry around. Fifty pounds minimum and you'd kind of attract attention."

"Smaller?"

"Dark Web time," he said.

He tapped and scrolled and said, "In some of those countries over there we don't get along with, there are stories that they've made some even smaller. Nothing confirmed."

"How small?"

"Damn small. They call them jewel boxes."

"How much oomph do they pack?" I said.

"Less in kilotons, you know, than Hiroshima, but they'd vaporize ten or twenty city blocks. The radiation would hang around, like Chernobyl. Any way you look at it, a jewel box nuke is some bad shit."

I said, "Has anybody had parcel deliveries lately?"

Judy said, "What are you implying, Theo?"

"Damned if I know. Nothing good."

The elevator dinged.

"On a Saturday?"

"Seldom on weekends," Judy said, sitting up straight.

44

I was the first one into the lobby.

Two guys came out of the elevator dressed in brown delivery uniforms. They wore shorts and their legs were the first things I noticed. The legs on the guy wheeling the hand truck were scrawny and scabby. He was around my height, had bloodshot eyes, and Rudolf's nose. He'd had hard miles on him and could be anywhere from forty to eighty-five. He had to put a bony shoulder forward and grunt to move the hand truck.

The guy behind him was holding a clipboard, a step off to the side. He was in his fifties, tall and broad-shouldered, robust, with hard eyes, everything his partner wasn't. He wore a sneer that said he knew something we didn't.

"I'm breaking him in on my route," the healthy-looking guy said. "I thought you big-shot lawyers were off on the weekends."

He was awfully eager to volunteer that, I thought. The hand truck held a cardboard box the dimensions of a case of beer.

Judy had arrived, a remote control in a hand.

"I didn't order anything," she said.

The healthy one presented a cold smile. "I can check. It's for someone else on this floor?"

"There is nobody else on this floor."

I pointed at the box. "Looks heavy. What's in it?"

The big guy said, "How should I know? We're paid to deliver is all."

He was oddly impolite. No customer-service training?

"Where's the address label?"

"It's on the underside."

I said, "Then how did you know where to deliver it? X-ray vision?"

He looked at me.

We'd attracted a crowd, the whole gang: Mom, Quetzal, the boys, Mike.

I couldn't tell who the rummy was looking at, even though he was looking right at me.

"Open it," I said. "Pretend it's Christmas morning and you asked Santa for CondorCake. Served with ice cream."

At "CondorCake," the big guy blushed.

"You're talking nonsense. I'll drop it off. You don't even have to sign for it. We've got a van full of deliveries to make. I'd like to be done and home before dinner."

"Open it," Judy said.

"Sorry. That's against company policy. We could get fired."

"What's your name?"

The spokesperson reached into a shirt pocket and said, "I'll show you my company name tag."

Stupidly, I took a step forward to look as he took a swing. I reacted quickly enough that his punch barely clipped my jaw, but it did put me flat on my back.

Quetzal screamed. Ty and Chris held her back and moved forward.

The guy went for the elevator, but Big Sis extended the remote and made the elevator door close.

"You can't take the stairs either. The door's locked."

I was on my knees by then and pushed off my back foot, catching him in the midsection with a shoulder, slamming him hard against the wall.

He swung wildly, but I was too close to take any damage.

I swung wildly, clipping his ear with my forearm.

I anticipated a counterpunch and pushed back and to a side, making room for Chris and Ty to stomp on him.

Instead of a blow, he pulled a short-barreled revolver out of a baggy front pocket, halted the boys by pointing it at them and aimed it at me point blank, the barrel the size of a cannon.

Is That All There Is?

"You're making me do it the hard way, fuckhead," he said, "All of you. You first, hero."

I heard a shot, a *pop*, but it wasn't my face was being blown away. A small red dot appeared on his forehead.

I released him to drop and staggered to my feet to see Mom holding a tiny automatic pistol, gleaming silver with pearl grips.

"Oh dear," she said. "What do we do now?"

"You saved my life, Mom."

Head down, pistol pointed at the floor, she said, "Will they believe me? If they don't and send me up the river, I'll be locked up with two-hundred- pound lesbian dope fiends."

"Not a chance, Mom." I looked at the deceased's uniformed companion. "I don't see any witnesses. Do you?"

He shook his head. "I don't want no trouble. All I want is a drink."

Judy took the gun from her. "Mother, where on earth did you get your hands on this?"

She wiped her eyes with a sleeve. "Your father gave it to me for my birthday in 1964. God bless him, he knew I'd need it someday."

"Mom, you're the greatest," I said, hugging her, both of us quivering, while a sobbing Quetzal held me from behind.

Then to Judy, Quetzal said, "Please, not the police."

Judy said, "No worries, no nine-one-one. I don't know what they'd do with Mother. I do know somebody who can take care of—him. Boys, please bring him into the office."

Ty and Chris, our Correspondence Supervisors, each took an armpit, as casually as if they were moving a case of office paper.

"And try to keep him on his back so he doesn't bleed all over the carpeting."

"You're worried about the rug?" Ty said, as the lifted him to a sitting position.

"I'm worried about evidence. Get moving."

"Wait. Let's check his pockets first," I said.

Chris fumbled around, pulled out a cell phone, and tossed it to Quetzal.

"This is it," he said.

"You," I said to the zombie-like rummy.

"What about me?"

"Are there others?"

"Other whats?"

"Others like you."

"No. Just three of us in the van."

"Yes? No?"

"Yeah."

"Jesus H. Christ. Who are they?"

"Just some guys."

"Guys like you? Do you know them?"

"I guess they're like me. We sleep in the same doorways sometimes. One guy, I see him holding up his cardboard sign. That's how I know him, his sign, saying 'God bless and disabled veteran'. I know he ain't no veteran'."

"Why are you here?"

"Him," he said, pointing down at the corpse that had been dragged off by the boys. "Him and these two other guys, they picked us up. You know, like they do when they want day labor."

"Picked you up where?"

"Where we sometimes hang out."

"Paying you what?"

"I don't have to give it back, do I? If he's dead, I can't—"

"Show me what he paid you."

He took out a wad of cash and a gift card to a liquor store.

I ran into Judy's office, looked down and saw a brown van, half on the street, half on the sidewalk, lights flashing. I ran back out, sidestepping the boys and their cargo.

"Get out of your clothes," I told the rummy.

"Theo."

"Theodore."

"Dude. Whoa."

"Hurry up, Goddammit."

He began, almost falling.

"My undies too?"

"Jesus H. Christ, no."

As I peeled off my clothes, my resplendent Quetzal said, "I'm afraid to ask, Theo."

"Please don't, doll."

Mike had the package unwrapped, revealing Styrofoam, which he tore away, revealing a dull metal cube the dimensions of a half-case of beer. Inserted on one side was a flat round clock."

"Yo, Jewel Box City."

I lifted it. "Heavy as lead."

"A timer," Mike said. "Gotta be attached to an explosive that blows the shit out of this thing. The markings stamped on it and the timer, look like Russian."

"Shielding for CondorCake?"

"Gotta be. Blowing the shit every which way. Deadly radiation."

"On Russia Day," Judy said. "Happy Russia Day, everyone."

"Two-part question, Mike. Can you defuse it? How long before it blows? Answered preferably in that order."

"Damn good question. Damn good questions."

"I know somebody," Judy said, phone to her ear.

"Don't wait lunch on me," I said, rolling the hand truck into the elevator.

"Hey, me?" said the bum.

"Go stand in a corner and keep your trap shut," Mom said.

"Don't do anything stupid, Theo," Quetzal said.

"Me?' I said.

<h1 style="text-align:center">45</h1>

I headed down the elevator, fully uniformed, replete with hand truck, hanging on to it white-knuckle-tightly to control my shaking, as I tried not to capture the scent of the new me. I had lots of things to concentrate on, plus what I really had to concentrate on if only I knew what it was.

Please let me make this perfectly clear, I am no hero. I am a semi-failed painter who had peaked or never would peak, biting off on a helluva more than I can chew. Russia Day could be the designated day, for whatever they were intending to happen.

I left the building by the service entrance/exit into a narrow alley, where I dumped the hand truck.

I was able to stoop and duckwalk behind the van without the driver seeing me and banged on the rear doors. One opened and I climbed in, my Saturday night special in hand.

Three more derelicts sat on the benches, hand trucks and packages identical to our delivery in front of them. A guy in his seventies was at the wheel.

I jabbed his neck with my Saturday night special.

"Mr. Condor the Eldest, I presume."

"Theodore Cleaver Smith, the hack artist. Where's my son and his companion?"

"Your boy's taking a break with his friend. He's got a killer headache. A migraine."

"He doesn't get migraines."

"Must be caused by the jewel-box radioactivity. Where'd you get the van?"

"At an auction. A million miles on it, but the body's straight and the paint's clean."

"How much time left on the timers inside those packages?"

"Four hours, give or take."

"Ample time for you to finish your deliveries and leave town."

"And ample time for downtown to fill with shoppers and visitors," he said.

No detectable emotion.

"How are you riding out of Dodge?"

"Private jet at Boeing Field."

"Very nice. Where to?"

"Los Angeles for refueling. A second refueling stop in Panama City, then on to Quito."

"I think I can guess what a CondorCake is, in general."

"Enlighten me."

"Not available in the cake mix aisle."

"Correct."

"Radioactive material shielded by lead."

"If you narrow your guess to enriched uranium and *plastique* with hundreds of fléchettes in it to spread the wealth, you'd be correct."

"Did this sail in on the *Bamsan Kiet*?"

"You've done your homework."

"So, as you stated, if the packages explode in several hours, there'll be plenty of people killed by the radiation."

He smiled. "Correct."

"I have to say, you are one sick, cold-blooded motherfucker."

Still smiling: "Sticks and stones. Everybody on earth dies sooner or later, Theodore. Why get your panties in a knot over the timing?"

"You are one demented cocksucker."

"There you go again with the profane insults. I thought you were classier than that."

"What have you got against my family? You want to kill millions of people, but are bound and determined to do us Smiths first."

"Have you ever seen a loved one with his head blown off with a shotgun?"

"You're not talking about Ernest Hemingway."

"No, but same method."

"Your old man, toe on the trigger. He'd be a sight for my sore eyes. I'd pay admission."

"That was in questionable taste."

"Why us?"

"Your father is why."

"He derailed your daddy's Hitler-esque scheme."

"Let us maintain decorum, shall we?"

"All these years, Condor. You must have a beaut of an ulcer, stewing."

"You wish."

"What's in it for you besides pleasure?"

"What have you done with my son?"

"Fuck you. Give me the keys. Game's over. Then we can talk about your boy."

I felt a bee sting to my neck and smelled the foulest breath I had ever smelled.

Condor started up the van, saying, "Don't move a millimeter, Mr. Smith, or your gusher will get all over your uniform."

46

The bee sting went away, allowing me to turn my neck enough to see one of the uniformed bums holding a switchblade well within carotid range. His hand wasn't brain-surgeon steady, but steady enough to drive his blade home.

Condor said, "Theodore, meet Rolan, the only member of the quartet with live brain cells. Rolan is not your generic derelict who lives in a cardboard box under a freeway overpass, are you, Rolan?"

"No sir."

"I got lucky finding you, didn't I, Rolan? And vice versa."

"Yes sir."

"Care to tell Mr. Theodore Cleaver Smith why, Rolan?"

"Yes sir."

"I'm waiting, Rolan. Theo?"

"Me too. I'm all ears."

Condor laughed. "You are unless I order Rolan to get frisky with his toad sticker and do a Van Gogh number on you. Let's hear it, Rolan. Let's go, boy. We don't have all day."

"Yes sir. Well, I am a high school graduate and I trained in an apprenticeship to be a tool-and-die maker."

"Who fell into the loving arms of Mr. Jack Daniels and lost it all, job, family, home."

"Hey, what's this Jack shit? I ain't no faggot."

"Imagery, Rolan. A metaphor. Please calm down."

"I like girls is all I'm saying."

250

"The whiskey brand, Rolan."

"My favorite's any brand I can get my hands on, sir."

"Moving right along, Rolan. As we discussed in your job interview."

"Yeah, well, I'm what you call your two strikes in a three strikes state and you're my jackpot, sir. I done time for shoplifting and assault. Shit they framed me for."

Condor laughed. "If they caught you for everything you've done, Rolan, you'd be ten strikes and still swinging."

Rolan's gap-toothed grin released fumes so toxic I came close to fainting.

"You got a wit about you, sir."

I said, "I'm properly intimidated, Condor. Why the pop-up and mission statement business?"

"A youngster's fun and games. Poking the hornet's nest to see what's what."

"Childish."

"But effective. By the way, tell me the truth, Theodore, now that we're bonding, establishing rapport. Stop the evasive wisecracks and tell me what you're doing with my son and what's this killer headache nonsense is about?"

I said, "Clumsy as he is, he took a hard fall, but he's fine. We're holding him for observation. That's it. Scout's honor. Until we get sick of his company."

"Then what? Tell me."

"Rolan puts away his knife, you let me go, and you call off your lunatic plan. You get your boy."

"If I don't agree to your terms?"

"He accidentally falls out of a window. Tragic death by defenestration."

Condor lifted a shoulder. "If he does, I'll miss him. Some collateral damage is to be expected. We must go forward."

"Born, wasn't he, on the day JFK was assassinated. Some timing, huh?"

"Circumstances altered our thinking. We had his mother cut open five minutes before midnight."

"Fate and a surgeon's knife. How did your loving wife fare?"

He shrugged.

"You haven't spoken of your ladies. Girlfriends and wives."

"Condor women, like any other females, are ejaculation receptacles and pressure relief valves."

"You're showing me a romantic side I never dreamed you had."

Condor laughed.

"You born on Pearl Harbor Day. Too bad it didn't happen on the deck of the USS Arizona."

He laughed again. "I'm reminded that your late father taught history."

"It's nice to be part of a loving family," I said. "I'm really curious about your ultimate goal. Care to walk me through it? For confirmation of how sick you are."

Condor turned the corner, looking at a GPS screen on the dash. "Certainly. World War Three is our goal."

"We assumed that. But why? Ideological? To wipe Russia and the United States off the map?"

"Of course not. Monetary. It should have been set into motion a half century ago but your father ruined everything and killed my father to boot."

"I read the obit. Your old man died because he was as crazy as a shithouse mouse. He tried to set up my dad as the worst monster in history. Fuck him and fuck you. I'd love to piss on your old man's grave."

Calmly, Condor said, "Your father actually did me a favor."

"How's that?"

"The payment was to be in gold, stored by a Zurich bank, a mere ten million dollars worth at the fixed price of thirty-five per ounce in 1963. Who knows what would have happened to the gold and me by now."

"Too terrible to contemplate," I said.

"*My* gold is worth close to four-hundred million dollars today."

"Mushroom clouds in order to collect. That's unchanged?"

"Armageddon is the key word. In the Southern Hemisphere, we can watch it on the news."

"Who's paying you, should your dreams come true?"

"Originally, the Chinese and Chairman Mao. They'd had a lover's spat with the Soviets and America was already an enemy. Recent developments make the same scenario attractive to them. The present leadership isn't directly involved, but if they do know what I have set into motion, I'm confident they'll stand back and enjoy the show. They haven't interfered, due to ignorance or acquiescence. It doesn't matter."

"Your old man visited China during World War Two," I said.

"That's no secret."

"The scarce metals gig."

"Yes."

"Did he meet the chubby Chairman in person?"

"Yes, ceremoniously, and then with some of his top functionaries to hammer out the details."

"The black market made your daddy rich."

"Do not say black market like it's an obscenity, Theodore. During wartime it's a necessity at times, to move vital materiel from here to there, and from there to here. My father had a crystal ball in his noggin. He hitched his star to Chairman Mao. He knew Mao would beat Chiang and his Nationalists. He knew that the US and USSR would be the big players and that Mao didn't appreciate being aced out."

"He saw his chance in late 1963."

"He did."

"You guys were the best choice to handle business."

"We were. Until your father ruined everything. Raining on my father's parade."

"Give Lee Harvey Oswald some of the credit, Condor."

"What that disturbed little man did was unforgivable too."

"How's your money holding out? It doesn't take a CPA to know that your expenses to orchestrate this insane stunt are high. How much longer will your seed money last?"

Condor didn't answer.

"I thought so. You're a geezer. How are you gonna live long enough to enjoy your prize?"

"I'll spend and spend and spend, like every day is my last. I'll bathe in the finest French champagne with Ecuador's most beautiful whores. I'll check out cryogenics too. Who says you can't take it with you?"

"Not a trip to Zurich first? It should be nice this time of the year."

"I can withdraw and transfer funds with the key word and password, and a click of a mouse."

"Care to confirm the recipe for your CondorCakes?"

"Enriched uranium and a malleable explosive ten times as powerful as C-4. In three and three-quarter hours, it'll blow out every window on your sister's floor and in a ten-block radius. A flattened mushroom cloud. You think nine-eleven was spectacular? Our other destinations, propelling the goodness outside too."

"Three other destinations?"

"Yes. Denver, Minneapolis and Charlotte. Four cakes distributed in downtown skyscrapers. We have each time zone covered by delivery firms that are innocents. We're hands-on here to be up close and personal to the Smith family, and—." He snapped his fingers. "By gosh and by golly, doesn't Ms. Smith have law offices in those fair cities too? Big towns, but not the biggest, where she might face oversight."

"Realrealityresearch. Your mole?"

"I have very clever tech support. A brilliant young man. I am so proud of him."

"You had to kill my dad to push the buttons and try for the rest of us. Why?"

"It's hackneyed movie dialogue, but *you know too much*. However, you and I can strike an alliance."

This verified that he had plans for me and Rolan's switchblade, his notion of an alliance.

"How much and why?"

"You don't interfere, you get my son released, and you'll be going for the gold too. A small percentage that will nevertheless set you up for life."

Everybody dead, friends, loved ones, strangers. Nary a visible emotion nor a change in timbre when he spoke.

I nodded, trying to buy time to think.

47

Condor pulled away and pointed a finger at the front passenger door.

"You are so quiet, Theodore. Look out the mirror at that baby-blue Porsche behind us on the next block."

Judy's 911? No, she'd be busy with her sons burying a body. But, then, nature did abhor a coincidence. In order not to say the wrong thing, I said nothing.

"I am a reasonable and generous person. I reward loyalty and efficiency regardless of race, creed, national origin, or prior affiliations."

"Yeah?"

"Play ball and help me finish on time and without interference."

"Why?"

"I'll pay you three-percent is why. Do you like that Porsche?"

"It's okay."

"You can waltz into the dealership and pay cash. Me, I can waltz into the dealership and pay cash for the *dealership*."

"Not a Seattle dealership."

"Come with me to Quito, Theodore. You can buy a Porsche there."

"That's generous of you. I sure could use the money and be alive to spend it."

"Survival is part of the offer. I thought you'd like my proposal."

He handed me a phone. "That's my son's number. Just push 'send'."

I did. "Busy."

"Try again.'

I did. "Busy."

"Why isn't he leaving it open like I told him?"

"How the hell should I know? He's your boy. Could be on the line with one-eight-hundred-porn."

Condor stopped in front of another office tower, a recent addition to Seattle's vertical building boom. I was too rattled to remember its name.

"Rolan, take one of the boys up to make the delivery."

"Yes sir."

I watched a bored security guard give Rolan and his pal a once-over and cock a thumb at the elevators.

"When things proceed will be soon enough. There will be finger-pointing and blustering before rockets are launched."

When things proceed. An unimaginable holocaust, hundreds of millions dead.

"Dr. Strangelove."

"My all-time favorite movie and our inspiration. It came out in 1964. An omen."

"Yeah, a portent, a sign," I said.

"I especially love the ending, with radioactive clouds sprouting like mushrooms."

"I'll bet you do. You and your Chinese pards."

"Naturally, the Chinese will be the prime beneficiaries. The Chinese renminbi isn't a hard currency, but it will be. With any luck, it will be the only hard currency. My gold will be worth a *billion* dollars."

"Lucky you."

"Chairman Mao is on some of the larger denominations of renminbi," he said. "Nostalgic."

"Make sure you keep one under your pillow," I said. "Face up while you play with yourself."

"I'll tolerate your sick humor," Condor said, drumming an unknown rhythm on the steering wheel. "My offer? I'll get your family out too if you give me an answer quickly."

Sure you will, Pinocchio.

I said, "Wow. You're making it very attractive."

The baby-blue Porsche 911 slowly went through the next cross street to our rear. Because of the privacy glass, I couldn't identify the driver.

Traffic was increasing: CondorCake recipients.

Rolan returned alone and climbed into the back with his hand truck.

"Like you said to do, I did, Mr. Condor, Fred, he's standing by so the package ain't disturbed or messed up in any way by nobody."

"Good boy," he said, pulling away. "Last stop. Theodore, make that call again."

I did. "Busy."

Condor tapped the steering wheel. "Why?"

"How the hell should I know? How big a payoff did you say you're offering me if I help you grease the skids? Three percent?"

"I'm raising you to five percent."

Clever. Not such a high increase that I'd believe he was lying.

"Since I can't stop you, I might as well join you. Can I include my mom, sister and girlfriend?"

"We'll work it out, Theo."

Yeah, right.

"Just curious. The guy in the parking garage with the fatal slice in the leg, was he anybody you know?"

"An underperformer," he said.

I didn't pursue the subject further. We stopped at a building so high that I couldn't count the stories in the best of conditions. Rolan and the last rum-dum went in. Rolan came back alone.

"Larry, he's keeping watch like you said."

"Good boy, Rolan."

Pulling over at another tower on Fourth Avenue, a couple of blocks south of the Seattle Central Library, he said, "You'll have to run up with Rolan. Any problem with that?"

I could think of fifty problems with that.
"Not at all."

48

We passed a perfunctory security check, rudely interrupting the guard and the screen of his smart phone, and got in the elevator. I humped the cart and Rolan kept right behind me. I estimated the range on my shit-breath-o-meter: three feet. Hanging that close, he hadn't lost all his marbles to demon rum.

"Rolan, you know how you'll end up. Like your comrades you left with the CondorCake, like the rest of us. He doesn't give a shit about you. Condor is one sick fucking puppy."

"I know he don't care. I wasn't born yesterday. My last check-up at the free clinic they made me when I got out of the can? This wise-ass medic, he said my liver was the size of Rhode Island. He said alcohol was poison to me, my next drink maybe my last. What I'm thinking, I got three or four good toots left in me, so I don't give a rat's ass if the world goes on."

So much for the logic of self-preservation. I don't think he was lying. The whites of his eyes were urine yellow.

We came to a stop on the top floor. At that point, I went docilely along with the program, I had between fifteen and forty-five seconds to live, fifteen if he had his blade already out.

The elevator doors halfway open, I pushed off my back foot and twisted around our cargo, pushing the cart over in front of him.

Rolan did have his blade out, slicing it though the air as he tripped over the hand truck. He was howling and cursing, ready to do what Benihana chefs do to entertain diners.

Rolan was half-kneeling and half-walking, his momentum taking him to the wall opposite the elevator. The safest place for me was directly to his rear.

I got him in a headlock and lifted him off his feet. Rolan was a Tinkertoy.

"I can't breathe, motherfucker. Lemme go."

"Toss your knife as far as you can and I'll let you go."

"You promise?"

"I do. You used it on the other guys, huh?"

"Mr. Condor told me to. *Arrrgh.* C'mon, man."

"Toss it."

"Lemme go."

I squeezed harder. "Toss it."

He tossed it. I did let him go, but as hard as I could, slamming him into a wall. I lost count of how many times I kicked him until he went down like a pile of dirty laundry, coughing and spitting blood.

I called Mike.

"Dude, what's up. We're scared shitless for you."

"I'm fine, I think. Where's Quetzal?"

"She's in Ms. Smith's land rocket, calling in your locations to us. I got our package neutered and these guys Ms. Smith called up, they're doing the others. They got bums guarding them. You believe that?"

"I believe. Not the cops or their bomb squad?"

"She didn't say and I'm not asking. You'll have company mucho quicko."

"Can I talk to Judy?"

"She's kind of, you know, tied up. Her and the guys, they're giving that scumbag a decent burial. A couple of guys dropped by to help out."

"Couple of guys?"

"Size of refrigerators. No necks. If you catch my drift."

I told him to warn Big Sis about her Denver, Minneapolis and Charlotte offices, and asked about Mom.

"She's standing watch over that ratty dude in the undies. Your sis has your mom's baby gun, so we wrapped the guy in duct tape. He's going no place and nowhere, no time soon."

"One last question, Mike. Can these things be set off remotely?"

"Damned if I know."

"Hang on."

I tore open the package and aimed my smart phone camera at it. What do I do?"

"Easy, just pull that silver thing off. It's gotta be the detonation mechanism."

I did and said, "How powerful is this?"

"Beats the shit out of me."

I scanned the bomb and timer slowly. "What else do you see?"

"The timer, you know, doesn't have hands like a Mickey Mouse, but does it go tick tock tick— ?"

"It does. What else?"

"There's a little square glued to the side, I think a chip."

I couldn't peel it off with my fingernails.

Mike said, "Shit, man. Might be one-eight-hundred-*kaboom*."

"Condor's phone?"

"Man, I wish to hell I could say no. To this and the other jewel boxes. Not even Spiderman could get to all of them in time."

"Mike, if I dunk this in water, will that defuse it?"

"Electricity and water generally don't mix."

"Great. Tell Quetzal that I'm on my way."

"Got you covered."

I went into the men's room even though the women's' room was closer—old habits— dropped it headfirst into a toilet, and rode downstairs with the hand truck as calmly as I could.

Quetzal was on the next block to the van's rear. I let loose of the hand truck and sprinted to her, hoping Condor didn't see me.

But he did, goosing the van.

I dove into the Porsche. "Follow that car. Van."

I was kissing her cheek when we heard an explosion. I looked upward at billowing smoke.

"Please tell me that's not the CondorCake," she said.

"Nope. I was clearing the mother of all toilet back-ups."

49

As Condor turned right on Fourth, headed toward First Hill, we kept a block behind him. He was struggling uphill, its dense, bluish exhaust as noxious as my Corsica's.

He crossed under Interstate-5, turned left, then right on Madison, then left on Ninth. We were deep in the heart of Pill Hill, so nicknamed for the profusion of hospitals and clinics.

"Where the hell is he going?" Quetzal said. "Oh wait. Look. That garage. The door's raising. He's slowing, turn signal on. A law-abiding driver. His pop-up digs may be the apartment right above it."

"Let's ask him," I said, finding his number. "Keeping him on the line too."

"Why?"

"Mike said he can phone in his Armageddon, with or without time fuses."

He picked up on the first ring.

"Jerome, are you okay?"

"Hey, asshole," I said.

"You—. The explosion?"

"No Armageddon for you today. The boom you heard, I was repairing a plumbing problem. The bomb squads and cops are all over this. Give it up. Game's over."

The next sound was a clunk, his phone being dropped on the floor.

Condor jerked the van ahead, took a left, than a right on Madison, a straight shot down the hill to the waterfront.

"Lean on the horn and don't give him an inch of room," I told Quetzal. "We can't let him pick up the phone. He has to be one-hundred-percent occupied with driving."

"You want to drive?"

"God, yes."

"No way," Quetzal said, downshifting and racing around a clueless SUV pulling in front of them from a parking garage at a hospital entrance. "Judy would kill me."

"You're no fun."

"Yes I am."

She smiled. "Yeah, you are."

50

Jerome Condor the Deuce hadn't an inkling where he was going. It was a shame that he couldn't stop and pick up his family at the pop-up, but it was every man for himself now.

That blue Porsche, its horn going nonstop. An unmistakable passenger, phone to his ear, middle finger of his other hand pressed to the windshield. Man-child Theodore Cleaver Smith.

Backtracking, Condor headed west on Madison, toward the waterfront. He recalled an immediate entrance onto Interstate-5 northbound. Put the pedal to the floor, hop on the freeway and take the first exit, leave this piece of metallic rubbish at the first available spot, hail a cab. Then once in the taxi, far out of town, dial the magic number.

But no, he was wrong. No immediate entrance. He'd have to turn right on Fifth to loop onto I-5 southbound. A tight two-hundred-and-seventy degree turn. It'd take forever. And they could box him in.

So he stayed on Madison, gaining speed, Puget Sound in view, a Seattle-Bremerton ferry boat coming in to dock. A light bulb went on. Bremerton, a Navy town. He could hide in a restroom for the hour's sailing, fade into the crowd, and be gone before anyone realized he left Seattle. On to Vancouver. Make other travel arrangements. On to Quito as planned? Or Perth? Cape Town? Riding out the thermonuclear shitstorm the only priority.

Madison Street was steepening. He braked to little effect. The pedal was spongy. When he bought the van at an auction, the odometer

266

was 108,177.4; miles and miles of uncountable stops and starts, the hardest mileage you can put on a vehicle.

He pawed from side to side for the seat belt, couldn't find it. The cell phone would have to wait.

Red light coming up. He laid on the horn and went on through, listening to screeching brakes and horns.

He took out the left front of an old Taurus trying to parallel park. Sorry about that.

Condor slalomed down the middle, sideswiping a Fiat 500, punting it onto the sidewalk and into a teriyaki cafe. The Porsche and its goddamn horn remained five feet behind him.

At Second Avenue, he smelled the brakes. They were smoking, virtually useless. He knocked down parking meters on both sides, like bowling pins. His most effective braking system was a BMW 528i he rear-ended, pushing it into the intersection, where it plowed into a Cadillac Escalade.

At First Avenue, he chanced a turn to the right, onto the straight and level. It looked like he had it made until he caromed off the left-rear corner of a Metro Transit articulated bus.

His van was no match for the bus, which budged six inches maximum. The collision deflected him across the street, through the picture window of an Oriental rug shop. Rolls of displayed carpeting served as air bags, but the unbelted Condor punched through the windshield.

In midair, his last thought before he sailed headfirst into a hardwood counter was that his grandson, their computer whiz-jokester, Jerome Condor the Fourth, would have to pick up the torch.

Born on September 11, 2001, it was the lad's destiny.

51

"Millicent is with child?" Mom said.

This an hour after we'd congregated and had a good wailing cry, hugging and sobbing, releasing the tears that the Smith stiff-upper-lips had held in for too, too long, beginning at Dad's funeral.

Judy's vet was making a house call after us bipeds had noticed her a little heavier and sluggish. Hopperd's next-door neighbor Ed, I thought. Cats digging in his flower beds at night. Doing other things too. Millicent among them, losing her innocence.

Judy had semi-forgiven me for my culpability in Mike's elopement with the girl of his dreams-girl of his mother's nightmares. Her name was Lilith Ann. A coincidence or a love child of Lil's? If I worked up the courage, I'd have to ask her.

Big Sis and I had a long, private chat after the end of the van chase. By the time the door to Judy's garage rolled up, we were hearing quadraphonic sirens. There'd be numerous questions to answer.

Judy assured me that no questions would be coming our way, with the exception of the restroom damage. A crew wearing coveralls without names or logos had repairs well underway.

"Cops? Bomb squads?" I said. "None? Nothing? Nobody?"

She said, "We're leaving that to the private sector. Police and fire people have enough on their plates."

"I see. Denver, Minneapolis and Charlotte too?"

"By some coincidence, CondorCakes were delivered to my other offices."

"Nature abhors a coincidence."

"Theo, please leave the aphorisms to experts."

"Your people can dispose of everything?"

"Worry not."

"Who?"

"When you scrolled through my client list, making snide remarks, you missed one. They're headquartered in Delaware, with branches in Bucharest. They do hazmat clean-up and disposal. The firm can react so quickly because they have a procedure unknown to me that can bypass the permit processes."

"Ah."

"Theodore, please wipe that supercilious look off your face. Read the Constitution. Everybody has the right to legal representation."

"Gotcha."

"This way there's no leakage to the media? No international incident. No missiles flying."

"That's my thinking," she said. "Our little secret."

Even if our cell phone conversations throughout all this could be linked to us, the phones were burners I'd liberated from the Happy-Happy Convenience Store, now pulverized in Smith, Hurlbert and Kraus LLC's industrial-strength shredder.

Mike and Lilith Ann had sent honeymoon selfies, framed by palm trees and backdropped by turquoise water. Mike looked—worldly. Lilith Ann glowed as brightly as the hardware she wore in her earlobes, lips, nostril, eyebrows, belly button. They looked happy.

We were happy for them too. Even my sister, who had promised Mike's mother that she had an annulment team standing by if the wheels came off the marriage.

Judy, her boys, and her unidentified associates of an unidentified client had given Mr. C the Three a decent burial, details of which they did not reveal. Nor did I ask. For all I knew, he was being mummified in the building's HVAC system.

The Condors' alcoholic underlings had been dressed in thrift-shop clothing, given a wad of cash, and directions to the nearest dive bar. After a three- or four-day blackout binge, they wouldn't be able to testify even if they wanted to.

Quetzal and I continued our sleeping arrangements at Judy's.

"Sis and her annulment team. Good idea for her if she's ever tempted to tie the knot again."

Quetzal shook her head. "Tie the knot? Theo, you can be deaf, dumb and blind about some things, you know."

"Why not? The third time might be the charm."

"Inge is why not."

"Huh?"

"Don't you remember your sister's comments on gay-bashing? How revolted that amazon blonde is by your irresistible leering?"

"No way."

"You haven't seen how they look at each other because you don't want to."

I stared at the ceiling that was too dark to see.

*   *   *   *   *

I got back to work in my pigsty/studio, working like I'd never worked before, as if the ghost of Edward Hopper was there, kicking me in the ass if I let up.

I took a glass-half-full approach to the Zorro-esque vandalism; it wasn't ruination, it was inspiration.

The remake of *WEATHER DELAY 2013* glued on plywood backing, was already ninety-percent done. I'd incorporated the slashes to the original, separating the sections slightly, a quarter-inch or so, like a hard-edged jigsaw puzzle. The passengers seeing their cancelled flights were being drawn apart from reality, nothing in their futures but lost luggage and airport purgatory, bad food, and the TSA.

I renamed it *A FIELD GUIDE TO ARMAGEDDON.*

My family raved about it and I think they were sincere. I contacted gallery owners I knew, and negotiated a show with the first one who didn't hang up on me. I planned to include the Hack Wilson triptych. It was time to clear out my inventory and move on.

Our ancestral home was being readied to be put on the market and Mom, not pleased by this, had grudgingly accepted it. Big Sis sweetened the deal with one glass and one glass only of merlot at dinner.

Christopher Theodore Polk and Tyler Lee Taylor resumed their duties as Smith, Hurlbert and Kraus's Correspondence Supervisors.

Unable to withstand Mr. Singh's begging and whining, I filled in part-time at the Happy-Happy until Lil was released into his custody, working at double pay.

Her and Mr. Singh had made some kind of payment plan. They didn't tell, I didn't ask. I paid close attention to his body language. His eye contact with her was at once erotic and terrified.

By throwing a tantrum, citing personal safety in this day and age of street criminals and dope fiends here, there, and everywhere, Mom retained possession of the baby Browning. The Glock 19 taken from Mr. Gull was loaned to me by Mom to me to carry at "that horrid excuse of a job," after giving me a thorough primer on it so I didn't shoot myself. It in one front pocket, my Saturday night booby trap in the other, robbers beware.

"More accurately, with children," the vet went on, gently probing Millicent's abdomen. "My guess is quadruplets."

"For certain, four?" Judy said.

"Ninety percent certain. I could do an ultrasound."

"Don't you dare," Mom said. "We've had our fill of atomic radiation in our lives."

The vet looked at her.

"Mother," Judy said, then to the vet, "My mother lived in Nevada during the above-ground tests in the fifties. She's naturally wary."

"If you say so," Mom said.

"You slut," I said to Millicent, listening to her purr as I scratched under her chin.

52

Meanwhile, to end this story, at this precise moment, after the day's commodity market closing, $372,111,854 in fictional gold sits in a fictional Zurich bank vault.

Waiting to be claimed.

ABOUT THE AUTHOR

Gary Alexander is the author of sixteen novels. *Disappeared,* first in the Buster Hightower series, has been optioned to Universal Studios.

He's also written 150+ short stories and sold travel articles to six major dailies.

One story appeared in *Best American Mystery Stories 2010,* and another in *Mystery Writers of America Presents Ice Cold: Tales of Intrigue from the Cold War* anthology.

On his last visit to Lisbon in 2015, Alexander walked where Harry Antonelli had in 1940, although somewhat less recklessly.

His website is www.garyralexander.net